EXPOSURE

ALSO BY THE AUTHOR

Shutter

EXPOSURE

RAMONA EMERSON

Published by
Soho Press, Inc.
227 W 17th Street
New York, NY 10011

Library of Congress Cataloging-in-Publication Data
Names: Emerson, Ramona, 1973- author.
Title: Exposure / Ramona Emerson.
Description: New York, NY : Soho Crime, 2024.
Identifiers: LCCN 2024026462

ISBN 978-1-64129-476-8
eISBN 978-1-64129-477-5

Subjects: LCGFT: Thrillers (Fiction) | Detective and mystery fiction. |
Paranormal fiction. | Novels.
Classification: LCC PS3605.M485 E97 2024 | DDC 813'.6—dc23/
eng/20240614
LC record available at https://lccn.loc.gov/2024026462

Interior design by Janine Agro

Printed in the United States of America

10 9 8 7 6 5 4 3 2 1

For Brenda,
my best friend in the stars.

CHAPTER I
GUNPOWDER GIRL

Nikon D2X • f/16, 1/8 sec., ISO 200)

THE LITTLE GIRL'S breath smelled of blood and gunpowder.

I've heard it said that children's souls ascend into the heavens without the tethers of recollection and the pull of longing that their mothers carry—the connection to their bodies and their blood and their memory. But sometimes they must stay behind—their little voices must tell us their stories. The grief is just too much to carry.

It was 3:15 in the morning when her cold hand squeezed mine. My apartment had gone so bitter cold that I could hear cracking glass coming from my window ledges. I pulled my blankets closer, my gaze traveling toward the darkness in the corner. Her eyes were bright and framed by darkened bruises. I stared at her as the moon fell on our faces. I had no idea who she was, but she pulled on me, my stretched skin stinging as she drew me toward her.

"We're waiting for you," she said.

I became aware of the six other sets of eyes standing in

the shadow, of the sound of their breathing like a collective wheeze, the liquid in their throats. I felt a sickness deep in my stomach—the pain of grief. There were so many of them, wheezing until their hearts went quiet. Time stopped as we stared at each other, fifteen minutes of their whispers on my skin. Our confrontation was interrupted by the sound of my phone ringing, the light bouncing on the nightstand. My heart was racing. I answered and the ringing stopped. "Hello."

The black eyes were gone and the room had begun to warm.

"Hello, Rita. We need you up on the west side." Samuels sounded strange. "Our specialist . . ." He paused long enough for me to check the blue reflecting light of my phone's screen. We were still connected. "Our new specialist can't continue."

"I still haven't been cleared with Dr. Cassler." I looked at the clock. It was now almost 3:30 A.M.

"We need you down here." There was a long and distant silence.

"Send me the address." I hung up the phone and looked around the darkness of my room. Even though the girl and her shadows were gone, I couldn't shake her or the smell of her breath. As I stood in my bathroom, water dripping from my face, I could smell smoke, gunpowder and the stench of burning hair, like it was billowing from my walls. I dressed, pulling my leg brace up over my thigh, the sharp sting of pain rolling down to my ankle. It did this every day. I told no one. It would be one more thing they would be able to talk about, another whisper around the water cooler. I would tell no one about my visitors this morning either.

7310 Platero Road NW, 4:14 A.M.

There were eight units already at the scene, mostly police vehicles and two quiet ambulances. Officers had the property taped off all the way through the end of the block as early risers stretched their necks over their fence lines. The air was still cold as I readied myself to begin another morning in my paper suit.

It had been an hour since the original 911 call. The report stated that a James Sandoval, pastor at First Desert Light Church, was on his way to the crime scene with the suspected perpetrator in the back of his vehicle. The suspect was a teenager, a Jude Montaño, the oldest son of Steven Montaño, a retired Albuquerque PD detective. Jude had come to the church in the middle of the night still holding a gun, blood splatter on his face. When Pastor Sandoval approached him, he raised the gun to the pastor's face and pulled the trigger. Luckily, there were no bullets in the gun. Pastor Sandoval called the police and drove with Jude straight to the boy's house, where they found every single member of his family dead from gunshot wounds—three girls, aged three, seven and fourteen; three boys, five, eight and ten; and both parents, Steven and Elizabeth Montaño, both forty-three.

Jude Montaño sat in the backseat of the patrol car, staring at me through the window as I pulled up. His back shook with every breath and tears rolled down his cheeks. He stopped crying when he saw my arm rise. I was pulled toward the house like a pendulum. I wondered if he could see her too.

The little hand pulled harder as I walked toward the crime scene. I looked down to see her bruises, the gunpowder freckles on her cheeks, the hole in her face like a honeysuckle bloom. Her mouth was bloody and swirled with white that leaked from both sides of her lips.

"I knew you would come," she said. "Can you play with us?"

All the dead children were outside on the playscape in their pajamas, cavernous wounds in their backs and heads. I watched them chase one another up and down the slides while the oldest stared at the people passing in and out of their doorway. She turned her eyes on me, her expression one of anger—of finality. I think she was the only one who wasn't confused about what happened.

The little girl never left me as I stepped onto the crime scene. Her siblings ran up and surrounded us, their voices unaware—a strange echo still giddy with childhood. The smallest one cried, raising her hands to me, wanting me to pick her up.

"Come play with us." A boy pointed to their yard, scattered with dolls and toys.

I looked toward the door where the techs were assembling. A few officers stared at me, as they often do. I pulled away from the children.

"Rita, over here." Samuels stood by a man with a graying beard. Sandoval, the pastor. The air was cold, the sun still behind the mountains.

"Rita Todacheene, photo specialist." I extended my hand, and Pastor Sandoval took it, never saying a word.

Samuels motioned to the responding officer, the first on scene, a senior investigator named Louis Giovanni, to join us. He was already making his report, checking the temperature, and calculating the times. He read out what he had already taken down as I loaded my camera. Giovanni was brand-new to APD after four years in Minneapolis and another five in Los Angeles. He had come to Albuquerque to replace Sergeant Seivers, who had finally retired and moved to California to be with her grandbabies. I liked Giovanni because he was committed, and he wore horn-rimmed glasses—there was a mad scientist buried in him somewhere. He was very tall, quiet and reserved, but always seemed to know what questions to ask on scene and how to leave no stone unturned. That was how Seivers used to be. They had found someone who was almost her equal. Giovanni wasn't privy to my special radar. Samuels still considered it compromising to cases. He never talked to me about it as long as I kept going to the shrink.

"Pastor Sandoval says the kid walked into the church and stood there silent, gun in hand. He knew right away something was wrong and drove them straight over here," Giovanni concluded.

"Did you go inside, Pastor?" I asked Sandoval.

"Yes," he answered after a hesitation. "But once I saw Steve, I came right back out. He was a friend of mine."

I ducked beneath the tape, two cameras at my side. I could see our new specialist sitting in the ambulance, her hands over her face. My leg muscles pinched and burned as I coughed the smell of old blood off the back of my throat and started to take pictures. I backtracked from the scene, framing the front of the house, the number by the door, the blood-sprayed porch. Photo one, marker one. I photographed everything in the yard, the toys and bicycles, the new vehicles and construction equipment. From this viewpoint, nothing looked out of the ordinary. I pulled my notebook from my bag and diagrammed the scene as I saw it, lines and circles marking bodies and distance. Then I moved into the house.

At marker three, a man lay on the floor near the doorway, his face an explosion of blood and bone. I looked up to the ceiling of the porch, right above where Giovanni, Samuels and Pastor Sandoval stood talking. Pieces of brain tissue, skull fragments and flesh sprayed the columns, some nestled in the white macramé yarn planter, others embedded in the peeling paint and wood slats. The tissue smelled already, the earthy, milky smell of brain mixed with sharp iron.

After framing the blood and tissue from the porch in my lens, I moved to the man in the doorway. He looked up at the ceiling as if his face was still there, some memory loading before he died. Whatever gun had made this wound was powerful. Judging from the spray on the porch and doorframe, he was shot as he entered, surprised by his fate. A spattered recliner faced the door, its arms and back dotted with blood. I took twenty-seven photos of the man—the father, a former detective, a husband—his surroundings and his wounds. Blood pooled behind his head, a ten-inch-diameter circle embedded in the tan carpet with a wide river of blood trailing toward the door, small streams branching into the fabric. The bullet had hit him right at the upper bridge of his nose, knocking his eyes out of their sockets and pouring them into the sides of his hairline. On his right hand, there was a hole —a jagged tear between his middle and index fingers, bruising on the knuckles and fingers and deep cuts on his palm. There was a distinctive blackening of his hands and another hole indicating where he raised his arm for cover. The bullet had cut right through to his skull. A 9mm gun lay by his right side, the television lights flickering on its silver skin. The man's ghost never came. When I photographed the wounds on his hands, I could smell gunpowder. Photo count eighty-seven.

I counted three rifle casings behind the couch, a .30 caliber ammo that was more suited to hunting animals. At this range, the man had no chance. The recoil of the gun could have caused the bruise on the boy's face. We spotted two more holes above the front door and at the edge of the ceiling. Most likely the other two rounds had been fired inadvertently, a product of the boy's inexperience with the gun's power. I could hear the kids outside laughing. The oldest girl was watching me through the open door, the baby tugging at her nightgown.

The gunpowder girl, still by my side, pointed at the man on the floor. "Jude shot Dad in his face." When she turned to look at the man's body, I could see the side of her head, a bloom of blood that took up half her skull. Blood flowed into her ear and down her neck, soaking her pink pajamas. She turned to look at me again, her smile revealing bloody teeth, then darted away toward the next room. She didn't seem too worried about her father's current condition. I pulled the camera to my eye and continued to shoot the slugs the officers found stuck in the cheap wood paneling.

Impatient, the gunpowder girl had returned for me. "This way. I'll show you. I'll show you." Her little hands pulled at my shirt until I followed.

Down the hallway, I saw two bodies lying in the kitchen, a woman and the oldest girl, whose ghost surveyed from the front door. They both lay on the floor, the mother holding the girl in her arms. Their wounds were brutal. Had I not seen the photographs in the front room, I would have no idea what Elizabeth Montaño looked like. Her face had been blown open right above her brow, skeletal segments pasted along the sink and the back wall draped with bloody long black hair. The gun had been right in her face, and her mouth was still open in midscream. Her bottom teeth were intact, but there was a huge cut on her upper lip, her two top front teeth dangling from the flesh of her gums. As I took photos of her injury, I figured that she had been hit in the face with the butt of the gun. The wound on her forehead was large, a fully open skull with some remaining tissue inside, the curve of the bone like an incoming wave. What was left of her face was speckled with residue and buckshot burns. Markers 90–145 indicated Elizabeth Montaño and the pieces of her spread around her well-kept kitchen.

The oldest girl had not been shot in the face. Instead, her mermaid T-shirt had been sucked into the blackened hole in her chest, a wound that measured more than three jagged inches. I turned to see her looking from the kitchen door, her injury exactly matching that of the body on the floor. The blood around her wound was dark and hardened, her heart cut in half by the blast of the gun. I framed the entire kitchen, every inch clean and organized and speckled with beads of drying blood. Mother's and daughter's bodies were unusually twisted together, falling into a coil after they were shot. I could hear the older girl crying close to my ear. They'd begged for their lives. Photos 145–183.

My companion in the pink pajamas appeared in the kitchen and watched her mother and sister on the floor. She never moved as I continued my work, photographing the bodies and the blood spatter. I could still smell the kitchen cleaner below the old blood. The girl sat on the floor with her mother's body as I finished and continued through to the next room. There were four shotgun casings scattered at the door's threshold, red plastic with bronze tops. One shotgun blast had pierced the white cabinet doors. I moved in and out of every angle until the room had been covered from corner to corner.

"The gun is under there," the little girl, still squatting in the kitchen next to the bodies, called out to me, pointing at the counter. I followed her finger, crouching and pressing my face against the floor. It looked like the gun had been tossed, slid across the tiles and came to a stop beneath the cabinets. I snapped four more photos and called in for someone to box the shotgun.

Down the hallway, the door opened to a small bathroom, decorated with fish decals and princess characters on the mirrors and shower curtains. A small girl's body lay in front of the baby-blue toilet, a bullet hole through the side of her head.

"That's me. I'm dead," she said, and skipped past me into the room. We found four casings in the doorway. She had been shot at point-blank range as she was brushing her teeth, probably never realizing that anyone meant her harm. Her hand still gripped her toothbrush, the blood coming from her mouth swirled with toothpaste. The little soul stared at herself in the bathroom as I took photos of her body, the casings, the spatter and the bullets still embedded in the blue toilet seat and the wall. Our yellow markers lay on the floor, 184, 185, 186, 187.

"Seven," she said, pointing to the last digit on the last marker. She ran out of the room in a breeze. I heard the officer behind me gasp for breath.

I framed the closed door to the first bedroom and looked for anything strange. Nothing looked out of the ordinary. When I opened the door, I found all three of the little boys' bodies still in their beds and under the covers, their ghosts huddled in the corner watching me. I can only imagine that they had heard the gunshots in their sleep and hid beneath the bedding to escape. Their brother had shot them right through the blankets. Once I'd photographed them in the position their killer had left them, I pulled the blankets back. Their faces were intact because the shots had come from the side, the blankets slowing the blow of the bullets before they embedded in their heads. There were holes behind each of their heads, the tendons of their neck muscles separated. I could hear the steady thump of their footsteps as their ghosts ran from the room, afraid of the reality beneath the linens. The sound of the blasts must have scared them, as their hands gripped their blankets. I hoped their killer, their brother, had some semblance of remorse. He couldn't look at their faces. He had even closed the door.

At the end of the hallway, there were two bedrooms. One looked like it belonged to the parents. There were gun cases laid out on top of a quilt covered in flowers. The ammo boxes were dumped and empty, a few bullets rolled into creases of the sheets. I photographed the bed and all of the ammo and guns. Five or six orange pill bottles sat open, a pallete of color laid out in capsules on the nightstand. The drawers were open, scattered change in the corners, as though other valuables had been removed. There were still three more rifles in the closet and one 9mm pistol on the bed. Judging from the ammo boxes on the bed, there was no ammo left for the 9mm. Photo 208.

The little girl appeared in the doorway, watching the flashes that emitted from my camera. She laughed as two of her brothers joined her, jockeying for position in the doorframe before turning and running into the room across the hall, the backs of their heads wide open. All three of their ghosts had jumped on the bed, their legs bouncing in unison. I could hear the springs from the other room, a hard metal scraping. I watched a technician come into the hallway behind me with large bags, cardboard boxes, and zip ties to remove the firearms. He paused to peer into the girls' bedroom, and I thought for a second that he could hear the springs too. He lowered his eyes and went back to work. So did I.

There was only one room left. The room was a sea of pink, every corner covered in sequins, light pink boas and Disney princess posters. A small white bed stood in the far right of the room with raised bed posts and pink bed skirts and duvet. The baby of the family lay in her crib, posed with her hands folded over her heart. A star-torn gun wound stood in the center of her forehead, a burned cross pulling the skin back into the bone. I photographed her as her baby laughter welled behind me, the three-year-old pushing against her older sisters as they played tag, the toddler unable to keep up.

I filmed the little soul as she lay in that crib. I wondered if she might have been the first. She had not shed one tear. She was perfect in her little white night gown. Her brother had posed her, angelic, like she was in her coffin. I looked around for casings.

"He shot her first." The seven-year-old appeared from nowhere at the bedside, making me drop my camera. My heart raced. She stared at her sister's body just as the littlest ghost came up to me, raising her arms in the air to be lifted. "She was asleep when he did it. It didn't hurt, though. Mine didn't."

I figured I would ask since no one else was around. "Was it Jude that shot you?"

"It was Daddy." She looked straight at me and smiled. "The bullet thing is right there." She pointed to the pillowcase, then looked toward the door and again pointed. The .22 caliber rifle lay on the floor behind the open door.

It was Daddy. The girl's words had taken my breath away. I began to think of everything I had just photographed, how the whole narrative was changing right in front of me. No one would believe it.

"How are things going in here?" Giovanni walked through the doorway and the two ghosts disappeared. "What a morning, Rita. Sorry to start your week off like this. We have OMI ready to come in once the scene is processed. Let me know when we're ready to move."

"I'm just about done," I said, looking around the room. Now I couldn't help but see the man in the front room, his gun raised to his own children, his own wife. I saw a single gold casing by the pillow, right where the girl said it would be. Photo 215. I took photos of the casing obscured by the pillow. I took another photo, this time from the other side of the bed, the blood pooled beneath her head, continuing down her back and creating a heart-shaped red shadow beneath her body. No wonder our newbie couldn't take it. Photo 223. I kept shooting.

There was a small bullet hole that pierced her mattress, and reddened cotton sagged through the hole, soaked. The bullet was lodged in the floor, its edge on the top of the carpet. The baby's ghost stood beside me, her legs thick and wobbly, the hole in her head black with blood. Her chubby fingers gripped her bed while the other hand reached out to me and cried. I zoomed into the wound of the toddler, the injury rife with abrasions, soot and stippling—her face a constellation of red, burns and dried tissue. My flash lit up the girl's room, the cold light on her face reflecting back at me.

"I think this room is done. I think all of them are done." I looked at the back of my camera for the image count—273. Now we had to wait for the coroner to remove the family from their home over to the Office of the Medical Investigator. Giovanni and I made detailed diagrams of every room and narrative notes for our reports. The gunpowder girl's words haunted me. My leg tensed with pain.

"Do you really think that kid did all of this, Giovanni?" I watched as OMI took the toddler from her bed, the back of her head absorbed into the bedding.

"You'd be surprised what kids are capable of these days," Giovanni said. "Some kids just won't take no for an answer."

"All of this over some kind of disagreement?" I knew that the little ghost had no reason to lie. "I'm not buying it."

When I came to the front room again, seeing the dead father

rotting on the carpet, my heart told me he deserved it. The heaviness weighed down the entire house as we moved in and out of every room and cataloged in silence.

It wasn't silent for me.

"I want to go see Mama. Why can't we go see Mama?" The kids squirmed on the couch as we did our work. The young boys watched the television screen, their mouths agape, their bullet holes leaking onto the sides of their faces. An officer walked by and touched the button on the front of the television, blanking the screen. The boys cried until the oldest one rose and turned the television back on. When the screen lit back up, everyone in the room looked at me. They rarely ever said anything about it, but the rumor kept stirring. They went back to work, leaving the television on. My nose began to bleed, an easy bleed that tickled instead of raged.

Each of the bodies was removed in a black-and-blue bag after I documented the scene, then loaded into ambulances and Suburbans from OMI and driven back to the laboratory for autopsy. I stepped outside the front door to watch the oldest girl herd the sibling ghosts into a line, walking them toward the grove of trees that separated the property from the edge of the river. I thought all of them had moved with her until my hand was gripped again. This little girl with the bullet breath stood beside me, her bloody teeth smiling, her fingers like ice.

Her little hand guided me to a small shed that sat off to the east. I looked around to see who on scene was keeping an eye on me, but everyone seemed to be busy doing their part. She walked me right up to the door of the shed and dropped my hand, smiling one more time and running into the haze of the bosque. I stared at the shed, then shook the doorknob. It was locked.

I walked back as the morning sun began to warm the front

of the house. We measured and photographed the scene again with the bodies removed, looking hard for any casings or shots we might have missed. We catalogued the weapons—an impressive twelve rifles, shotguns and handguns. Looking at the report, I could see that the three girls were Neveah, Margarita and Marisol, and the three boys were John, Samuel and Mark. Steven Montaño and his wife, Elizabeth, had been married for eighteen years; their wedding photo was speckled with blood in the living room. Their oldest son, Jude, the last family member, was still sitting in the squad car. This city seemed heartless on days like this, and I was getting tired of photographing babies and children. These scenes usually brought me to tears or forced me to gather myself for a day or two. I looked at my watch. It was only 11 A.M. No tears ever came.

I had not stopped thinking about the shed on the side of the house. I felt the little girl around me still, the ice on my fingertips. Once the photos of the vacated scene were done, I knew I had to find out. I walked over to the crime scene unit, where Officer Hope sat bagging evidence.

"Officer, do you have a way to pry open this shed east of the house?" I pointed toward the shed. It sat off to the back of the yard, obscured by dried honeysuckle bushes and a primer-gray Chevy truck with its engine on the outside.

"I hadn't even noticed the shed. What kind of lock are we looking at?"

"It looks like a standard doorknob. No deadbolt."

I followed Officer Hope to the back of the unit, where he grabbed a crowbar.

The door popped open quickly, flooding the shed with light and dust. I turned my flashlight toward the corners of the room and saw a cramped storage unit packed with boxes, clothes and old furniture. I knew that the girl's ghost hadn't brought me over without a reason. I felt cold on one side of my face, like a rush of air inside that closed shed, turning my head. I pulled at the drawers of the black file cabinet in the corner, rocking the metal back and forth. The top drawer opened.

Inside, there was a scattered collection of old bills and papers stacked into files, and an old blue silken box way in the back. I pulled the box out and opened it: typical family photographs of the children and Mrs. Montaño, their faces smiling. The bottom drawer was filled with more neatly stacked photo boxes. I pulled the first one out and opened it.

"Oh, Jesus." Officer Hope focused his light on the first photo. A naked photograph of the oldest daughter in the very same shed we were standing in, an uneven backdrop hanging on the wall. I looked to the floor and saw the same gray backdrop rolled into a flat cylinder, lying on the dusty floor. There were dozens of photographs in the box—of various children, some naked, some posed in sexual positions, a few with damp, crying faces. I closed the box and looked at Officer Hope.

"This case just hit a whole new level."

"You think the kid did this?" Hope moved his light around the room looking for more.

I pulled one more photo out of the stack. In the same room, the gray background pulled tightly against the wall, a young Jude with a red tie around his mouth, his hands bound with handcuffs. Behind him a mirror reflected back the Polaroid camera around Steven Montaño's neck.

"Somehow, I don't think so," I replied. I could still feel the cold of the little girl's hand in mine even though she was long gone. "Let's lock this shed down for processing. This is going to take some time."

. . .

I FOLLOWED A few officers to the station to turn in my report and to back up my work. I knew they were taking Jude in, and I had to be there to photograph him before he was booked. I went to the cold linoleum and wasted blue light of booking, and photographed him wearing a slightly large flannel shirt, baggy jeans and white Converse sneakers speckled with deep red blood. The close-up photos showed small and medium blood spatter on his face, and flecks of tissue in his hair and on his clothes. We found five empty shotgun shells in one pants pocket and ten more unspent rounds in another.

He had been crying. As I photographed him, he waffled between a strange, understated giggle and a quick and heaving cry. His hands were red and cut, shredded with scars and scabs.

"How did you get these wounds on your hands?" I pointed to the cuts and bruises. Jude just stared into space, saying nothing. I photographed his wounds and all the pieces of flesh in his hair, and blood that hardened to a dark, shiny skin. He started to laugh again.

When all of his clothes had been removed and placed into individual paper bags, Jude sat there in the cold white booking room like a child. I photographed his back; it was full of bruises. He slowly put on the white paper suit we gave him, pulling the hood over his blood-hardened hair. They took his mug shot, and I watched him move through the three barred doors in the jail. I didn't know what to think of the boy, but I knew he didn't kill his whole family.

The three officers opened the holding cell and began to remove all of its contents. Suicide watch. I took another photo of him in his paper suit and moved closer.

"What if I told you that your sister says you didn't do it?"

He looked at me, his eyes like glass. "What did you say to me?"

"You heard me."

His breath labored and wheezed as he looked straight at me. He was trying not to cry.

"The man deserved to die after everything he put us through," he said. "I was trying to save my sisters, but I was too late." His body was frail and malnourished, his soul resting on the outside of his skin. "If I had been there an hour earlier, he would have been the only one dead."

I looked at Jude Montaño and thought of the little girl and the dust-covered shed.

"I believe you," I said.

Two guards came in and dragged him from the holding cell, his arms twisting away from them.

"Tell them!" he yelled. "Tell them you believe me!"

His echo followed me out of the building.

MY DESK INSIDE the crime scene unit felt desperate and lonely, my coffee getting cold as it sat by the hard drive while I backed up my SD cards. I was tired. I sat at my desk in silence, looking down to see dots of blood on my desk, two, then four, then six. My nose bled hard, filling the philtrum above my lips. My heart raced as I thought of their faces. The dead were everywhere, and I couldn't unsee them. Their souls gathered inside of me.

I saw Samuels sitting with his feet up on his desk, his head stuck to his phone, so I approached, wiping the blood on some napkins from the collection on my desk.

"Samuels, can I head home?" I knocked on the window. He pointed at his phone. Samuels, and most men in this office, could only do one thing at a time. I waved and placed my drive on his desk, leaving him to his phone call.

"Rita, just a minute." He lowered the phone to his chest. "Rita!"

I pulled my head back into his office.

"I have to put you back in rotation tonight. I'm sorry." He lifted the receiver again. "Hold on, please." He pointed the receiver at me. "We lost our newbie today. I knew it was too early to send her into a scene like that right after training. So, my fault."

"Samuels," I said. "I still haven't been cleared by Cassler. You know this, right?"

He went back to the phone. "Hope for a slow night."

I walked back to the parking lot, two rolled-up napkins inside my nostrils, and sat in my car for a few minutes, near sleep. The sun fed me, moving into my bones and into my leg. I had to get some sleep before the sun set.

CHAPTER 2 | 15°

"To everything there is a season, and a time for every
purpose under heaven: a time to be born, and a time to die; a
time to plant, and a time to pluck up that which is planted."

ECCLESIASTES 3:1-2

WINTER MAKES GHOSTS of us all.

I am the cold, icy river that evil flows into, a wild tributary in which I bathe.

There is a reason I was sent here, that I was born and molded for this life and baptized in this blood. I know you won't understand. But my story must be told, and I will tell it. I have no idea how much of this I will remember, even now my mind is aching with pain, but you need to know the reasoning behind it—the guidance that propels me to my work. Sometimes I forget, I admit. I confess here and now, as 2006 nears its own death, that I have killed for God, and I will kill again.

My hands are guided by something so much bigger than all of us. I have been sent here in this human realm, where evil lives right alongside good, where life breathes and death leeches, to guide the most innocent into the arms of God. Though my hands may be awash in blood, it has been God's work. I have been blessed.

This winter the streets came alive with unusual force, the gutters running rivers down Coal and Aztec. The avenues have turned white, live bodies huddled under any bit of cover. I don't mind the snow. I've become used to the bitter weather in this town, making my grid through the alleyways and sidewalks, watching the Navajos move through the streets at night, far from their homes and the lives that they remember. I remember them. I can say their names and see their faces.

For the last month, I've watched them move with the season, the cold just starting to make its appearance in Gallup's swift transition from summer to winter. The bars and hotels are rife with pulses, blood still warm and supple in the cool fall. Since November, they have dug themselves into the dirt for warmth or moved into empty boxes or discarded cabinets in abandoned buildings—hiding from the cold. I've watched them sleep in the winter. For years now. Seven degrees. Zero degrees. Below zero. I tick like a clock. They don't hear me. I just sit and listen to them breathe. Their bodies changing, hard then soft, blue then white. Alive then dead.

That winter, ten years ago now, I took my first angel. A man they called Hoskie, almost blue from death, offered his coat to me, his skin bare underneath.

"You look cold," he said.

I gave him the flask, the liquor blended with poison, and he drank it, happy to escape the cold, happy to be free of this horrible place between the train tracks and the sky. He went that night with the stars wrapped around him for warmth.

He was the first of many.

I found him the next morning before the sun came up, curled into the earth. His face was pain. I gathered his death like dry sticks and pulled their scratching skins into my body. His coat was gone, his bare chest the same color as the dirt.

It didn't take long for me to learn their routines, their hide-aways. I've watched their sufferings and wondered how anyone could ever live a life so hard. But they've lived it, many with histories that most of us could not even comprehend, many as heroes of a country that forgot them long ago. Now many are years into their twisted dreamworld, their bodies muddled, their skin hardened, their eyes blinded. They need a way out of the nightmare, a way to ease into the next iteration, a way out of the fog and into the light.

I wait for my Rosemary now, and as I do, I will tell my story. They may never understand what I've done, and what guided me to it, but I'll write it anyway. I feel the walls closing in on me. But my purpose is clear, my mind finally steady and cold and focused. I can already feel my wings emerging from my back, black and smooth, their breeze cooling my legs. As I wait, all I can do is write it all down. Every memory that comes to me.

May my words be my penance, this story a chronology of my ascent into heaven.

CHAPTER 3
GHOST IMAGE

Sony Alpha 100 35mm • f/1.4, 1/60 sec., ISO 1600

THESE STREETS ARE filled with ghosts. I drove home through the frontage roads, circumventing the old parts of town and the memories and histories that continued to stagger through the streets. So many meshed into the lives of the living, sitting at bus stops, staring from street corners, filling the lobbies of hospitals. I dreaded the hospitals. The voices in those blue-and-green corridors rushed into my ears, their death pressed into my skin, the oil seeping. They were the shadows and the empty blackness. They were the blurs that hovered in front of me. They were the figures in the hallways that no one saw.

After my scene in the valley, I came home numb and rode the newly repaired elevator up to the top floor of my apartment building, Downtown Village. Lately my home life had become just as haunted as my work. In the months I had spent in the hospital, many of my elderly neighbors had made their journeys. Now, every day when I returned home, their ghosts walked angrily through the corridors, swinging their aged arms through the young people who came to move in to their apartments. With so much turnover, the landlord had begun to upgrade the building with new paint and new rental rates. The elders hated the new tenants.

I never bothered to make my apartment a home again after it was trashed by my ex-colleagues last spring. My walls stood cold, white and bare, the windows bleeding from the spring light as I lay alone every day. But I was never alone. Never. They came all the time. They mostly came to tell their stories to someone who would listen. Some were just lonely souls, while some came with messages they wanted me to send a loved one. I wasn't here for that. Not anymore.

The top floor felt cold and hollow as I walked to Mrs. San-tillanes's door and knocked three times—our code. As I waited, I felt a pain in my leg and leaned my body heavily against my cane. I still carried it with me most places, even six months after my injuries. At my first assignment after returning to work, over two months ago, I took about fifty pictures before I hobbled back to my car and grabbed my cane. I still needed physical therapy before work every other day, but I had given that up. My leg would never be what it was before. It felt like a lifeless log most days, but at night it came alive, the tendrils of nerves moving and crackling inside of my skin. Sleep didn't come easy. The doctors told me it would resolve itself in time. I was reluctant to believe them.

"You okay, Mrs. Santillanes?" I knocked again. I waited for a reply, but all I could hear was the drone of her television. "You need me to get anything for you?"

"I'm here, *hija.*" I heard her voice moving toward the door. When she opened it, I was relieved. She looked good, her hair up in curlers, her nails polished. "They brought me a tray from the senior wagon a little bit ago, so I'm all full. But gracias." She hugged me deeply, then pulled away and looked into my eyes. "Get some rest."

I worried about Mrs. Santillanes, alone in her apartment, and checked on her every day, no matter what. I brought her food to make sure she was eating something; I often had a feeling she wasn't. Grandma was the same. As people get older, I guess their bodies and their stomachs shrink along with their will to be on the planet. Feeling the pain in my leg every day reminded my body that its fate would be the same someday. I was already feeling the dread of that pain in me.

I staggered back to my apartment and let myself in. The air was sterile and still. I still had groceries in my refrigerator from Shanice, who had taken responsibility for me the last few months, but who had just left for a job on set in southern New Mexico. I pulled some potato salad and a beer from the fridge, then checked to see if I had any new messages from Grandma.

There weren't any, but I had talked to her just yesterday. Her breathing had sounded labored as she answered on the eighth ring. I envisioned her running toward the phone from outside or from a distant part of the house and felt guilty for not insisting that I get her a wireless phone.

"For what? I'll just lose it somewhere anyway, like in the refrigerator or out in the cornfield," she'd teased. "I'm fine."

I'm fine. That is what she always said. Last night she talked about her new dog, whom she had named Barkley after her favorite basketball player, and the rows of corn in her yard that needed to be stirred back into the soil. "Next year is going to be a good year for the corn, Rita. I can feel it. And Mr. Bitsilly will come over every day to help me water."

"It sounds like he's taken a real liking to you, Grandma," I teased back.

"Oh, hush," she said. We laughed until I felt the warmth of tears in my eyes. I missed her every day and tried to check in as much as possible, and when I couldn't, I sometimes replayed her voice on my answering machine. I never erased her messages.

I sat myself on the couch and turned on the television. On the screen was a local news report about the very place I had photographed that day. I changed the channel to find a woman singing some tune I had never heard before.

A voice came from behind me. "Do you remember that crash up there on I-40?"

He was here again. I couldn't even eat bad food and watch shameless television in peace.

This was my new reality. The dead stacked up in my office, sat in every available seat in my car, their random voices fighting to get my attention. I stayed quiet. The more I recognized their presence, the more they had to say, until they flooded me with words and thoughts. They didn't relegate their visits to my work hours—they came into my home or found me at the store. Some of them never left. This all proved what I'd known all along: there are no rules to the world of the dead.

The man in my apartment now was named Irvin, over two years dead, who had lost his wife and son to a car accident decades prior. His memory must've died the day his wife and son left him, because it was the only day he seemed to remember. He had followed me home from the hospital.

"It was on a Wednesday in the spring of '87. Do you remember the big crash up on the hill on I-40?" He waited for me to respond. "Do you remember?" His voice grated in my ear, fingernails on a chalkboard. He persisted. Day after day, he persisted.

"Do you remember?" His voice was a daily reminder of my

lingering responsibilities. He asked me the same question every time.

"Do you remember?" He rubbed his brow, his powdery skin speckled with red dots and liver spots. For months, the same question. I could be sitting having coffee in my kitchen and "Do you remember?" would come out of the corner. I would walk into another room, ignoring him, day after day.

One morning, exhausted from a sleepless night, I heard him again. He was looking at me in my bathroom mirror as I brushed my teeth.

"Do you remember that accident in 1987, way up on—"

"No. I don't remember," I interrupted. I glanced into his eyes, realizing my mistake. His eyes were suddenly lucid and alert. He'd heard me. He hasn't left since.

"It was the worst accident they had ever seen out there on the interstate." He stared at me now as I sat in front of the television, poking my potato salad with a fork. "They never had a chance."

I couldn't get rid of him, or any of these ghosts, including the ones that lingered in my head. Every single dead person living in my hard drives or stacked in file cabinets at the office. I didn't know how long I could keep this up, how long I could extend the charade. But one thing I knew was that I couldn't go home to Grandma until I had taken back more of my life and had better control of my own body. Now was not the time.

I needed sleep. I had scheduled my first work evaluation with Dr. Cassler that week—the evaluation I should have had two months ago—before they'd put me back into circulation. I wasn't sure whether I'd be able to fool her into thinking things were back to normal, but staying up with ghosts all night wouldn't help. I finished my pseudo-dinner and went to bed, so exhausted

I could barely see. I slammed into the mattress, fully dressed, only kicking my shoes into the corner, their tongues still tied down by laces. Grandma had told me never to leave my shoes tied because I would never get enough rest. I needed to shake off this day, this whole scene and all the death; it just weighed down my body and pushed me into dreams.

I closed my eyes.

"Do you remember that accident up on I-40?"

I pulled my pillows over my head and screamed as loud as I could. "Go home, Irvin!" I yelled. "Go home."

"Where is home?" Irvin asked, then a long silence. "It was one of the worst accidents they had ever seen on I-40."

CHAPTER 4 | 13°

"For the one in authority is God's servant for your good.
But if you do wrong, be afraid, for rulers do not bear the
sword for no reason. They are God's servants, agents of
wrath to bring punishment on the wrongdoer."

ROMANS 13:4

WHEN I WAS a boy, I saw the soul of an Indian move into
the sky after my father hit him through his head with an axe.

We lived in a white wood A-frame on a sprawling farm
in Delmont, South Dakota, with a full stable and an equipment building to its south. Our house was surrounded by
alfalfa and cornfields and a tall row of oak trees just beyond
the fence line. We had apple, apricot and pear trees, too,
on the far west section of our five acres. It was just the three
of us at first: me, my father and my mama. My father was
a decent man with shoulders like the ends of a clothesline.
He had deep brown eyes and a pastor's stoic disposition. He
quoted from scripture almost every day as we ate breakfast,
and at night, he'd send me to bed with the worn leather
Bible that his mama had given him—a beautiful thing, with
a bright red ribbon to mark the page. Mama was slight but
strong, with determined eyes and a steel will. I have never
seen another human being with eyes like hers, the color of
the lightest blue skies, surrounded by ocean foam. She doted

on me when Father wasn't around, but when he was, she worked me as hard as he did.

Most days, Father had us up early doing the chores for the farm. We had over twenty chickens, two hogs and five horses, and it was my job to feed them before the sun came up. The chickens laid eggs like clockwork, even in the bitter cold, and I often filled several baskets for Mama to sell at the market each week. It was how she made money, which she'd hide away in an old stocking tied to a pipe under the sink. My mama saved things: dying animals, wounded men, money.

I learned, in long days of labor, to catch moments of stillness whenever I could. I spent hours on our farm, watching the sun trickle through the branches and leaves, shifting between light and shadow. At night, after hours of harvesting alfalfa and corn, and lining the drive with the fresh bales of hay, my shoulders screaming from exhaustion, I would lay myself down on the cool, wooden floor of the house and find silence. I would look to the screen door and turn my face to the chill of the night. On many occasions I fell asleep there before I could manage to get my aching body to bed, and Mama would have to wake me up and bring me to my room.

At a certain point, just before Father left for the war, he brought a man named Wapasha to help us during planting and harvesting seasons. Wapasha was from Yankton, just south of the farm. He was tall and had his hair cropped short, right to the collar of his neck. He sometimes spoke to me in English, his pronunciation polished from the years he spent at St. Paul's Indian Mission School. His clothes were always clean, but his hands were calloused and scarred, the marks planted there by the "hate of a million sisters." Wapasha told me many times that God was never behind the evil of the church. They were wicked all on their own. I wasn't sure, as a child, what he meant by this. But still, after everything he seemed to have endured, he never showed fatigue. He worked harder than anyone I ever knew and still managed to smile at the end of the day. I don't know why he worked for my father. I'm sure we didn't have a lot of money to pay him.

To this day, I still try to remember the man my father was before he left for Vietnam. He didn't drink then and was young and vibrant, his body still intact, uninjured. I recall his approving smile, his scent of dusty oil and Old Spice. It was spring when he left. He went from planting on his seeder wheel straight to the bus for basic training. I remember him giving my mama a kiss on the cheek, and then he was gone. It was 1970, and I was seven years old.

I spent my summer that year working like my father, in his stead. I woke early in the morning and helped Mama with the animals. Wapasha would arrive soon after to help with the watering and weeding. He maintained the corn and alfalfa fields as well as our garden, where Mama grew onions, peppers, potatoes and turnips. It was a difficult season without Father, but together with the help of Wapasha's wife and two brothers, we managed to pull in over two hundred bales of hay, a significant crop of corn and enough vegetables to fill our storage pantry with jars throughout the winter. As we finished our harvest, Wapasha's wife was only a month into her pregnancy and was already rubbing her belly. She was beautiful, with long black hair that she wore in two shiny braids, one on each side of her neck. Looking at her, and how Wapasha would care for her, and looking at Mama too, whose work was tireless, I felt proud of our accomplishments.

Father returned seven months later with hatred in his heart.

He never showed me or Mama, or anyone for that matter, an inch of love from that point on. My mama knew from day one, when we went to the bus depot to pick him up, that something had changed in him. She hugged him, pulling him to her chest. His arms stayed heavy by his side, his left leg dragging. He remained quiet and just stared straight ahead. As we drove home in our old pickup, Father held his rucksack tightly to his chest. I noticed that his hands stayed clenched, his knuckles and fingers were scraped and torn, almost like Wapasha's, and two fingers on his left hand were nothing but nubs of skin.

We got back to the farm and watched Father limp up the stairs in silence. He stayed in his bedroom and slept for two days without moving. We didn't dare make a sound while he rested, tiptoeing around our creaky house while we did our chores. Mama and I stayed in my room, and we said our nightly prayers in a whisper. We prayed for Father. We prayed that we would hear his voice once again. We prayed that he would really find his way back to us.

When Father awoke, so did the demon. It was the first time I ever saw him hit Mama. I remember the cold of the wooden floors on my bare feet as I ran downstairs from my bedroom to find where the clamor was coming from. Eggs and bacon smoked on the stove as my mama, a fresh bruise below her eye, pulled herself off the floor. Her nose dripped blood.

"Get off the floor and turn off that fire. You're burning the food." Father kicked at the chair. "Get the fuck up, you stupid whore." He slapped Mama hard, sending her body flying into the stove. I could hear the sizzling of her hand on the iron surface. He looked down at me, his eyes red with fire as he swung his fist at my head. The thud was unbearable. I fell to the floor and cracked my head against it. Mama flung the hot skillet toward the table, hitting my father in the thigh, and grabbed me by the arm as she ran out of our screen door. We ran and ran, my neck still stinging from Father's blow, until we couldn't hear his voice and the barn was just a speck on the horizon of our country road. Father struggled to run after us, but the injury to his leg prevented him from outpacing us. Our lungs had pushed out every breath by the time Mama slowed to a walk.

"It's another couple of miles, baby." Mama wiped her bloody nose. "We can do it."

We had to drink water out of the creek on the way there, the murky brown liquid gritty and sour. Our bare feet were caked with mud, the dry dirt pulling blood from our skin. The sun made my head spin, the pain piercing when I opened my eyes too far, making me throw up several times along the path. By nightfall, Mama and I had made it all the way to her sister's house in the next town over. We had kept off the road most of the day, making paths through the harvested cornfields and the fence lines of the larger farms and warehouses that were on the outskirts of town. Once we rounded the corner, we saw Father's pickup, the dented '65, sitting in front of Aunt Belle's green farmhouse. Mama and I hid in the bushes across the street for two hours until he finally left, screaming and cursing into the night.

When Belle saw Mama, she began to cry and said she'd put us up in her dead daughter's room. She cleaned Mama and me up with a washcloth dipped in warm water. I wished badly that she could wipe away the incessant, painful ringing in my head. I looked out the window, expecting Father's truck to pull into the drive. Father didn't come back that night, but I felt him deep within me.

I was awoken the next morning to the sound of his truck's rattling engine. I turned to the other bed to wake Mama, but she was already in the kitchen, watching him approach the house. She looked terrified, but met him outside, maybe to protect me. I don't know what they said to each other out there. They never told me. But Father drove us back home. I rode in the back of the truck in silence, loose hay and alfalfa pricking my skin the whole way.

We didn't see Father's demon again for months. He hid from us whenever it came, and Mama asked no questions. As long as he never hurt us, I didn't ask questions either. I just kept my head down and did what I was told. The same was true for Wapasha, and for anyone else who encountered Father. Even the men at the farm store started to fear him. There were rumors about his time in Vietnam, stories of burning flesh and machetes and the horrible things that our soldiers there inflicted on the world. Our small town had four other men who went out to that jungle and never returned. Father had made it home, but in some ways, we knew he hadn't. Not the man we remembered.

The fields were the only place I could find peace. On most days it was only Wapasha and me, as Father sat with his belly to the bar or any place other than the farm. As we worked, Wapasha taught me about the real history of the land before strangers came and stayed for good. When Father would stagger home in a rage, Wapasha would hide me away from him, by the river at the far end of our property, where I couldn't hear his pain, or feel his anger.

"My father came home like that too," Wapasha told me once. "It was a different war but the same hatred. But we are still here. The two of us. For a reason. Do you understand?" I always understood Wapasha. "The world has a place for you, boy."

Just then, I remember, a raven landed in front of us. A dark angel with shiny black wings. I stared at it with childlike awe.

Wapasha, noting my reaction, told me stories about the raven—
its lore, its trickery, its power of shape-shifting.

"There is a legend about a white raven," he said. "A white raven
who could trick the buffalo, lure them away from the hunters.
He'd save entire stampedes from the hunters' weapons. Without
meat, the men became starved, desperate. Until one day, one of
the holy men grabbed the white raven and threw him into the
flames. That is why these birds sit here today with charcoal on
their backs." The raven's eyes looked at us as Wapasha told this
story—and after that, I'd notice ravens accruing in the trees,
carrying on conversations with each other as the sun set and the
night moved in. "They're watching you," Wapasha said to me.
"They watch you, always."

BY THE TIME I was eight years old, I was working most
of my days in the field. I had stopped going to school because
Father had demanded it. He said that they were filling my mind
with evil. My head was full of honey, anyway. After that lick
Father gave me, I would sometimes drift away in my mind,
waking up in the dirt of the fields and unable to remember what
happened, my head an open wound. I learned to live with, to
adapt to, Father's abuse. I developed a blackness of heart and
started absorbing his pain like dry earth. When I saw his violence coming, the darkness would move in and wave its prayers
upon my skin. I learned not to feel it. Not to feel anything.

Mama could never manage to cave to the darkness like I did.
She took his punches like a bag of sand, but later, when I would
see her, she would share a wide smile, her lip bruised, her eyes
swollen. She remained steadfast in her duties, even as Father
accused her of the evilest things—all to justify his rage and his
abuse.

It all came to a head one morning. That awful morning. Wapasha was a few minutes late to help us with tilling the alfalfa fields, the usual work we did before the spring planting. The sun had not yet tipped over the horizon. Wapasha stood with his hat in his hands and explained that his wife was sick, that the new baby was not doing well either, that she had taken a bad turn. Mama took pity, of course, but Father listened to none of it. He just walked to the barn in silence.

I knew what was in the barn. We all did. Father's tools—an entire arsenal. His cutlass blades, hog scrapers, pickaxes, axes, stone grinders, hand tillers, apple pickers, sickle blades and knife reapers. The bolo he brought back from the war. We watched as Father—not Father, but the demon—came out from the barn with his axe in one hand and bolo in the other. His boots stomped in slow motion as he moved toward us in silence.

"Run," Wapasha said. "Run." He stayed there with his feet planted in the soil as I stepped back.

Father hit Wapasha in the side of the head with his axe so hard that the bit and the heel of it got stuck in his skull. Wapasha dropped to the ground, a thud in dust. I went to Wapasha's side as Father ran into the fields with his bolo.

Wapasha's face and body were still moving on the ground, the axe handle pointed upward in the air. His eyes looked into the dawning sky as he sang words to a song I couldn't understand. Eventually his singing turned into a somber gurgling. And then nothing at all. He looked at me with a strange, vacant peace on his face. I thought of his beautiful wife, who had worked in our fields, now alone with their child. The darkness refused to take over; I began to cry. That's when I heard Mama scream, her echo flooding into the pasture.

I ran into the fields after her. Father was gaining on her, his heavy feet creating dust blooms behind him. Mama tripped on one of the rows and fell, her dress billowing in the wind.

"Stop it, Isaac, please," Mama said on her knees. "Why are you doing this?"

"Because it is what God would want!" he screamed.

Father lifted his blade into the air and stabbed it into Mama's shoulder with such force that her body shook and raged against it. Then she fell forward, her face planted in the cornfield. Her body was lifeless and still. Father stood over her in silence. He grabbed the bolo's handle and dislodged it from her shoulder and turned it over and over in his hand with a thump. Then he turned to me. As he approached, I took off toward the sun. My eyes stinging from a well of tears, I left Mama's and Wapasha's bodies in the dirt behind me. The darkness took over again, and I shut out everything. The sounds of Mama pleading, Wapasha's gurgling mouth. It all vanished. I ran.

As I rounded the corner toward the country store, I heard it. The gun shot rang deep into the fields of Delmont, stirring clouds of birds into the sky. The starlings rose and spiraled into the horizon; a raven's wings dug deep into the air. The sound made me stop and turn around, not unbound from the fear, but called back by the force of my mother's love. I ran as hard as I could until I came into the cornfield again and saw Mama lying in the dirt, her face still buried. I turned her body over with my hands until her eyes were fixed to the sky. I couldn't move. I held Mama's hand as her soul ascended toward God. It was the first time in my life that I wished for death. I sat in the rising sunlight and waited for Father to come take me too. He never did.

I walked back to the house quietly, minding the sounds of my shoes against the dirt and then the steps of the porch. Nobody was inside. Moving toward the edge of the porch, I saw Father lying in the dim yellow of dawn near Wapasha's body. The gun had set the demon free. His face lay open, flesh curved like an orchid stained the color of blood.

I heard a cry so loud and so fierce that I thought it may not be a cry at all, but the screaming of birds in the sky, or the animals in the barn warning of trouble. But it was none of those things. That cry was coming from my own throat, louder than the approaching sheriff's siren. Louder than the scalding of earth. The starlings flew overhead, keeping their distance, while kingfishers gathered around the gates of the farm, not daring to come closer. The ravens were unafraid. They began to circle, a perfect dance around me and around the death of us. One swooped down right beside me. It was the day they told me I would one day get my own wings. It was the day that I began to believe them.

CHAPTER 5
1101 CAMINO DE SALUD

Office of the Medical Examiner

Hasselblad 500 C/M • f/8.0, 1/250 sec., ISO 800, EV 11

"SO, YOU COULDN'T stay away," Dr. Blaser said, not bothering to look up as I walked through the doors of his lab. It was early morning, but it was clear to me that he had worked through the night. The smell of old, burnt coffee filled the fluorescent-lit room.

"I guess not," I answered. "Neither could you."

"Duty calls." He looked up from his paperwork and smiled at me through his mask. I could see the skin crinkled at the corners of his eyes.

Mostly out of habit, I started my day here, at OMI. I had spent the last few months on limited duty, helping Dr. Blaser and his deputy medical investigator with autopsy photography, perched above cadavers to record their final form. During that time, I developed a respect for Blaser—he was one of the good ones, someone I could trust.

He turned his head, directing me to the five blue body bags that occupied his exam tables, two already unzipped.

"The Montaños," I said. "Where are the others?"

Dr. Blaser pointed toward the lab at the far end of the OMI hallway. I could see there were three small body bags waiting in the dark.

"I started to do the initial anterior and posterior on the two younger ones here, but my deputy investigator won't be here for a couple of hours to help with the rest."

"I guess it's good I came in so early, then," I said. I grabbed the investigator's camera and the scraped green lab stool from the corner of the room. We were going to be there awhile.

I helped Blaser as he took each of the three remaining bodies out of the bags and removed what was left of their clothes, their jewelry, their shoes. I photographed each clothing item, front and back: every pair of pants, every blood-stained T-shirt and pair of nylon pajamas—all laid out and measured, numbered and documented. Then I went through the clothes and photographed any stray belongings we found in them—wallets, pens, packets of gum, money, lipstick, car keys, keeping the items organized by case number. The older girl had her report card folded in her back pocket, half of it red with blood. There were five A's and one B.

Next, we laid each body out in an anatomical position, arms at their sides, palms up. I photographed them again in this posture, free from their hardened clothes—their fingers and hands, their naked torsos, the areas surrounding their wounds, both anterior and posterior, in portrait and landscape. I looked into Mr. Montaño's lifeless eyes as I took his photo. He didn't look back. His face was a tangle of muscle and bone, his eyes looking in opposite directions. Dr. Blaser helped me tip his heavy frame onto its right side, and as he did, he examined the posterior. "I think we need some photos here." With my camera active, I walked around the table to take a closer look. His blood was pooling in his back, his arms bruised at the biceps and forearm, his knuckles bruised and cut, black speckles along his thumb, forefinger and the back of his hand.

"They definitely know how to throw you back into rotation," Dr. Blaser said, resting Mr. Montaño's body back on the exam table. We kept moving, inspecting and recording each corpse with precision. This brought us well into the late morning. When we finished the initial examination, Dr. Blaser then scraped under their nails, combed through their hair, and reexamined every inch of every victim as I recorded. I would have to do this all over again once the bodies were thoroughly washed.

"What's your take, Rita?" he asked as he returned to his notes. "I'm always curious about your opinion."

"On the record or off?" I said.

"Off the record, Rita," he said, looking up at me and lifting three fingers in the air. "Scout's honor."

"Everyone is convinced that his son did this," I said. "I think the former Detective Montaño did most of it, and the son came in to finish it by killing his father."

Blaser didn't say anything. He was waiting for my story.

"I know you know about me, Dr. Blaser." He never broke eyes with me. "I know you hear what people say."

"Is it true?"

"Yes," I said. "You know me. Why would it not be true?"

"I'm a doctor, Rita," he said. "I believe in science."

"I do too, Dr. Blaser." I pointed toward the small blue body bag that waited for us down the hallway. "And I also believe the little girl in that bag. She told me that her dad was the one who shot them all, including her. She was shot right through the face in the bathroom. It was cold and heartless."

Dr. Blaser filled the room with his silence, his face sullen beneath his mask.

"There is so much more to the story than what is in that report they gave you, Dr. Blaser," I said. "I was there. I saw it. And that is the kid's story. He killed his father, but I'm beginning to think it was self-defense."

"Those are big allegations, Rita. Do you know the ramifications of what you're saying?"

"I do," I said. "Crooked and perverted police officers don't scare me."

"Well, they should, Rita. Let's keep going. There's still so much to do."

He was right. I already had 565 photographs, and there were still three bodies waiting in the other room.

IT WAS NEARLY evening when I drove home. My body smelled of OMI, like the walls and the old carpet and the tables and autopsy tools. We had documented every part of the Montaño family, their final images now filed in yellow and green folders and beginning to move through the justice system. Dr. Blaser had been doing this for years and I had no idea how he'd survived it. Every time I came home from OMI, I had to scrub my skin raw, but I could still smell it—the heavy odor of death. I rubbed Vicks inside my nose, brushed my teeth and doused myself with body spray or perfume or anything I had with me.

As I drove, the light was changing from the harsh white of afternoon into the soft yellow of sunset. Something about the quiet of that moment made me think of Sergeant Seivers and the last words she'd said to me. She told me to get out, to get away from this life that we both lived. She told me to go and take pictures of things that were still alive, the things that could bring light to our memories instead of framing the moments nobody wanted to remember. What was I doing aside from depositing a paycheck and driving myself into madness? I had no friends, no boyfriend and no life, really, outside of work.

When I got to my apartment, I could hear the gentle hum of Mrs. Santillanes's television, the shuffling of Irvin in my hallway, the noises of the street down below. I stared at my mother's Hasselblad sitting in front of my television, only two photographs burned into the negatives inside of it. Almost an entire roll of film left unused. I could hear my mother's voice in my head, her laughter, and her words.

"A true photographer is never without her camera, Rita."

I hadn't picked up a camera for anything other than work in months and I could feel it in my heart. I had lost the passion for something I'd once loved. That thrill of catching fleeting life, of preserving the line and color of memory. It was gone. The job had taken that away from me. At work, I took hundreds of photographs almost every day, and they served a cold purpose: to document, to make sure lies couldn't be told of the dead, that the narrative of truth couldn't be bent. I realized that now, and that was why I stayed. But I knew there must be something more for me than this kind of life. There was once something so intimate about capturing another human being through my camera's lens, so exhilarating about appearing in the reflection of the subject's eye. An unbreakable sense of trust was forged, in that moment, between photographer and subject. But the dead never gave permission. Their eyes had lost their ability to reflect back to you.

The lens of my mother's Hasselblad felt my loneliness in that moment, the pain in my body and mind. My lack of sleep was no doubt playing into my paranoia, but my body raged on, unable to sleep. I could feel the cold in the room, Irvin's shadow standing inside of the kitchen. "Do you remember?" I couldn't bear to hear his story for one second longer. I pulled on my coat and grabbed the Hasselblad, looking to escape my solitude and the voices of all the people who couldn't move into whatever was waiting for them next. As the elevator took me downstairs, I could hear them in the hallways, their feet shuffling on staircases, their cold hands pressing into the doorways. At least outside, there was so much more to distract them, to keep them from noticing me and what I could see.

I drove up to the west side of Albuquerque and waited alongside the river for the light to change. The first chapters of winter had unfolded in Albuquerque, lining the river with dying cottonwood trees, a gentle frosting on their leaves. A storm was approaching on the other side of the Sandias. The mountains were capped with snow the color of ripe watermelon flesh. I perched the camera on my tripod and looked through the viewfinder, spinning the silver lens until I had my focus. In the silence, I pressed the shutter, holding it open for a few seconds as I watched the clouds move.

I had loaded Mom's camera with 120 film, so I knew I had only twelve chances to capture something meaningful. I took a few shots of the landscape, which in this place never ceased to inspire and deliver, then drove deeper into the city. The driving kept me awake and away from the eyes of this world and the next. I parked by the university and walked through its streets with my camera around my neck. It felt good to take pictures again, to wait and listen for the perfect moment to press the button. I found a few reasons to lift my lens: old neon signs flickering, restaurants billowing steam into the streets, Central Avenue filled with cruisers, their low riders, hopping and shining into the beginning of evening. I spotted an old woman with a bag of laundry heaved up over her shoulder. Her legs bowed under her, her hands raw and red from the wet and cold. I took her photo as she stood below the white neon of University Laundry. Her eyes met the lens at the exact moment I pressed the shutter button, her soul framed perfectly in my six-by-six box. She smiled at me, and I helped carry her laundry to her scraped and tattered car a half a block away.

I stood in the median in Nob Hill and looked down the long path of Route 66, the dim lights on each side of the highway framing the adobe buildings and rows of sycamores. The streets were bathed in the gold shadows of sunset, their closing beams rolling through the alleys. I held on to the shutter again as lights turned and people walked through my frame, their bodies trailing with light. It nearly fooled me.

It didn't take long to notice that ghosts were walking among people downtown, the trailing entities not translating to the viewfinder. One woman sitting on a bus bench looked straight at me, her face obscured by the dark hood of her winter coat. I kept my eye on my viewfinder hoping that she was real, that her black form would muddle the photograph but not the force field that was my camera frame. "That is where I sit," the woman said, matter-of-fact. My heart raced. I closed my eyes and pulled my camera into my coat. I refused to engage. I just needed a moment for myself, a few minutes to catch my breath in the sometimes-unbearable space between the now and the later. I turned the camera on myself and pressed the shutter button. The woman disappeared.

As I put the Hasselblad back around my neck, I thought back to a morning, years ago, when Grandma took my photograph up in the mountains, and my grandfather's ghost light came into the camera frame. Back then I never feared life or death or thought about such things. I yearned for those days again—for the safety of home, for the protective walls of Grandma's house. Out here, I felt exposed.

The rush of fear had made my body tired. I walked back to my car in the dark, listening to the distant trains arriving downtown, the buses hissing and clanging up Central Avenue. At almost ten o'clock, the streets were alive with cold and despair, some people still looking for a place to sleep between the buildings and trees. I was lucky I had a place to go.

I sat in the driver's seat, the heat on full blast. I caught my breath, hoping the ghost woman hadn't followed. For a moment, I sat in silence. What had become of me? The pain, the loneliness—it was something I had never experienced before. I had grown cold, my body shutting itself down to the emotions surrounding this job. It had always been okay to spend a moment in that sadness, back when Sergeant Seivers was there to lend a sympathetic ear or at least give some reverence to the moments we had been thrown into. But I hadn't been the same since the day my body decided to return to this world. It was like I was suspended between anguish and apathy, in pain but unable to shed a tear. I could feel grief building inside me like a blocked artery, the plaque and blood and bone leaving me with only pockets of air or drops of blood to keep me alive.

I couldn't explain to myself why I continued to stay here, to fill myself with sorrow and anguish every time I filled my camera frame. No one in the department wanted me there. I was a snitch as far as they were concerned. This Montaño case was going to cement that fact for them, I just knew it. Cops protect their own. They were going to find a way to cover for Steve Montaño the same way they covered for Garcia. I thought of all the kids in that house, their last moments of terror. No measure for what they had endured during their short lives. My report wasn't even finished, and I knew what was coming.

My reentry evaluation with Dr. Cassler was tomorrow, at long last. I didn't know whether to show the panic and fear on my face, or to hide it. To be honest with her, or try to pretend like things were normal. I didn't know if I could bear this place anymore. I knew the girl with gunpowder breath would haunt me for the rest of my days if I didn't figure out what happened, but my need to get them justice was beginning to play second fiddle to my need to survive. I felt like I had one foot still in the grave, my quick trip there last year leaving a footprint trail right back to it. There was nothing left keeping me here but death, and now death was depending on me. But it might be time to leave it all behind.

I arrived home in the dark and willed myself into my space. I put my mother's camera back in its place in front of the television. I eased my brace off, feeling the release of tension in my leg muscles, then popped a few pain pills. Irvin was sitting on my windowsill, looking out onto the streets below, but saying nothing. I slid into easy, restful sleep.

CHAPTER 6 | -8°

"Yet what we suffer now is nothing compared to
the glory he will reveal to us later."

ROMANS 8:18

A MEMORY OCCURS to me now, the horrific story of the
end of my family. It was a winter as unrelenting as this one, five
or six years ago. I had just finished a shift at the Sacred Heart
outreach center, which we'd just opened in Gallup, and I was on a
drive to clear my mind. During these winter nights, I often travel
the streets in silence, watching the beautiful contrast of snow and
darkness, the streets reflecting an amber glow from the lamps
overhead, death hiding in the shadows. The train forever bellows
from the middle of town, the metallic screech in my ears a constant drone. On that night, the night I'm telling you about now, I
left the outreach van on the side of the highway and stood in the
street to listen, as if God had guided me right there, as if the sound
of the train was a sign the brothers had sent me from the *morada*.

I saw a man standing there, right in the middle of Route 66.
It was like he was waiting for someone. He was singing a song
in Navajo as he looked up into the sky, a constant stream of
white ice and gray night. One lonely car maneuvered around
him, the snow beneath the tires forcing an uneasy swerve back

and forth. I waited until the car passed, then walked over and stood in front of him.

"Are you okay?"

"Do you see them up there? Look!" He pointed up into the sky and resumed singing. I could see them. The ravens called, and the swallows dipped and swerved in the sky. It was something only the two of us could see.

"What is that you're singing?" I asked, thumbing the needle in my pocket.

"It's a blessing song." He looked straight at me for the first time. "They are here for me, and I have been waiting. They've called for me in battle. Like in the old days, before my mind and body became the dirt and the street."

"Are you ready?"

"I'm ready."

No one saw us as we walked into the dark edge of the trading post. I pushed the needle into the meatiest section of his leg and watched him slowly go to sleep.

"Thank you," he said.

Thinking of this man drifting into death brings me back, full circle, to the day my soul left this world—when I found myself alone on the farm as Mama, Father and Wapasha bled into our land, our soil. Mama's eyes were the color of the sky, her skin white and veiny. I talked to her as I watched the birds circle us. It was their way of honoring my mother, of welcoming her soul into the sky. Wapasha's too, whose soul would be lifted from this evil purgatory we call life, but whose next world was something I would never know or understand. I looked at the ravens marching in circles on the ground and the starlings, hundreds of starlings, swooping and speaking in agreement, lifting their souls out of the dirt that swallowed our hopes and dreams. The one soul they would never take still lay stiff in front of the house, nothing left of him but rotten flesh.

I had been jostled back to life by the arrival of the policemen, who had come to examine the carnage. They pulled me away from my mother's body, and though I tried to keep her with me, I was too small to fight. I watched my life stripped from me, the corners of my mouth red and open from screaming. The men dragged me past my dead father, his mind gone and his flesh dead, the crows and the vultures ready to pull his evil into their beaks, into the caverns of heat and fire. Even as I mourned my separation from Mama and Wapasha, I hoped I would never see that house again except in my memories and dreams.

I stayed at Aunt Belle's house for four days. She spent her mornings making the biggest breakfasts I had ever seen, eggs and ham and gravy. She would let her plate get cold as she watched me eat from her perch at the windowsill, her hand circled by smoke from her cigarette. At night, we watched television and ate dinner out of silver trays, meat and vegetables neatly separated, covered in sauces and accompanied by hardened cake. We went to the funeral home on the third day. Aunt Belle came back from the office, her face flooded. There wasn't going to be a funeral. There was no way Aunt Belle could afford it.

Her husband, back from his job working on the railroad, demanded that she get rid of me. Mama never liked the man. She'd told me that he used to drink just as much as Father, then beat my aunt into sleep. He'd beat her so badly that she would never have babies. I think she was hoping that I would be the baby she never had, someone to replace that void in her and offer her new hope. She was so kind to me, those four days. She didn't want me to end up in the dirt like Mama and Wapasha. She wanted me to live.

My auntie dropped me off at the orphanage as the snow began to turn the plains into white sheets of nothing. As we approached, I could see the towers of St. Joseph's grow larger and larger, until the small black silhouette turned into a massive church, flanked by two large three-story buildings. The one on the right would be the place I called home for the next ten years. My aunt walked with me as the sisters brought me, and my bag of what was left of my life, into the dormitory. There were ten small beds lined up on each side of the stone walls, all with white rounded headboards and the same dark gray blankets pulled tightly over each mattress. A nun named Sister Jean led us through the dorms as the rocks in the soles of my boots scratched the brick floors.

Aunt Belle kneeled in front of me and hugged me, shaking with grief.

"Be good for Sister Jean and everyone here. They will take good care of you." She cried like she had no breath left in her lungs. As I watched her walk away, I finally let myself cry too. I knew that if I cried in front of her, she would always remember it. Sister Jean put a hand on my shoulder, but I broke away and ran down the hall to the front window. I watched Aunt Belle's car recede into the horizon until I couldn't see any trace of her—until all that was left of her were tire tracks in the snow.

Sister Jean's demeanor changed once my aunt was out of range. It was almost instantaneous. Her eyes narrowed and her brows pulled down into the center of her face. "It's time for you to settle in, boy." She grabbed my arm and led me back to the dormitory. She was tall and thin, her skin a pale covering over her bones. Her fingers dug into my flesh.

Other boys had shuffled into the dorm by then and taken their places in that cold room, which fell silent as Sister Jean pulled me through the door.

"Boys. We have someone new in our midst. Do try and welcome him here, will you?" She pointed to the last bed in the corner, the one nearest the door. "That there is your new home." Sister Jean turned and left.

As the door creaked closed behind her, all of us let out a collective sigh of relief.

"She put you in the bed," said the boy standing by the bed next to mine. "Father Saren will visit you."

I curled up in the bed, my bag the only thing to embrace. I thought of Mama and Wapasha and cried myself to sleep. In my dream, I remembered something Wapasha told me, only days before Father sent him to God. Even in the dream, I was angry with my father, tired of his hatred, a persistent ringing in my ears. I wanted him to die.

"We all live on the edges of death," Wapasha explained. "You can only honor your father with the memories of his goodness. We're all good, until something in this world hurts us. You will need to work hard to honor him, his goodness, your mother's love." He smiled at me and lifted me onto the porch. "You're my son now," he said, then walked off into the fields alone, his feet picked up by the light.

CHAPTER 7
1025 MEDICAL ARTS AVENUE, BUILDING EIGHT

Behavioral Sciences Department—Dr. Cassler's Office

2 Megapixel IP Camera / IQInvision

THE WALLS OF Dr. Cassler's new waiting room were painted a bright blue, with blinding white baseboards. It was trying to be a livelier version of its former self, with the department surveillance cameras in the corners of the room turning every nineteen seconds. There were actual living plants on the tables, which were covered in glass, a step up from the aged Formica in her last office. Old copies of *People* and *Psychology Today* lay fanned out on them. A short woman was quietly sitting in the corner, staring out of the large windows that took up the whole north wall, I-25 shimmering in the view.

Dr. Cassler's receptionist remained the same, and I wondered if the wad of gum in her mouth hadn't changed either since the last time I saw her. I could hear her pop it between her teeth, counting the seconds before another bubble rose to burst. The telephone rang, and the receptionist answered.

"Dr. Cassler will see you now," she said passively. Her lacquered nails tapped on the keyboard. The other woman in the lobby never released her gaze from the highway outside. I wondered if she was a ghost.

Dr. Cassler's office smelled like canned cinnamon and burnt coffee. She stood by her filing cabinet, pulling a few files from her drawers. She had grown her hair since the last time I had seen her and the suit she wore seemed a little more tailored, clipped at the cuffs and the hips, giving her a refined, almost confrontational look. It suited her.

"Hello, Rita." She put what I assumed to be my file on the desk in front of her. "Thank you for coming in to see me. I know we were scheduled to have this meeting a couple of months ago and I apologize for the delay."

"It's fine. I wasn't in a real hurry," I said. There were two chairs behind her desk. Dr. Cassler was in one, and there was a woman in the other behind her.

"So, how have the last two months been treating you?" Dr. Cassler sat down and began to scribble in her notebook. I already felt pages of notes being added to my file. "I hear you were on the scene down in Los Ranchos yesterday. That must have been tough, even for someone like you, Rita."

"Encountering that much death in one place can be a little overwhelming." I stared at the chair behind Dr. Cassler. The woman scratched at her wrists, at two deep lines etched down the center of each arm. I forced my attention back at Dr. Cassler. "It was a change from working at OMI. Lots of death, but a sense of finality in that place."

"What do you mean?"

"Death surrenders at OMI," I explained. "Nothing is ever settled when you're still on the scene."

There was a long silence. The woman continued to scratch her arms.

"Do you feel like it might be too early for you to return to duty?" She met my eyes and I looked away. "Physically? Emotionally?"

"I don't know," I admitted. "Physically, I will never be the same." I felt my leg, a dull pulse. "I don't seem to be affected otherwise. It's always been the same. It will always be the same."

"And the hallucinations?"

"I don't have hallucinations, Dr. Cassler."

"I'm sorry." She looked at another pad of paper on her desk. "Your visions."

I waited for the scratch of Dr. Cassler's pen to stop its digging into her brittle paper pad.

"I see death, Dr. Cassler," I said. "It hasn't grabbed hold of me yet, so I guess my only choice is to keep going."

Dr. Cassler put down her pen. "This type of work seems to disturb you, Rita. It puzzles me that you would actively want to jump back into duty so quickly. Maybe you would be better suited at a lab, like OMI. You could do great things there."

Dr. Cassler was right. My body fought to find peace, and I was resisting it at every turn.

"I have obligations here," I said.

"You mean at work?"

"At work. At home."

"Maybe some time back at home would be a welcome reprieve for you, mentally and physically," Dr. Cassler said. I could feel her trying to find my gaze. I avoided eye contact. "Do you have any friends that you can confide in or spend some time with away from work?"

"My friend Shanice just moved away a few weeks ago for a job. So, it's been quiet at my apartment. It's nothing. I'm used to silence."

Dr. Cassler started writing again.

"Any relationships that you're in or any thoughts on a family life?"

Her question startled me. It was something she had never asked before.

"I thought I might have a relationship, but it didn't work out," I explained. I thought of the day Chris had come to find me in the hospital and the days that followed. It was the closest thing I had in my life to a glimmer of love. After two weeks of visits, he got a job three states away. It was always a nice thought. But I'm sure Grandma wouldn't have approved after the way she met him. "The guy moved away. Simple as that," I said.

"After hearing about everything that happened, I have to say that I'm surprised you haven't just moved back home," she said. "Your . . . visions concern me, Rita. I think it's all connected to what you've gone through. It's okay to admit that you might need help."

"My neighbor also needs me." I pulled at a hangnail on my thumb until I could feel it begin to sting. "I have cases to finish. Things I've started that need to be resolved." I stared at the woman behind Dr. Cassler. Her eyes were fixated on the back of Dr. Cassler's head; her arms were red from ceaseless scratching.

"Are you close?"

"Yes. I think she saved my life a couple of times."

"What is her name?"

"Mrs. Santillanes."

Dr. Cassler wrote that down. "How did you meet? Well, aside from being neighbors."

"She's watched out for me since the day I moved into my apartment."

The woman with the scarred arms stood up. Her blood-stained

hands gripped the leather headrest of Dr. Cassler's chair. I couldn't help but watch.

"Rita." Dr. Cassler pulled my gaze from the woman. "You need to heal—from not only the physical trauma of your incident, but also the emotional and spiritual trauma that you continue to experience." I sat silently, looking at the floor, unwilling to share a glance or to acknowledge the smell of blood that was beginning to fill the room. There was nothing that Dr. Cassler was going to say to change my mind. "I don't know that I can clear you. I think you need to give yourself a few weeks before fully returning to duty. The work, it could trigger the issues with these visions you have."

"There is only one thing that hurts me now, Dr. Cassler," I said. She seemed surprised to hear me say this. "It's not the visions. It's the voices."

"Your visions are . . . speaking to you?"

I struggled to find the words. "Doctor, do you know how it feels when you have to look over your shoulder at work? If I was in danger, or out on a questionable case, do you really think that the officers I work with would go out of their way to make sure I was safe?"

"Well, I've heard that Dr. Blaser has found you to be a great help over at the OMI and that the new field investigator"—she paused—"Specialist Giovanni, has put in glowing work reports about you ever since you've been in the lab. I'm finding it hard to see where your worries are confirmed here. Have you had any kind of retaliation or threats made against you since you have returned?"

"No. But I feel it. I see the way they look at me. I can hear them whisper. I see their faces."

She stared at me, quiet taking over the room. I could tell she was still thinking about my *visions*, as she called them. I knew that the word "ghost" was scribbled all over her notepad.

"Why don't you just ask me?" I said.

"What do you want me to ask you?"

"I know you want to ask me if I'm still seeing ghosts. Isn't this what all of this is about?" I looked up at her camera turning in the corner. "Don't you all want to prove that I'm crazy? I have no idea what that is going to prove but if you need some kind of validation, that is not what I'm here for."

"Rita. I'm not going to lie to you. After the Garcia incident, some officers have stated that you are"—she opened another file on her desk and read the words as they appeared—"quote, 'Depending on her paranormal issues to introduce evidence into cases.'"

"That is what they're saying?" I sat back and did my best to hold back a chuckle. "Well, they can say what they want, but evidence speaks for itself."

"Have you been using your abilities to solve cases, Rita?"

There was a long silence. I didn't know what to say to her.

"I'm pretty sure that you have some kind of ability. I don't believe in it myself, but I think there is something about you that gives you a real sense of, I don't know, intuition." Dr. Cassler tossed the files back on her desk. "I just want to know if it's real. I want to know if *you* believe it's real." I looked at the woman behind Dr. Cassler's chair. She was still standing there, the wounds on her arms now angry red flesh.

"Did one of your patients die in this room, Dr. Cassler?"

The ghost let out a faint cry. Her shoulders shuddered slowly. Blood dripped from her arms and pooled on the floor.

"What?"

"Did you have a patient die in your office, Dr. Cassler?" I

stared at the woman, her cries becoming louder and gritty with anger. "A woman?"

"How do you know about that?"

"She must have slit her wrists. I can see her pulling at her wounds."

The woman was now wailing. I closed my eyes, unable to bear the sounds of it. My skin felt cold, and my nose began to drip blood.

Dr. Cassler stood up from her desk in stunned silence. Her eyes were wide open, anxious. She handed me a few tissues.

"Thank you," I said, wiping the blood from my nose and lips. When I looked up again, the woman was gone. "Does that mean I can get back to work?"

My phone began to ring.

CHAPTER 8 | 5°

"Lord, give me chastity and self-control—but not yet."
PRAYER OF THE YOUNG SAINT AUGUSTINE, C.380 A.D.

SAINT JOSEPH'S ORPHANAGE was a cold and miserable place. Our childhoods came to die here, to burn in the furnaces of the basement. We were there because our parents were dead or because they didn't want us, and it was instilled in us that we should feel lucky for what we had, that we were not living out on the streets. They provided us with a roof and enough food to keep us alive—porridge, goat milk cheese and bread. On occasion, they brought us meat, but it was never enough. Most of us walked that land with our bodies eaten by hunger, our ribs a xylophone of flesh. We were meant to be grateful for this.

There were only five nuns and one priest—Father Saren, who ruled the campus with an iron fist. There was not one kind word among them. I wondered how God could dispatch these wicked souls to watch over the twenty children that had no place but here to call home. Father Saren was stout and fat with long white hair that jutted out from the sides of his head. He wore a long black cloak with a large wooden cross around his neck.

When his feet poked out from the bottom of the cloak, we all could see that he only had six toes, five on one side and one on the other—right in the center. The sisters, in their long black cloaks with white collars and habits, never spoke to Father Saren, saving their sharp and heavy words to spring on us before they handed out slaps.

The boys were right about the bed. Father Saren tried to visit me for days after I arrived. I fought him, the first night kicking him in the face so hard that his jaw became swollen and blue. He tried again and again, and each time, I hurt him. Each time, my punishment was worse: working with no water or food, taking lashes with the horse bridals and hand paddles to the palms, spending hours holding Bibles above my shoulders. They were designed to break me, but I never broke. A lifetime of torture would only have made me stronger, and Father Saren's desire to take advantage of me slowly began to die. Even after the visits ceased, I stashed a small, folding harvesting scythe under my mattress, in case he ever came to my bed again.

The threat of Father Saren was replaced by a harrowing, unending winter. Months of snow and ice, relentless winds that pierced the drafty schoolhouse at the center of campus. We nearly froze to death. Winter was the only season we spent in the classroom, studying the Bible and the words of our saints. We learned entire passages by heart, because Father Saren said it was the only thing we ever needed to know. There was no time for math, or for books that would taint our hearts with dreams of the world outside the orphanage. We were there to work and to earn our keep. Father Saren saw the strength in my hands and the oak of my back; he had not forgotten how I'd refused his advances. After Bible study every night, I was sent down to the basement and spent two hours pushing coal into the furnaces and chopping wood for the classrooms, cafeterias and the adjacent convent.

In the spring and summer, we worked on the farmland owned by the diocese, ten acres of every vegetable known to grow. We woke at four every morning, our rakes and shovels in hand, and walked to the fields. When fall came, we harvested for three weeks, stacking all the vegetables in neat and tidy rows, just like the nuns taught us. We weren't allowed to speak to each other while we worked, but sometimes deep in the fields where they couldn't hear our voices, we would talk. We learned each other's hometowns and histories, and dreamed of the days ahead when we would be set free.

In secret I hoped that I would wither and die from overwork, but my body rejected that wish. Instead, I became stronger and stronger, until my heart had hardened right alongside my muscles. Years passed, and my young body turned to stone. I spent my days tilling the fields until I could barely stand, my nights in the basement working until my hands bled. I learned every word of the Bible and repeated the scriptures in my head while I nursed my own insecurities. By the time I was twelve, I had four years of God and hard labor carved into my history. The tenderness of Mama's love, of Wapasha's sacrifice, was by then a distant memory; I was beginning to look more like Father.

In those four years, the orphanage had taken in ten more unwanted children, a collection of boys ranging in age from seven to fifteen. They came, as we all did, with various degrees of neglect and trauma. We older ones tried our best to shelter the younger ones from the overwork and abuse. Father Saren and the sisters kept their grip on us, though, and any complaints or cries were met with a cedar paddle that the sisters had us fashion for their work.

One of the youngest boys at St. Joseph's was named Cleveland.
He was a gentle soul who would make us laugh as we labored in
the fields. He told us about baseball games and television, about
music that we weren't allowed to listen to, about presidents we'd
never heard of. He made us realize just how much of the world
we were missing. St. Joseph's was a place where time stood still,
that gave us no need to look toward a future.

Even though Cleve was a few years younger than me, I felt
a strange connection to him. He was like the brother that my
mother was never allowed to birth. We looked similar and
both came from farming families. We shared stories about
our upbringings as we harvested. I told him about Wapasha,
how he'd come to our farm when I was young and passed
on his knowledge of the land. I told him about Father, and
what he'd done. I told him about the ravens, too, and what
Wapasha had once said about them as they gathered near
us: "I think they know that you are special. They only gather
around those who are worthy of their knowledge. Don't dis-
appoint them."

As I told him this story, Cleve's eyes widened. He always listened intently, and he seemed to understand what I was saying.
I assured him that the ravens had so much more in store for the
two of us—that we were special. I gave him the raven feather I
kept in my Bible. I'd found it my first week at St. Joseph's. Cleve
trusted me wholly after that. He followed me everywhere and
stood close to me when his fear stirred.

At night I would lie in bed and dream of my escape from St.
Joseph's. I plotted my journey across the miles of fields around
the perimeter of the school. I imagined taking Cleve with me, of
finding somewhere safe for the both of us. I couldn't wait until
I was eighteen. It seemed like an eternity to me. The other boys,

they slept their futures away after long hours of labor. I wanted mine back.

But six months after Cleve came to be with us, he began to be swallowed by the suffering of this place. A malevolent spirit seemed to have ripped his tongue away from him. He turned to silence. We begged him to tell us more stories, to sing us songs he'd heard on the radio, to teach us all the newest dances, but he began to move sullenly, refusing our requests. I knew something was happening to Cleve. It wasn't just the cloistered existence that was getting to him. His light shone too bright for that.

One day I saw the bruises. I begged him to tell me where they came from, but he only cried, deep and fearful tears, pulling away from me when I tried to get a closer look.

At night I stayed awake, staring at the blackness of the ceiling, waiting to see how the darkness affected Cleve, until I finally understood something I should've already known. Early in the morning, long before the sun rose, I heard the sounds of creaking wood and footsteps in the dormitory. I watched as Father Saren's silhouette guided Cleve into the rectory next door, his hand over his mouth, tugging his small arms to keep him moving.

I put on my boots and pulled the harvesting scythe out from under the mattress. I followed them in silence, quietly closing the door to the dormitory so as not to wake the rest of the orphans from their sleep. Behind the door to Father Saren's rectory, I could already hear Cleve crying, his lungs fighting his fear. I looked through the small window and saw Father Saren, his robe pushed open, forcing Cleve into the cloth.

It only took seconds for me to make my way inside. I forced the old priest to his feet, knocking Cleve into the ground.

"Get out, Cleve," I yelled. Father Saren stared at me vacantly as Cleve pulled himself to his feet and ran, his cheeks stained with tears. The priest was weak and old, his skin the texture of dry corn husks. It was easy to walk up to the old man. He backed away, feeling the heat of my rage, my thirteen years raw and unloved. He tried to make for the door behind us, but his frail body was no match for my call for revenge—for what he'd done to Cleve, and whoever else had fallen victim to his evil. He was lucky that he had not had his way with me as a boy, or his death would have arrived even sooner.

I grabbed Father Saren by his robe and pulled his slender neck into the crook of my arm. He tried his best to free himself from my grasp, but my hatred pulled him closer. He screamed to his brood of heartless sisters for help. I put my hand over his thin lips and drew the scythe across his neck, feeling the warmth of his blood pour down my arms. I let his limp body go, his face hitting the hard brick of the floor. His blood gave penance to the earth he'd made us toil. His evil soul was released into the darkness. There would be no angel wings for that man. I left him to rot in his rectory.

Then I went to the pond that sat alongside the fields and washed the blood from my face and my body. I threw the bloody scythe in and watched it sink to the bottom. I stepped in after it and I dipped my head under. The water wrapped around my body and filled my lungs. I was ready to die, to end myself just as my father had. The ravens wouldn't allow it. They swept down from the sky and stood watch around the pond's perimeter. They reminded me to come up for air, but I fought against their attempt at salvation. I wanted to drown.

Heaven felt like my mother's embrace. I could hear her voice just beyond the horizon, beckoning me to come with her. The sweet smell of her skin, the bright light of summer sun. She grabbed my hand and took me running above the soil of our farm. Laughing, dancing circles around me, even as rain began to fall. I wanted to stay, to melt into those warm memories and let my earth body sink into the pond.

But on the weathered posts of our farmland, the birds gathered still. The brightness of those moments fell to the gathering of clouds as the rain continued to fall. Mama faded into the fog and mist. My body became cold and heavy. Two tall and bright angels, their skin a blur of glitter and blood, pulled me from my memory and dragged me with gentle arms to the pond's edge, where a flock of ravens cawed and stammered. I thought they might've been there to peck out what was left of my soul.

Instead, the ravens told me a story.

I kneeled there, at the altar of God, and listened.

God had chosen me to hide in the shadows to see the evil and the goodness of men, they said. To bring them to death or to usher them to life. The world was rife with those who needed their souls guided, straight to hell or to salvation, and God had seen fit to make me their guide.

My throat burned from death, the water still dripping from my body. It was then that the angels stabbed black raven wings into my back and sewed them into my skin with golden needles.

The ravens watched me in the dark, their wings clapping in the night. The priest was dead.

I could taste years of blood on my tongue. It was a taste that I would get used to.

CHAPTER 9
GALLUP — NIGHT

Sony Alpha 100 35mm • f/3.5, 1/500 sec., ISO 400

IT WAS HARD to leave Dr. Cassler in midsentence to answer a call from Samuels, but I felt no need to explain myself further. She was trying her best to figure out how to recommend me right out of a job. It made me wonder how deep it all went, if somehow even Dr. Cassler was in on a joke that I was missing. But she had her own problems. That ghost was probably going to be with her forever, and I wasn't in the mood to get involved.

"Rita, they're gonna call you down to OMI to go with Giovanni for a DB in Gallup," Samuels told me. "They have their first real homicide of the year and no staff to process it." On the other end of the line, he pushed some food into his mouth and sucked in his cheeks. I could hear all of it. I hung up.

Silver Stallion Bar, West Route 66, Gallup, New Mexico

It took just under two hours for me and Giovanni to streak our way to Gallup in the crime van. The sides of I-40 were wet with slush, but it hardly slowed us down. Giovanni sat in the passenger seat with his head slumped to his chest the whole way there, his reading glasses clasping the end of his nose. I knew when he asked me to drive there was a nap in his future.

I was used to the drive from Albuquerque to Gallup. It was the same route I took to get home. I hated to be so close to Grandma, and to Tohatchi, without paying her a visit. But who knows how long we would be in Gallup. Evening was making its descent.

For a place that didn't have a full-time coroner, Gallup was having an influx of violent crime, and was short on investigators and detectives, their resources and personnel increasingly drained. There was plenty of death, most of which would never be investigated. In Gallup, there was a genuine famine of empathy and a lifetime of greed to guide it. The streets were deadly for our relatives. If they didn't meet their ends in Gallup, they could punch their ticket in any of the surrounding desolate communities on the reservation.

As we pulled into town, I could see the band of neon lights to the south of I-40, the last artery of Route 66. The Silver Stallion was on the east side of town, only a few minutes from the first exit. It was a shabby-looking bar made from red bricks and tacky wood tiki paneling, a jail with neon beer signs in the windows. The Gallup police had the bar taped off, cutting off traffic from the main road. The still half-packed parking lot was to the west with dumpsters lining the back gates. They waved us into the parking lot just as Giovanni snorted back into reality, wiping the sides of his face.

"Sorry, I must have dozed off."

A man approached us on our right as Giovanni rolled down the window.

"Are you all from Albuquerque?" The man looked like he was twelve, his smooth face like a child's. He wore khaki pants and a coat that was too thin for this kind of cold.

"Yes," I said. "We're from OMI. I'm here to help the investigator."

"I'm the new deputy field investigator for McKinley County. Deputy Taylor." He extended his hand to Giovanni and sent me a wave. "You can park anywhere over here. The vic is over by the trash bins and I estimate that he's been dead for over twelve hours."

"Do we know it's a homicide?" Giovanni rubbed his hands together.

"Yes." The deputy pulled his hat off and scratched his head. "His throat is cut. Nearly clean off too. I have doubts that he did it to himself."

We pulled the van up and gathered our gear, stuffing ourselves into our coats. I pulled my fingerless gloves out of my camera bag as we approached. I got right to work as Giovanni interviewed other officers on the scene and a woman not in uniform who was standing with them.

The victim was between two blue trash bins in the alley behind the bar. Two tattered, fire-stained barrels sat off to the right. The ground was covered in dirty ice, leftovers from the snow Gallup had endured yesterday and the day before. I worked my way to the body, which was twisted into the cold itself, arms splayed in awkward positions, legs crossed at the ankles. Photos twenty-five through thirty-six framed the man as he lay there between the dumpsters, absorbed in a pool of frozen blood and snow. His body had been frozen into the ground, his clothes clasping the frost with a solid seam of ice. His limbs were stiff, either from rigor mortis or the temperature. Photos thirty-seven through fifty framed the man's hands, curled up like claws in front of him, the skin wrinkled and damp but frozen.

His head was dangling from his neck, leaning heavy on one

side, the wide strap of sternocleidomastoid muscle from his neck peering out like a bulging river. The snow around the body was stained red, but any potential footprints had been buried under last night's six inches of heavy, wet snowfall. There were now about four or five sets of footprints in the snow surrounding the scene. The usual—nosy witnesses and early police arrivals, obscuring any evidence that might have been left behind. That took me to photo sixty.

"So, the woman who found him opened the bar this afternoon." Giovanni was standing beside me as I continued taking photos. "She closed last night, too, and that was the last time she saw him. She says she figured he went home. Nothing out of the ordinary. But that means that our vic had all night to freeze solid."

Photos sixty-one through seventy covered the rest of his torso. His shirt and jacket were saturated with blood, the dark liquid hardening his front and sleeves. His shoulders were turned into the ground, forcing his head and face into the frozen asphalt. It was going to be difficult to identify him without turning him over, even if we were pretty sure that this was Mr. Emmitt Gurley, the former mayor of Gallup and the owner of the Silver Stallion, according to all the local law enforcement on scene and his traumatized bartender. One of the detectives from Gallup had been filling in the blanks for us when we needed them. I had forgotten what small-town life was like, where everyone knew one another's business. When I zoomed in, I could see that his hair and beard were just as thick with blood as the rest of him, his whole upper body turning into a black-and-purple scab. He had lost a lot of blood.

Giovanni and the field investigator prepped the gurney and the body bag for transport, then waited until I had captured everything. When they saw that I was finished, they approached.

"Detective Arviso, I'd like you to meet Rita Todacheene with the crime lab in Albuquerque."

I reached out and we shook hands. Her grip was loose and unassuming, which surprised me. I had almost gotten used to the tough pull and push of the city handshake.

"Nice to meet you," I said.

Detective Arviso looked perfectly pressed, even out here in the unrelenting cold. She had high cheekbones and a perfect tsiiyéél tucked beneath her hat. Her eyes were steady and deep, her face beautiful but stern.

"It's good to see someone from home at the detective level here in Gallup."

"There're only two of us detectives, you know." She blew into her cupped hands. "We don't get the kind of action you all get in Albuquerque."

"Are we ready to see what's on the other side, deputy?" Giovanni motioned to the field investigator as he dropped the flat gurney in front of the dumpsters. Deputy Taylor and Giovanni pulled hard to extract the victim from the frozen ground. The rip and crack of his frozen clothes echoed back off the bricks and concrete in the alley. When they finally turned him over, we could see the deluge of frozen blood coming from the cut of his neck. I zoomed in on the wound and its placement on the body. His face was darkened and purple, lined with blood streams that ran into the creases of his neck.

"Wow. You don't see something like that every day." Giovanni shook his head.

"Thank God." Deputy Taylor covered his face with a gloved hand.

When Deputy Taylor and Giovanni pulled Mr. Gurley from the ice, he had been dead for hours. But the cold preserved him well, not allowing for the smell of decay. His eyes were pulled open by the thick stickiness of his bloody eyelids and brows, the pupils staring up into the sky. We had 289 images for his scene. Detective Arviso scribbled into her report as she walked the perimeter, and snow began to fall again. I stopped and looked at my watch. 4:23 P.M. As Giovanni and Taylor lifted the man into his death sleeve on the gurney, his ghost appeared right next to it, his eyes meeting mine.

My skin tingled just as a bitter, strong smell of decay began to squeeze my throat. His teeth were bloody, his gums turning black with death. His stench wafted closer to me; his breath heavy with iron.

"You can see me, can't you?" His voice was a weak, gurgled hiss. His face was only inches from mine now.

"Are you okay, Ms. Todacheene?" Detective Arviso grabbed my arm.

"Talk to me, you little Navajo bitch," he said in a hollow whisper, blood spewing from his vocal cords. I could feel his spirit touching my face, making my skin burn in the cold. My coat felt like a snake, coiling in tighter as my body froze. I could hear the rattle of the gurney as Giovanni and the deputy moved his body into the medical examiners' van.

"Are you okay?" Detective Arviso searched for what my eyes followed, but she saw nothing but blankness.

"Talk to me," his ghost hissed. His words pushed themselves into my body with a force that seemed to bruise me from the inside. I dropped to my knees, my heart racing.

"Rita?" Giovanni moved back toward me as Arviso pulled at my arm to help me off the frozen, wet ground.

"I'm okay," I said. I lied. I looked beyond their concern to see the man still staring at me, his eyes hollow gray, his mouth caked with blood. He breathed like his heart was dying. His head was loose and uncontrolled, the cut in his neck freeing it from its tendons and muscles.

"I can feel you," he continued, his voice like a hushed chorus of gravel. "Who did this to me?" His body was tight with shock. "Tell me who it was!" His rage burned my face.

"I understand," Arviso said to me. "Death is never easy for us, is it?" I nodded as Arviso helped me to the van. I looked back at the scene and saw the crimson stain on the snow. It was all that was left of Mr. Gurley.

"Thank you," I said. "I'm just tired."

"Take care," she said. She closed Gurley's body into the ME van and walked back to her cruiser.

"You okay, Rita?" Giovanni said, looking at me with a genuine concern that I had never seen before. He was usually all business.

"I'm fine. Let's just get back home." I looked again at the back of the van. The ghost sat sneering into me.

"Did you think I was just going to let you leave alone?" His voice rattled in my ears.

My guess was that he wasn't.

CHAPTER 10 | 10°

"If, however, a man acts presumptuously toward
his neighbor, so as to kill him craftily, you are to take him
even from My altar, that he may die."

EXODUS 21:14

I WILL NEVER forget Father Saren's blood on my hands,
the intense stream of warmth that continued down my arms. It
was my first taste of the razor-sharp edge of God's will. He had
a purpose for me, illustrated in the lightning of that night, my
body washed in Father Saren's blood. He could have let me die,
let the water soak into my lungs. Instead, he pulled me from
death to face my new life as his servant.

The sisters found Father Saren's dead vessel that morning
right where I left him, his eyes turned to the ceiling. His blood
had melted into the stones like black iron, dragging him down
into the hell he deserved. The sisters came into our damp
dorm rooms wracked with panic, their cries echoing in the
halls. The boys rubbed their eyes as the sisters screamed Father
Saren's name through the corridors of the school. I sat in my
bed and watched. I hadn't gone back to sleep; my clothes were
still damp from the baptism of death. Cleve stared at me with
drowsy eyes, his soul robbed of sleep. I didn't know what he
had seen. It didn't matter. Father Saren wouldn't be touching

him ever again. And Cleve was in no hurry to talk to anyone about what I had seen. His terror and embarrassment would keep him silent.

We marched our tired feet into the kitchen. As we passed the window, I turned toward the pond, looking for Father Saren's black soul hovering above the water. I didn't wonder what would become of me if anyone ever found out about what I had done. The police had made their way to the rectory, had searched through our campus to find clues as to what had happened to Father Saren. But by the time they came, the sisters had scrubbed the blood from the floor and had moved Father Saren to the chapel to prepare his body. No one questioned it.

They buried Father Saren by the pond in an unmarked grave. I felt safe in knowing that God had protected me, had shrouded me in an invisible cloak. He had used their own sins against them. I knew eventually I would join the angels in heaven.

After a month, the orphanage found a new priest to take over the job as headmaster. Father Benildus was a pious and generous man with a full and heavy laugh, who greeted all of us on his first day with blessings and the largest and best meal we had had in years. I loved him immediately and wondered what God intended to show me with this wild paradox.

Father Benildus broke our days up into sections with only a few hours' work in the fields. He could see that we were all desperately behind in our studies. He taught us about Saint Benildus, a nineteenth-century French priest who worked to educate children and adults of all backgrounds, making sure everyone had a chance in life. Our Father Benildus wanted to give us the same thing.

I admired Father Benildus because of his devotion. He played football and baseball with us on the weekends, kicking up dirt on his robe and running in his work boots until his feet turned to logs of mud. He was a thoughtful man, his face a cavern of history and his hands a valley of callouses. Every morning his voice bellowed to the boys of St. Joseph: "Remember, boys, it's up to you to make a future. You have the power to direct your own destiny." He would ring a tarnished gold bell attached to a worn, oily handle. "Today is the first day of the rest of your life."

On occasion he told us stories about his own childhood on the East Coast, a state called Maine that he said was way up in the corner of our country. We looked up at him in wonder as he told us about the desperate, gray Atlantic Ocean and about his life helping his father, who worked as a lobsterman. Father Benildus knew he wanted to be a priest when he saw a miracle—the rebirth of a man who had drowned in the tumultuous waves. While his father and the other men on his boat had tried to revive the man, Father Benildus watched the man turn gray under the blue summer sky. He dropped to his knees and asked God to save him, and the man spurted a spout of water from his mouth and sucked in a breath from God himself. Everyone on the dock stared at the boy—the young Father Benildus. He knew that he had found his life's work.

As I listened, I wanted to tell Father Benildus about my own experiences with God, about the birds coming down to help me usher my mama and Wapasha into the heavens. I wanted to tell him about Father and the crows and his journey into the underneath. Instead, I did as the sisters told us, I listened and kept my mouth shut. I learned more about God and about benevolence from Father Benildus than I did from four years of seminary school and all my years sitting in the creaky wooden pews at church every Wednesday and Sunday.

By the time Father Benildus had been at St. Joseph for a

year, I was lamenting the fact that I only had a year left at the orphanage. Some of the other boys had been adopted, including Cleve, which gave me a particular feeling of solace. He had gone home with an older couple who had lost their son in a farming accident. I sometimes imagined him growing strong and able on their land, his thoughts of that horrible time forgotten forever, along with his memories of me.

I imagined my life outside of the walls of St. Joseph, living on the streets and begging for farm work in the summer and fall. I dreamed of a different life somewhere else, a life of service to something bigger than myself. Out in the fields, it was hard to think of anything but my own father's hands, hardened like bones, digging in the dirt just like me; of his hard eyes.

That last year, there were only fifteen of us left at the orphanage and I was the oldest. Father Benildus worked alongside us with vigor. One night, we worked harder than we had ever worked. My muscles seized as we stacked our sickles and shovels in the barn next to the rectory. When I did my headcount, there was one missing.

James had arrived from a family of abusive alcoholics. He was happy to be with us. I watched over him as much as I could because I understood the road he had taken. He was willing to do anything just as long as there were no beatings. His skin was fragile and thin, his strong chin jutting out into the world, unafraid and adventurous, ready to work. When I saw he was missing, I knew something was wrong.

I ran back into the fields as fast as I could, my shins on fire as they sank into the soil. The last haze of orange was setting on the rows of stalks and leaves left back by the harvester. I looked down each row frantically. I was responsible for the little lives that worked the fields with me, just as Father Benildus watched over all of us. I felt guilt and panic rushing through me as the darkness descended. Then I saw his feet, the toes of his boots buried in the dirt.

I rushed to turn him over. He was not breathing. I cleared the dirt from his face. His eyes were caked with soil, his mouth full of mud. His heart was not beating. I pressed my hands into his chest, watching it rise and fall with each push. His body was hot as I breathed into his mouth, the taste of clay on my tongue. When Father Benildus had finally caught up to me, I was breathing into little James with all I had, and nothing was happening. Father carried a bucket of water with him, and I scooped out handfuls onto James's hot face, washing the dirt from him with every roll of my hand. Nothing happened. I pulled James up from the ground and prayed. As the last of the sunset dug into the dust, I could hear the swirl of the starlings above my head. Their flight swarmed left and right and off into the dusk, their murmuration so loud that even Father Benildus and the other boys couldn't help but look into the sky with me. Everyone felt the breeze of their flight on their faces. Crows had gathered in the trees, cawing deeply to warn us of the approach of death. I squeezed James so hard at that moment, holding his heart to my own and begging them all to bring his soul back to earth. That is when Father Benildus and I heard James's cough, a muffled gasp from the depths of my embrace. The starlings bent into the sky and dipped toward us as James looked into our eyes, his lashes thick and separated from the earth and water.

"What happened?" The other boys were gathering around us, their flashlights tilted into the dust. "Can I have some water?"

I carried James back to the barn and we loaded him into the old ranch truck that Father Benildus kept for our weekend sales at the market. I listened to little James breathe as he slept in my lap all the way to the hospital. The doctors told us that he was severely dehydrated and had had heat stroke, and for someone like him with a heart murmur, this could have been fatal. No one had been told about James's weak heart—probably no one knew, not his drunk father or absent mother.

Father Benildus and I drove back to the orphanage in the morning. There was a long silence in that truck as the heartlands streamed past us, until finally he spoke. "You were sent here to save that boy's life; do you know that?" He sounded serious, a dip in his voice. "The boys told me you guard them from evil. Did you know they talk about you like that?"

I had no idea. My face burned as I wondered—panicked— that word had gotten out about Father Saren and Cleve, or that someone had seen me that night washing Saren's blood from my body.

"I'm the oldest," I said. "That's why they say that."

"It goes far beyond that, boy. What are you going to do when you leave this place?"

"Farm work," I answered. I knew no other path.

"You have a calling that you can't see." Father's face was lit up blue from the morning. "God is calling you. Do you hear him?"

"How do you know what God is doing, Father?" I said, then was embarrassed immediately. "I'm sorry, Father. I meant no disrespect."

"I know. I just think you need some direction, and you showed me that you are ready for that voice to be part of your life. I could feel your trajectory calling from heaven. You brought little James back from the brink and did it without even the vaguest of reservations."

I sat in silence. I feared that if I did speak, I might say the wrong thing. I had no desire to disrupt the plans of God himself.

We pulled into the orphanage, and I knew I had to say something to prove I was giving thought to the dreams he was holding.

"What do you want me to do, Father?"

"That, son, is up to you." He shut off the engine. "When I brought a soul back from death all those years ago, God came and spoke to me, and I knew that I should spend the rest of my years in his service. What you do with your knowledge is up to you. What do I always tell you boys?"

"Today is the first day of the rest of your life?"

"Well, at least someone was listening."

The battered truck was barraged by the boys looking for James as I opened the door. They gripped my body, their bright energy pulsing. At that moment, I worried about my own future and that I wouldn't be there much longer, leaving them unprotected in the world and in this lonely orphanage.

I fell asleep that night dreaming of the sky. I envisioned myself as a raven joining a group of other teenaged ravens. People referred to this as an "unkindness" of ravens, a group of young and unruly gangsters still looking for their lot in life. I dreamed of myself in the trees, my wings and my strong, hard feet grasping the branches. Above me in the red skies, the starlings congregated, calling for me to join them in their movement. I left the branches and moved above the other ravens gathered in the trees. I felt small and fast, my wings forming into smaller and sleeker arms in the air. I felt so free in that moment, circling in the sky, fast and exact—we were all moving together, our wings buzzing.

At the end of my dream, I felt my feet hit the ground with a force I had never felt before. The dust from my landing rose up around me until I could see the crows watching me, circling me in formation, looking to see what I was going to do next. I was a human then. At that moment, I felt it: the first piercing pain of my wings pulled through my skin. My wings were a shiny raven black that touched the back of my naked feet. I stretched my wings out to the side and up, showing my family of birds what I had grown from my human form, the stitches made with golden needles the night I had killed Father Saren. The cacophony of songs from every bird rang in my ears.

The clouds built around me. The angels gathered, their iridescent skin making my eyes burn and tear. I could feel the pain in my head, and my legs and arms stiffened in my bed, but the dream continued. The angels held me down against the clouds as they examined my wings, the golden stitches red and irritated. I could see their hands rubbing on the wounds until the holes became clear and white. My pain stopped long enough for me to realize I had been dropped from the clouds and was plummeting, heavier than iron.

I woke from my dream in a sweat, feeling my shoulder blades for the long, black wings. I felt pain and sadness knowing that they were not real, that they only existed in my dreams. This was the closest to God that I had ever felt. The anguish of heaven had been bestowed upon me while I slept. I was God at that moment, with the ability to see the evil in men's eyes and the goodness of men's souls. I had been put here to sort through it all, to decide who was meant to stand in what line. Who would I save and who would I kill? I didn't know yet. But God would tell me soon enough.

CHAPTER 11
MRS. SANTILLANES

Hasselblad 500 C/M 150mm • f/16, 15 sec., ISO 6400, EV -1.9

AFTER WE DROPPED Mr. Gurley's body at OMI, I drove home. The energy of his ghost had swallowed me whole. His voice, the entire ride home, a constant presence. I thought of Erma and her determination, and knew that a man like Gurley would never relent. I adjusted the rearview mirror in my car, half expecting to see him in the backseat. For now, he seemed to still be figuring out what was going on, waking up in that body bag in OMI. I was glad to leave him to his own mystery.

The ghost residents of Downtown Village were on alert. The second I walked through the door, they were quick to turn their attention to me. Three of them sat in the lobby, playing cards like it was just another day in their old lives. One was still attached to an oxygen machine. I tried to ignore their ghost bodies, and thankfully, they went back to their game.

"You can't play that card." Mr. Evers was angry, just as he had been in life.

"Oh. I'm sorry." Mr. Alvarez picked up the card and shuffled it back into his hand. "How about this?" He slammed a different card on the table.

The elderly ghosts laughed in unison and continued to play their cards, slapping them down with force. Down the hall, angry Mr. Taino banged his wrinkled hands on his old apartment door, begging the new couple inside to let him in. He stepped through the door like a curtain, then I could hear him screaming.

"Get out of my home!" His voice wavered between rage and despair. "Get out!"

I arrived at the elevator doors, now adorned with a sign that read OUT OF SERVICE. Two weeks of service and broken again. The world's progress was moving in reverse at breakneck speed. I made my way to the top floor the old way, slowly, nursing the harsh sting in my leg. The whole way up, I could feel him there. Mr. Gurley. A steady presence of death. I pushed the thought of him away as my nose began to bleed again. I pinched my nostrils together with the cuff of my coat, trying to stop the warm stream of blood down to my lips. His anger sparked fear in the pit of my stomach.

The green light bulb above Mrs. Santillanes's door was flickering. It made my heart sink. I knocked, but there was no answer. Instant panic settled in my throat. I felt that old anxiety of encroaching death—a childhood spent with my ear pressed against my grandmother's door, listening for her breath. I banged the wood like old Mr. Taino downstairs.

"Hold on," Mrs. Santillanes said from the other side. "I'm coming. Hold your horses." She pulled open the door as the green bulb continued to flicker above our heads. I stepped over the threshold and squeezed Mrs. Santillanes with all my strength.

"*Mija.*" She looked at me, her eyes full of concern. "Are you okay? Come in here."

As she took me into her kitchen, I felt the beat of my heart slow down, but I was still enveloped by anxiety. I looked behind me to make sure nobody had followed. Nothing—no Mr. Gurley, with his black teeth and horrible breath. I hated to think of Mrs. Santillanes's ghost in this building, trapped forever with the angry old men from downstairs. Tears lined my cheeks. I didn't even realize I had been crying.

"Your nose, *mija*?" She sat me down at her table then handed me a paper towel she'd run under cold water. I held it in place as she put the kettle on the stove.

"I just got scared, that's all." I wiped tears from my eyes and watched as Mrs. Santillanes shuffled back and forth in her kitchen, then stopped to stir a steaming pot on the stove. It smelled of red chile and posole in the entire apartment, and I hadn't even noticed. She came and sat down at the table beside me and held my hand, looking straight into my eyes, a stare so deep and intense that I almost looked away. But I couldn't. I met her gaze, the gentle folds of skin heavy on her lids.

"I had a craving for some posole," she explained as she used a wet cloth to wipe blood from my chin. "I'm so glad you came to enjoy it with me. You are always so busy." Her gaze never wavered and her grip on my hand became tighter. "You're seeing them still, aren't you? I can see all the darkness around you, Rita. It's like a swarm of bees. And the nosebleeds . . ."

"How do you know what I'm seeing?" I swallowed my fear deep into my throat.

"*Mija*, I can see your soul is melting away in all of this. You have crossed a line that you should never have crossed." The kettle began to scream. She didn't break our gaze. "You must get out of here. Do you understand?"

"Why are you saying this to me?" The scream continued from the stove.

"Because I want you to live." She looked away and walked to the stove to take the kettle off. She walked right back to me and grabbed my hand.

"How is your grandma? And Mr. Bitsilly?"

The questions sent tears down my face again. I was ashamed that I hadn't checked on either of them all week. The murders were unending, a plague of death and violence that had descended on the city. The gunpowder girl, the clear and detailed images I'd taken of her, still haunted me. Her, and now Mr. Gurley, his nearly severed head wavering from his neck. Guilt and terror enveloped me.

"It's okay, Rita." Mrs. Santillanes wiped my tears with her embroidered handkerchief, a tangle of red roses and green vines made of thread. "You have to go home. You need to forget about this place just as easily as it became a part of your heart."

"But what about you, Mrs. Santillanes?" I gripped her hand. "I can't leave you here in this place alone. After everything you've done for me."

"Don't you worry about me, Rita." She rose from the table again and pulled two bowls from the cupboard, then ladled large servings of posole into them. "I am more worried about you." She placed a bowl in front of me. She already had a comal of tortillas on the table, still steaming fresh. She scooped a small spoon of soup into her mouth and opened the comal. "You died, Rita. You moved into the spaces of the dead. I can see it and I can feel it inside you." She took a piece of tortilla and dipped it into the broth. "So can they. They can see you too."

She took a bite. "Oh. I have been craving this like crazy! I can't eat chile anymore. It just doesn't agree with me. But sometimes you just have to go for it and give your body what it wants." She waited for me to take a bite. I did, and felt the hot spice of the broth spread on my tongue. I grabbed a tortilla to tame the heat. After the first bite, I couldn't stop. I ate quickly, in silence, the food filling my empty body. I realized right then that I hadn't eaten all day.

"You know, your soul is just like your body, Rita. Your body is weak and frail, so your soul can't be much different. It's starving."

"I have so much work to do here," I explained, repeating the same thing I'd told Dr. Cassler earlier that day. "There are so many cases to be solved, and I can't trust these police here to do the work or to see the people who walk among us." As I swallowed my last bite of posole, I added, "It's my job."

"It's not your job to regulate the world of the dead," she said. "There is nothing that you can do for them now."

"Except to bring them justice," I said.

"There is no real justice in this world." Mrs. Santillanes wiped her mouth, then rose again to fill two mugs with hot water from the kettle. I pulled a couple bags of tea from the canister on her table and began to shovel sugar into my mug. She laughed.

"I can feel that my co-workers have a real hatred for me," I said. "They are protecting their own. That is what they do. I have a feeling that is why they won't give me my disability. They say I need two more years to qualify. I hate to throw all these years I've earned away, but I may have to."

"They are more dangerous than death." Mrs. Santillanes was right. I had already come so close to death that I felt it around me every day. I remembered, then, the easiness of moving into it. The release of pain and torture when you entered the portal.

I'll never forget it. It made me wonder why any ghost lingered here in this world when the other side seemed so sweet and warm, so comforting.

"I will go home to see Grandma and Mr. Bitsilly as soon as I get these cases closed," I promised. "If I don't finish these cases, then six children will never find peace, and this man who we just found murdered will scare me to death."

"Six children?" Mrs. Santillanes made the sign of the cross and went to her altar, the cedar table in the corner of her kitchen, its legs carved into gentle claws. I could smell the wax burning, the smoke rising above the candles. The last one she lit was my candle—the candle of Saint Victoria, her face distorted by the rise of heat. She walked to her bedroom and came back with a small wooden box in her hand. Inside was a white pearl rosary. She grabbed my hand and put the rosary in it.

"I know you don't believe, Rita." She closed my hand around the pearls. I felt the edges of the crucifix on my skin. "But this will protect you. I have prayed protection into it. Keep it with you always."

"What about your protection?"

She was staring into my eyes again and I felt the heat of her gaze. "God will protect me, Rita." She smiled. "And I will protect you."

I WOKE EARLY the next morning and scanned my bedroom, half expecting Mr. Gurley, or the Montaño family, to be in the room with me, still unwilling to let go. But there was no one there except Irvin, who was in the corner, sadly staring out the window.

"It was the worst accident they had ever seen . . ." he muttered.

I didn't engage. I got up from the bed and went into the bathroom. I wasn't looking well. I still had dried blood beneath my nose; my eyes were puffy and unrested. I thought about Mrs. Santillanes's words the night before. I wondered, after my meeting with Dr. Cassler and all that I'd said to her, if I even had a job waiting for me at the office. What had she told the department?

I grabbed my phone from my nightstand. No calls, no voice-mails, no urgent dispatches. If I'd been fired, they hadn't even bothered to call. Judging from what I had said to Dr. Cassler, I doubted that she would let me keep working. I didn't know if that was good or bad, but it was bound to happen.

I headed out the door anyway, almost stopping to check on Mrs. Santillanes when I left, but I looked down at my watch: 6:15 A.M. I figured it would be best just to let her sleep. It was strangely—thankfully—quiet in the hallways. Even the ghosts were sleeping, wherever they were. Outside, it was freezing. If the last few days had offered glimpses of winter in Albuquerque, now it had arrived in full force.

No one else was at the crime scene unit except Mr. Flores, our maintenance worker. I switched on the computer at my desk. My phone sat idle. It was nice to have some silence—to have a morning without being called to attend to someone's last moment. It gave me time to catch up on work from the days before.

I broke down all the digital images from the Montaño crime scene, sorting them into discrete files and labeling them into sequences. Camera type(s), dates/times, orientation of the scene, specific locations, shutter speeds, aperture, environmental conditions. It was the same for every case. Most case photos were taken in the daytime, but the Montaño scene was in the dim light of the early morning. I had used long exposures for their overall photos, with speed light flashes and an ISO at 200. We had a few oblique photographs on that scene, some shoe prints that led from the Montaño house out into the shed, where we found the father's stack of photographs. The light caught his movement patterns and his kids gave me the rest of it.

Flipping through the photos, I revisited that awful scene, thinking the whole time of the little girl, Margarita Montaño, with gunpowder breath. The surface of my palms still ached from the touch of her tiny hands. Her voice passed through my fingers as I labeled each group of photographs—her father in the living room, her mother and sister in the kitchen, her brothers in their bedroom. My typing stopped when I came to the bathroom. There she was, the little girl, a toothbrush still in her hand, her baby teeth gnarled and her swollen cheek punctured with a hole.

"That's me. I'm dead." That was what she said to me. I'll never forget it.

I pulled out extra report sheets when I returned to the last groups of images: the baby in her crib and the stacks of photographs in the father's shed. I only had a chance to film a fraction of the photos that were in that man's file cabinet. I could make out a few quite clearly as they were his oldest daughter with no clothes on. I counted about twenty photos that I was able to get before the lead detective closed the scene and decided to turn the entire shed into an evidence room, a lock around the door. I hadn't photographed any portion of that shed since. I began my final report.

"The scene was secured on Thursday, November 30, at 5:56 A.M. A full documentation of the scene indicated that Mr. Montaño entered the home on or before November 29 and killed his wife, his three daughters, and three sons. The fourth and eldest son, Jude Montaño, entered the residence soon after and killed Mr. Montaño in his living room. Additional evidence concludes that Mr. Montaño was abusing his daughters and perhaps other members of his family. Please find attached images from the scene that documents these conclusions."

I turned to the murder in Gallup next. Victim one, Emmitt Gurley, found with his throat slashed after twelve hours of lying in the snow. From what I had read about him, he was a heartless man—but this fact made the photos no less difficult to stomach. In total, there were 289 shots of the scene and surrounding area. Those were taken in the late afternoon—the reflection of the sun on the snow helping to illuminate the horrific details. Gurley's throat was such a brutal sight I felt the muscles in my neck tighten. I thought about the strength it took to cut that deep, and the kind of tool that was used. We didn't find a weapon on the scene. It was somewhere in Gallup, sitting in a public trash bin or still in the killer's pocket. The images I took of him filled up my screen as I typed my report.

"Bar employee found the victim when she came to work in the early afternoon. He was in the alleyway behind the Silver Stallion Bar on 276 W. Route 66 in Gallup, New Mexico. The victim was identified as Mr. Emmitt Gurley, owner of the Silver Stallion and former mayor of Gallup. He was found dead with a deep cut to his neck. Investigation is underway at Gallup Police Department and NM State Police. Body sent to OMI, Bernalillo County."

It didn't take me long to figure out that Mr. Gurley had joined me. His smell arrived before he did. I looked around the office, the empty desks, the blinking of computer screensavers and flickering of fluorescent lights. The wind howled outside. I could sense his presence, but there was nobody there. I worked the moment away.

The office was bustling by the time I looked up from my desk again. It had to be around ten. Detectives moved in and out of the office, the different labs going about their business. Samuels's office was still empty. I imagined Dr. Cassler telling him what I'd told her, recommending that I should never have been allowed back into circulation. I had no proof of what the woman was saying, but I was convinced I'd scared her. All I could do was turn in my final reports and move into my future, whatever that was. I left the unit that afternoon not knowing if I'd ever be back. There was one more person I still needed to talk to before this whole thing was settled.

1101 Camino de Salud – Office of the Medical Examiner

The clock in the OMI lab was stuck at 5:30 P.M. and no one had ever bothered to change it. Dr. Blaser was examining paperwork in the adjacent lab, turning pages and drinking black coffee from his old, cracked coffee mug. Inside the body bag, Mr. Gurley lay lifeless, his neck connected by skin and decay. I knew that these things I saw had no way of hurting me. But Mr. Gurley scared me. He made my heart race.

Mr. Gurley's bloody and bruised ghost appeared, staring at the maroon bag with me. I kept my eyes ahead, no matter what.

"I'm still here, you know." Gurley's raspy whisper seemed to echo through the lab. I pulled my camera out of my bag and pretended not to hear his voice. But I felt his anger next to me like a raging fire.

"I know that you can see me," he said. "And you should be afraid. I will hurt you if you don't help me."

I stayed silent, staring at his body, unwilling to budge. I wasn't going to let him control me. Gurley's ghost rushed at me, pulling his face into mine. His stench dragged bile into my throat. Sheets of paper scattered out from the desks. I stood there, trying my best to regain my composure—but my heart was beating out of my chest.

"Everything okay, Rita?" Dr. Blaser had entered the lab. He stopped and stared at me, finishing off his coffee, then set down his notes. "You look like you've seen a ghost." I didn't even hear him coming into the room. "I didn't know you were coming down here this afternoon."

"I didn't either," I said. I saw Gurley watching from the corner of the gurney, an arm's length away from Dr. Blaser. I held on to my camera. "Do you need help on this one?" I pointed to the body bag.

"He came in late last night." Blaser went around the other side of the gurney and looked at his tag. "Mr. Emmitt Gurley, McKinley County."

"I know, I helped bring him in with Giovanni." I felt the bag. "He's still cold."

"Yeah, it's going to be hours before we're able to do much. He's still thawing out." Dr. Blaser moved to the body bag and unzipped it down to Mr. Gurley's chest, pulling the vinyl outward.

"I think he may have freezer burn. Might have to leave him out on the counter." He pointed out the pool of blood and melted snow puddled beneath his body. He zipped the bag back up. "Everything okay, Rita?"

"I don't know if I can do it anymore, Dr. Blaser," I said. "I think I might be on my way out."

Mr. Gurley watched.

"Are you quitting or getting fired? Because I haven't heard anything." He stood with his arms folded in front of him. "Is there anything I can do? Rita, you know you always have a job here if you want to transfer."

"I know, Dr. Blaser," I said. "I want to thank you for that. I just might have to take you up on it. We'll see."

"I understand," he said. "This job isn't for everyone, and you've had an injury that not a lot of people come back from. But I think you're worried for no reason. What would the unit do without you?"

"Well, apparently a lot," I said. I looked toward Mr. Gurley. "And there's not much I can do here anymore. I guess that decision is in the hands of the department and the shrink. I don't even feel safe going home anymore."

Dr. Blaser tossed me a half smile, then put a hand on my shoulder. "Well, I'll give you a holler after Mr. Gurley here thaws out. I'm not sure what's going on, Rita. But just know that you do good work here. If you decided to quit, you would be missed." He paused, gesturing to all the bodies lying in the morgue. "By all of us."

I walked out of OMI heavy with worry. So many people in that building had stories to tell and I was becoming too weak to tell them. I was tired of fighting so hard to translate for the living. I drove home, the drone of the crooked and cracked asphalt beneath the car the whole way.

The hallways of my building still sat silent by the time I arrived home. As always, I checked on Mrs. Santillanes before I went to my apartment. I knocked on her door as hard as I could. No answer. I pressed my ear into the door, hoping to hear the shuffling of her slippers or the screaming of her kettle. But there was nothing. Only silence. I banged on the door again and called out to her. Still nothing. Desperate, I tried to force the door open with my shoulder, then with my foot. I didn't want to make the call, but I knew if I didn't, no one would.

My heart beat, empty.

CHAPTER 12 | 7°

"But those who hope in the LORD will renew their strength. They will soar on wings like eagles; they will run and not grow weary; they will walk and not be faint."

ISAIAH 40:31

GALLUP IS UNFORGIVING in the winters. Sometimes as I watch them die, I wonder about their families. If there is someone at home wondering where they are. There could be a child out there in the darkness watching a door, waiting for the familiar return of their father, or their mother. Instead, they are on the streets. That kid of theirs will be waiting the rest of their lives. At least I was lucky enough to know that my parents weren't coming back from what happened to them. I was on my own.

I could see my path by the time I aged out of the orphanage. I had stayed to help Father Benildus on the early planting duties, showing the older boys how to run the till and drive the orphanage's aging tractor with the trick ignition. That farm would miss me, and I knew it. So would Father Benildus. In his heart he wanted me to stay and work for the orphanage, but in his mind, he had already decided there was more for me. He helped me to apply to his alma mater, Holy Cross, and a few other local colleges. He wrote glowing letters of recommendation. He told me every day that I was destined for something much bigger—to bring hope and life. When I was accepted at Notre Dame, he beamed like he was my father.

"I have never met another like you," he told me on the day he dropped me off at the bus station with my one small bag. "You too will earn your wings someday." He grabbed my shoulders and smiled. I watched him walk back to the farm truck from the inside of the old Greyhound bus. I never saw him again.

At college I studied mostly biology and theology, two strangely entwined subjects. I thrived there. My body became stronger. My mind built itself up like a city, the numbers and formulas stacking like bricks, the windows and doors leading back to my faith. Father Benildus had shown me the way to serve, and I felt myself ready to make a complete commitment to God. I worked at the church after classes and prepared myself to move into service immediately after graduation. But I didn't see myself as a priest. I didn't feel the call to preach and to dispatch the sacraments. I had another charge.

I battled to serve in those years that I studied. There were many people who deserved to have their blood drained from their bodies. It was hard to ignore the cruel ones, to let them continue day after day in their selfish and bitter lives, but I let them live. Meanwhile, I sometimes found myself fumbling in dark dorm rooms with young girls, yearning for the taste of their blood, or for the feeling of their blood on my own body. I felt no guilt in my thirst. I took their bodies, soaking in their flesh, their lust, my lust. Eventually I grew tired of the sins of sexuality. I grew a stronger will from the flesh, a mistake to never return to. God would call me when real blood needed to be spilled.

I MOVED TO New Mexico in the summer of 1990, around fifteen years ago now. I spent that first year with an old man who lived and worked at the top of a long and treacherous road at the Truchas Morada. Lozaro was part of a small, secret brotherhood, a crumbling network of Penitente churches. Their faith was extreme, a devout and often violent form of worship. These were my early days of brotherhood, when I still searched for meaning in my faith, a way to escape the distress I lived with. I think Lozaro saw that I needed guidance. What he taught me was patience and penitence. He rarely spoke, but he was devoted to God in the deepest sense, willing to shed his own blood to honor His sacrifice and to truly atone for his sins. His *disceplena* was made of yucca and rope, hardened knots pulled into the strands. In the Truchas Morada, Lozaro took care of everything, and for the year I was there, he taught me all that he could. He taught me about the history of the Penitentes, explaining to me the reasons why they decided to live in secret. On the first day I arrived, he looked at me with tangible mistrust.

"You would not be here had I not received that letter from the archdiocese," he said. "I know you are studying to be a priest."

I wasn't. But I didn't argue. "I'm here to work, to be of service before the archdiocese stations me somewhere in New Mexico." I tried to explain myself, but I seemed to be digging a bigger hole.

"I'm going to make sure I get all of the materials I need while you're here," Lozaro said. "You're young. And you can carry it." He laughed. He was not joking.

I worked with the man every day and he never tired, even though he was well into his seventies. He chiseled wood for hours, spending days painting gold leaf on a new retablos honoring Saint Michael. "My favorite saint," Lozaro said. The harder he worked, the more he proved his devotion to God. There in the silence of that distant community, on top of a mountain overlooking this new place I was going to call home, I began to understand the path Lozaro was clearing for me.

I worked harder those months than I ever had in my life, mostly helping Lozaro put together new elements of the *morada*, the chapel and the house he was building for himself. Much of my work was helping to lift and install the work Lozaro had already completed; only later did he move me into craftsmanship, really teaching me how to work the wood. Most importantly I learned to have faith.

"I know you are joining the church, and I'm glad," Lozaro said. "But remember that you serve God, you don't serve the church. It wasn't that long ago that the church turned its back on us, sending us into exile." He looked at me and left a long swath of silence. "We must never forget that. For as long as I can remember, they have rationalized their hatred and justified their own sins." He patted me on the hands. "Do what you're doing for God."

During Holy Week, the brotherhood walked the treacherous path toward the ancient adobe *morada*, still standing from the 1600s. On the most sacred day of worship, they invited me to be a part of the stations of the cross. Our bare feet walked for miles, crosses on our backs. We visited the *calvarios* one by one, worshiped at every station and prayed for forgiveness. On Good Friday, the brothers would strike themselves at the stations of the cross, shedding their blood on the grounds of the *morada*. I spent two years with them, finding my own journey and learning how to truly give myself over to God.

On their day of penance, they removed the boards from the old building and prayed. The building was still fragile and Lozaro only opened the *morada* for Holy Week and during *Las Posadas*—the Christmas holiday. We tended to those in the community who were still part of the brotherhood, following the long traditions held in the small communities in New Mexico. Even now, I still aspire to that kind of devotion. I sometimes think of those years and the blood we spilled to mark the sacrifice of the flesh, the crosses we carried until our feet and hands bled like Christ.

I helped Lozaro that year as he completed his altar, a small room he had carved by hand, wood panels made from aspen and cedar and pine, the faces of saints carved into the logs. Carved panels, in symmetrical shapes, spirals of color covering the wood. He hung retablos in blues and yellows around the walls, just like he did at the *morada*. Inside the altar, Lozaro had photographs of family draped in rosaries, bookended by burning candles and small carved crosses with straw inlay and bright colors. There was only enough room for a man to pray alone, to atone and to offer. That was his space, and I was blessed that he trusted me to help, to spend months with him as he crafted his masterpiece with little to no resources. He had carved every part of that church, creating an exquisite example of craftsmanship and engineering without a day of schooling or training.

Eventually, I began my outreach work with the brotherhood under Lozaro's instruction. I made my way to all of the communities that surrounded Gallup—Zuni Pueblo, and, of course, all over the Navajo land around us. The church is embedded deep in these places, like a hook in flesh, the corruption and terror written indelibly in the memories of all the Natives that live here. They celebrate the days they cut priests' throats. Seeing what I've seen, I would have been there to hand them the knife.

Nevertheless, I was invited to feast days and dances. I sat at the table with Pueblo families and laughed at their stories. I did a majority of my outreach on Navajo land, visiting elders in distant canyons, helping to haul water and serve meals on the weekends. At the start of fall, I'd spend my days of solace at the ceremonial night dances, soaking in the last of the warm weather. It was beautiful to see all of these Indians together in one place. They were welcoming and kind to me, even though I represented the church. They shared their stories with me, teaching me Navajo words, then teasing me when I said them back.

After a few years, my service to God led me to this valley, to the dark and frozen streets of Gallup, New Mexico. I landed at Sacred Heart, where I've been put in charge of the community outreach center for the homeless. Gallup is not a happy place. Over the years it's become dangerous. Something out of control. I suppose this makes sense. The town was birthed by colonialism, by the movement of strangers heading west toward the ocean, guided by the steel of the railroad and the encroachment of greed. Gallup was named after a white man, the paymaster of the railroad, Mr. David Gallup, the hardened boss of the western stations. When only years before, the Navajo lived in coexistence with the other pueblos and tribes along the corridor of trade and religious freedom, the steel beast had moved itself in. That is what this town was built on. The descendants of those early thieves and colonizers still run this town, and run the people whose land they live on, into the dirt. So much of their money has been made in the liquor trade, the poison that tricked so many into submission.

I see these Navajos here on the streets, forced to sleep on the sidewalks on their own land that was stolen from them, and their suffering is a beacon to me. My purpose has become clear. It is God calling me, showing me how to make this world a better place with the gift of grace for his angels. I can hear Wapasha in my ear too, another guidance from the other side. He will see that I'm doing the job right and completing the task set before me. He will understand that I have been sent to protect them from their constant pain, from the loneliness of another day on the streets, or in prison, or lying along the train lines.

And what is my reward? To go with them. I'm ready to make that trip and have been for a very long time.

IT IS IMPOSSIBLE for me to write about my early days in Gallup and not mention my Rosemary. In my thirteen years serving this community, I watched a beautiful, young-eyed run-away grow into a weathered survivor of the streets of Gallup. The men fear her, as she is known to carry weapons. I spoke with her once as she sat on the sidewalk outside the bar on Aztec. She must have been on the streets for five years by then. I couldn't help but watch the side of her neck, her soft skin pulsing with the blood beneath it. The night before, she had survived an attack by stabbing her would-be killer in the face. I found the tale hard to believe until I saw the man, days later, with a bandage instead of an eye. When Rosemary passed the man on the street, she would point to her left eye to remind him that she had taken it. When they found his dead body two weeks later, I had taken his other eye.

But that wasn't the first time we met. In fact, we'd arrived in Gallup around the same time and I'd noticed her during my first winter of outreach. It was a Thursday, and the old bank clock on the corner of Hill and Coal blinked between the snowdrifts, telling us that it was only nine degrees. I saw her standing in line over at Allsup's, her arms full of candy and chips, a six-pack of beer dangling from her middle finger. She looked alone and way too young to be fending for herself. I could see the men in the store staring at her, vultures all. They glared at her as she unfolded her money from her fist and walked out into the Gallup shadows.

"Do you need a ride?" I stepped out of my van, adjusting the tab in my collar. Two men, who followed her out of the store, turned the corner into the parking lot, but pivoted when they saw me. Two wolves, avoided.

"Can you take me all the way to Mentmore?" She followed my eyes, unaware of the danger she had escaped.

"Of course." I opened the door for her, moving some of my paperwork off the seats.

"Thank you, Father," she said. "I didn't know how I was going to get home."

"It's Brother." I pointed toward the beer. "Are you old enough for that?"

"I know the guy." She looked out of the window as we headed toward the highway. "I'm not quite old enough, but I'm close."

"When was the last time you ate?" Her arms were as thin as bone.

She looked out the window. "I had something to eat yesterday morning at my aunt's house in Mentmore," she said. "Right before she kicked me out."

"I haven't eaten since this morning." I said. "Let me take you over to Jerry's before I drop you off." She looked at me suspiciously. "I promise I won't bite."

When we got to Jerry's Café, the crowd was thinning, and the heat was swelling inside the foggy windows. I always sat next to the window so that I could people-watch. We sat together quietly, Rosemary still looking at me without an ounce of trust. I told her to have whatever she wanted, seeing the hunger in her eyes. I ordered a chicken sandwich, and she ordered a burger with everything on it.

"Are you sure that you want me to take you to Mentmore?"

She gazed out the window. She was so beautiful, long dark hair and haunting eyes. She wore a thin turquoise necklace with unevenly spaced shiny brown beads. It curved around the edges of her collarbones.

"If you have no place to go, then why should I take you back there?" She turned her head to look at me, and I could see her wondering if she should share her story with someone like me. I smiled. "You can trust me, Rosemary. I'm here to help."

"I've been out there my whole life," she said. "My mom died about a year ago and it has been real hard to find a place. My Mom's old house is a shack. Nothing works, no water, no electricity. So, I stayed with my auntie. But I can always go back to Mom's house if I need to."

"How old are you?"

"I'm nineteen." The food came and Rosemary ate with one eye on me. I was glad to see her eating instead of pouring her dinner from a can. "Thank you for the food. I didn't know I was so hungry."

"The streets of Gallup are no place for someone like you, Rosemary," I said. "I've just moved here myself. I'm over by Sacred Heart. Please let me know if there's ever anything I can do to help you."

"I know about the streets of Gallup," she said. "They kill people here with alcohol and hate."

"This community is facing hardship," I said. "The battles of addiction never end."

"That's all anyone ever talks about when they talk about Gallup," Rosemary said. "Addiction. The Navajos and their addiction." Her face contracted in anger. Her plate was nearly clean. "Like that's the whole story. They never tell our history."

"I've read about it. There is a huge amount of history, both good and bad."

"Did you know they once killed a Navajo man for trying to save Navajo lives?"

"I'm not sure I've heard about that."

"In the 1970s, when my mom was my age, there was a man named Larry who kidnapped the mayor of Gallup because he owned a horrible bar out on the Rez where people would go to die." When Rosemary told me the story, her body spoke of her fear. "They would find women raped, people murdered, Navajos frozen to the ground in the wintertime. But that man refused to close his bar. He was making too much money off their deaths."

"I've heard only a little about him. Larry Casuse?"

"Yes," she said. "He and another man kidnapped the mayor to make a statement, and they shot him for it. All these people care about is money. It has been that way since the beginning, and it will always be that way."

"You can change it, Rosemary," I said. "By not being another statistic."

"That's easy for you to say, Brother. God takes care of you." She was right.

We sat in silence as Rosemary finished what was left on her plate. Her teeth were well cared for, her skin smooth and unscarred. I could only hope that she would stay this way, that someone close to her would love her.

"What do you want to do with your life, Rosemary?" I asked her as I opened my van door and watched her pull herself into her seat.

"I just want to live," she said.

We rumbled down I-40 as the sun disappeared, the cracked windows of the church van whistling, the aluminum food trays in the back alive with movement. I looked at Rosemary, the darkness falling on her face, and hoped that I wouldn't see her in Gallup again, not the way I saw her that day—without sleep, without food and in the clutches of the men that walked the same streets with her. But Mentmore was only a thumb away from Gallup.

"Thank you for the ride, Brother," she said.

"Anytime, Rosemary," I said. "Don't be afraid to ask if you ever need help. That is why I am here."

She smiled and closed the creaky van door, walking off into the darkness toward the faint light coming from a distant trailer window. It was no place for anyone to live. I knew right then that I would spend my days in Gallup looking for her out of the corner of my eye and keeping her dreams in my heart. For years, I would find her asleep on the streets sick from drugs, smoking cigarettes as her feet dangled over roaring trains, or hitchhiking between the Indian hospital and Zuni, her body bandaged. Her smooth, gentle face became hardened, her skin only a cover for bones.

God has always helped me decide. Tonight, I know the temperatures will be well below zero. I don't have one more moment to waste. Neither does Rosemary.

CHAPTER 13
THE LAST REASON

Hasselblad 500 C/M 80mm • f/16, 15 sec., ISO 6400, EV -1.9

MR. CLARK, OUR new super, arrived at the top floor of our building five minutes after I called him. All I could do in the meantime was call Mrs. Santillanes's name, rattling her doorknob and trying to force myself through the door, past splinters of wood and into her front hallway. I pushed my mind to think of her coming into her kitchen, wondering what the racket was all about. Brief solace from my deepest fear. Mr. Clark had to shake the keys in my face to get me away from the door.

We could hear the television in the other room, but nothing else. The apartment looked like it always did, immaculate and organized—but I could feel it. The life of it was gone. We slowly walked into the kitchen, both afraid of what we would see. There was nothing. One single bowl filled with water in the sink and one spoon and coffee mug. Her salt and pepper shakers and napkin holders were perfectly balanced in the center of her kitchen table, not a crumb to be found.

"Mrs. Santillanes?" I walked toward her bedroom. The door was open. "It's me, Rita. Mrs. Santillanes? Are you here?"

The light beside her bed was on, giving her bedroom a warm glow. It looked like she was sleeping, her quilt pulled up to her shoulders. Her reading glasses and an open paperback lay at her side.

"Mrs. Santillanes? We're here to check on you."

Mr. Clark looked at me. I think we both knew. I approached her bed and stared down at her. She looked so peaceful, but I knew she was gone before I even touched her neck. Mrs. Santillanes had a life force so strong that I could often feel it from my apartment next door. Sometimes, I could feel her protecting me from miles away. Now, that energy was gone.

I hadn't felt so alone in a very long time.

I reached out and felt Mrs. Santillanes for a pulse, but there was none. She was still just a little warm. I must have just missed saying goodbye.

"We're going to have to call an ambulance." Mr. Clark took off his hat and shook his head. "I'll call 'em, kid," he said. "I know you two were close." He shuffled out through the hallway until all I heard was the echo of his footsteps.

I couldn't move. I just sat on the bed with Mrs. Santillanes and held her hand until the ambulance arrived. I knew that Mr. Bitsilly would probably scold me for doing it, but Mrs. Santillanes was my friend and I just felt like staying with her until the last second that I could. I imagined that she was happy wherever she was. She deserved to be. She had faith like no other and did nothing but heal and protect everyone who came within her reach. Now, she was at peace, as they say. Whatever that meant. After what I had seen in the last few days, I knew there would be no peace for me for the rest of my life.

It was at least a half an hour before the EMTs arrived, hot and out of breath thanks to our broken elevator. They confirmed what we all already knew and took Mrs. Santillanes's body away from Downtown Village forever, her body traveling like another ghost through the corridor. I followed her all the way to the ambulance. Mr. Clark watched from the window as I made my way back inside.

"Have you ever met her family?" Mr. Clark was beginning to look frail himself there in the lobby light. He was a spindly man—long and thin limbs in a baggy, sleeveless undershirt and jogging shorts, no matter the weather. "They didn't come by very often."

"I never had a chance to meet anyone from her family, Mr. Clark," I said. "I keep strange hours."

"Ah, yes." He started to walk toward his office. "The photographer."

"She talked about her sister from time to time. But I don't know her name." I felt ashamed that I didn't know her sister's name. Mrs. Santillanes probably knew everything about me, but I felt like I knew too little about her.

"I have her number," Mr. Clark said. "I'm going to give her a call now and let her know what's going on." He opened the door to his office, a pale cube filled floor to ceiling with white cardboard boxes and lopsided stacks of paper.

"If you reach anyone, please let them know I'm willing to help. If they need anything, tell them I'm next door." Mr. Clark nodded and gave me a flat smile. I turned to leave, my vision bleached by his fluorescent-white office, and made my slow journey up the stairs. I was surprised by the silence of the hallways. A few residents peeked out their doors, some giving me a quick smile, then retreating inside. The ghosts were quiet. Maybe they were honoring Mrs. Santillanes, giving her the quiet that she deserved, and passing that blessing on to me.

The top floor was so hollow without that horrible, green light. Our light.

My apartment was like a tomb. I sat in my living room, enveloped in silence, and felt the walls collapse around me. There was no stopping my grief or my loneliness. Every corner of my space looked darker, and every second became a slow and hollow tick. I ran into the bathroom and was sick but had little more to throw up than spit and old coffee.

Here, now, in my immense grief, the spirits stayed away. I remember what Mrs. Santillanes told me on our last night together—that it was her turn to protect me. At first, I didn't know what she meant. Now I did. I could feel home pulling me toward it like an underivable force, visions of my grandma and her laughter, of the barren but beautiful bluffs behind our house and that lovely feeling of ease that comes from familiar places.

I grabbed my phone and dialed Shanice. I needed to hear a trusted voice, to be close to someone who knew me and loved me anyway. After three rings, a sleepy voice whispered into the phone.

"Rita? What's going on? What time is it?" Shanice let out a cough.

"Mrs. Santillanes died, Shanice," I said. My breathing became labored as I fought back tears.

"Oh, sweetie," she said. "When did this happen?"

"It just happened," I said. I couldn't breathe. "I should have never gone back to work."

"Wait, you're working?" Someone was talking to Shanice in the background, a muffled conversation that I couldn't make out. "Do I need to come up there? I can. My gig ended a couple of days ago."

"I never thought I would say this, but I need someone, Shanice," I said. "I have no one, and there's no way I can handle this. And Grandma can't know. It would kill her with worry."

"What about the other stuff?"

"What other stuff?"

"You know what I'm talking about," Shanice said. "Don't pretend like I don't know."

"Yes," I admitted. "It's still happening."

"I'll be there as soon as I can," she said, and hung up the phone.

GRANDMA CALLED ME within minutes, her throat full of grief. Shanice had told her. The panic in my voice earlier must have scared her.

"She'awéé, talk to me," Grandma said. "Are you okay?"

"I'm okay, Grandma," I lied.

"I'm coming to get you, Rita." Grandma's voice was stern even if I could hear her heart breaking through it. "Mr. Bitsilly and I will be there in the morning. Take your corn pollen and pray, she'awéé. We are coming to bring you home." I hated to admit it, but I didn't even know where my tadadíín bag was.

Losing Mrs. Santillanes had finally broken me, and everyone could feel it but me. Being pulled from duty had become the least of my worries as I felt a sickness moving in, the same feeling I had when Seivers took me to the hospital because my body was breaking down. The last place I wanted to go again was the hospital. There was nothing they could do to fix me now. Nothing can fix you when your soul is cracked.

Shanice was at my door within a couple of hours with a box of takeout. She took me into her arms and held me as I cried. I couldn't help myself. I was relieved that I wouldn't have to spend another night in this cell on my own.

"Thank you for coming, Shanice," I said. I collapsed on the couch, unable to move. Shanice handed me a beer from the fridge. "How long have you been here?" I didn't feel hungry, but my body drove me to the sesame noodles Shanice brought. I ate them straight from the box.

"I just got in," she said. "And you called at a good time, because I'm homeless again." We laughed. "But seriously, I'm moving back here. I actually got a real job here at one of the schools. A real job, Rita. Not a gig. I just need a place to crash until I find my own."

"Well, you can have this place," I said. "I'm quitting my job."

"You're kidding. What happened?"

I caught Shanice up on everything—told her the whole story about Mrs. Santillanes, about Mr. Gurley, about the cases I'd been working on. The Montaños, the corruption. How it was all piling up, becoming too much to handle. "I've decided not to fight them anymore, you know? The ghosts. The cops at work. All of it. Now that Mrs. Santillanes is gone, I have absolutely no reason to stay. There's nothing left for me here."

Shanice understood completely. "It's about time you left this place," she said. "It's like a tomb, and you're still working that job with all the shitty men who don't like you. There's no shame in going home. It's the one place that will always take us. Things are changing, Rita. Things will change."

I inhaled another forkful of food and so did Shanice, both of us eating like we'd been on a hunger strike. My shirt was covered in scattered noodles and sauce.

"We need to get you a bib." Shanice laughed. It was good to hear some joy in my apartment.

"Oh. Also, I brought home a stray a couple of months ago." I looked around the room waiting for Irvin to make an appearance.

"Like a cat?" Shanice looked around the room.

"Like a ghost," I said. "He followed me from a suicide case I had, and I've been dealing with him ever since. I think he had Alzheimer's, because he can't remember that he's dead."

"Anything else I should know?" Shanice drank down half her beer.

"Yeah," I said. "I'm sick. I don't know how to explain it. My soul feels dirty."

"Jesus, Rita," Shanice said. "Things just don't change, do they?"

It was good to have my friend with me, to be able to smile and let go, despite all the heaviness. I think it somehow recharged my spiritual energy. We talked until we bored each other with stories, buried beneath covers on my overstuffed couches. I crept to my bed in the early morning, while Shanice slept peacefully on my couch. I was happy for the first time in a long while.

When the sun came up the next morning, the silence was broken.

"It was on a Wednesday in the spring of '87. Do you remember the big crash up on the hill on I-40?" Irvin wavered at the kitchen counter, looking up into the ceiling. I stared at him.

"Go home, Irvin," I said.

"You okay, Rita?" Shanice was standing in the doorway, still half asleep. "Who are you talking to?"

I turned to see him again standing at the window. Then he was gone.

It was time to pack my things, to move on. I got out of bed and started to load boxes with books, papers, whatever else would fit inside. Shanice helped clean out my closet and organize the clothes I'd take back to Tohatchi. As we packed, I felt more and more assured in my choice of moving on.

By seven that morning, Grandma and Mr. Bitsilly, our

medicine man, his leather bag in his grip, were at my door. The sight of them broke me down again. Grandma hugged me for five minutes as I sobbed, and Mr. Bitsilly sang and prayed for me. His smoke rose up for me and for Mrs. Santillanes, the sweet smell filling my apartment. Grandma fed us all breakfast, the television filling our faces with the hollow light of the morning news.

Grandma and Mr. Bitsilly stayed behind as Shanice and I went around Albuquerque, closing any connection I still had to this place. Ghosts, I found, were everywhere, their presence hot and sticky in the winter cold. I counted three of them at the post office, their bodies wandering through the concrete walls as I told a postal clerk where to forward my mail. There were two more at the bus stop outside the gas company, where I transferred the utilities account to Shanice's name. Each ghost bore witness to my last days in their midst. Their collective gaze clung to my soul like a sickness; they could see me, taste me in their dead mouths.

By the time we returned to Downtown Village, Grandma and Mr. Bitsilly had my life packed into a stack of cardboard boxes. I felt shame in seeing all the work they'd done for me— their hands sore from packing away my grief and my pain. But Grandma just seemed happy to see me, relieved that she could be here for me in my need. She fed us beans and red chile for dinner, but I found that I could barely eat or engage in conversation. They discussed the plans for the next day as I moved a spoonful of beans back and forth on my plate.

Mrs. Santillanes's sister had arrived while Shanice and I were out. Mrs. Santillanes would be laid to rest tomorrow afternoon at one of the oldest churches in Albuquerque, a fitting place to welcome her to whatever came next.

"That church is so beautiful," Grandma said. "I remember

going to Mass there years ago. I'll bring white flowers for her. How does that sound, Rita?"

Shanice nudged me with her elbow. I looked up from my plate to the three staring at me, concerned. "Rita, will you try to eat?" Grandma said.

Mr. Bitsilly took my hand. "Grief is part of life, Rita," he said. "Mrs. Santillanes would want the best for you. She'd want you to be happy. She knew you needed to heal."

"After her service, we're taking you home," Grandma said. "I hope you know that it's time for you to come home."

"I know," I said, breaking my silence. "I'm ready to let go of this place. I'm ready to let go of all the pain."

THAT NIGHT I lay awake, unable to move my body past its grief. I listened to the echoing sounds of the night: the sirens, the fight that broke out by the bar two blocks away, the stuttering of a shopping cart being pushed down the street as the sun began to come up. The clock blinked on the microwave. It was 5:53 A.M. I didn't bother to shower, afraid that I might wake Grandma in my room, or Mr. Bitsilly on the other living room couch, or Shanice in her sleeping bag on the floor. I changed into a fresh pair of work clothes, pulled my hair into a knot and quietly slipped out of my apartment. I only had a few hours to close this chapter in my life, these seven years, to end the only thing I had devoted myself to. Mrs. Santillanes would be happy to see me close that door, to be swallowed in the love that waited for me at home. I could feel her there as my body stiffened with heartache. I needed my life back. The police had taken more than their share of it.

CHAPTER 14 | 14°

"Who comforts us in all our affliction so that we will be able
to comfort those who are in any affliction with the comfort
with which we ourselves are comforted by God."

2 CORINTHIANS 1:4

I CAN FEEL time slipping away from me, and yet there is
so much more that I need to confess. As I write this, my head
screams for clarity. There is an agonizing pain in my back from
my lashes of penance. The pen is shaky in my hand. I force
myself to steady it. I need to keep going. There are so many
more memories, so many more angels whose stories need telling
before I leave. Questions that I know people will ask. How do
I choose them?

I wait in the shadows. And as I do, I watch them move through
the white landscape, the blowing snow, thick and heavy. Sometimes the door to the Silver Stallion opens, a body appears and
looks up into the sky, the heat and noise from the bar escaping
into the streets. Then the door slams behind them, leaving the
streets quiet again. My feet hover above the ground. No one
notices me. If they catch a glimpse, I change the angle of my head
or move deeper into a crease of shadow. I am just something they
thought they saw. I don't know how many I've taken while I've

been here. I've lost count. All these years and not even a hint that I could be caught, that I could be brought to judgment.

Two angels come to mind now. Their names were Merlin and Eliana, and I first saw them in the train station the day I arrived in Gallup. The old man, Merlin, walked with a limp in his left leg. His companion, Eliana, always stood on his right side so he could steady himself on her shoulder. Merlin's face was chiseled and brown, slight lines running down the side of his cheeks, but Eliana never aged. I offered them food that day, but they would not take it—they were offended by the gesture.

"We're not homeless," Merlin said to me that first day. "This land is my home. You're all living on my land, on our land. Right, Eliana?"

Eliana, always by his side, nodded in agreement.

They never took any food I offered. Sometimes they'd take money. But never a lot. And only when they were desperate. Over the last few years, though, I read about them in the police blotter, breaking and entering abandoned buildings or loitering in front of storefronts where Indians aren't allowed. They mostly were arrested for trying to survive. You could see Eliana's hope fading. She never did say much, and as the years went on, she stopped even nodding in agreement.

The middle of the month was a telling time, when most of the disability money had run out and people wondered how they would get by until the next check came. I knew, especially as the snow began to fall, that Merlin and Eliana would be making their way to the railway bridge just east of Gallup, where they could find dry ground and make a fire that could not be seen from the highway.

I found them at the Silver Stallion one night, buying a bottle of vodka from the bartender, a known bootlegger out on the

Arizona–New Mexico border who worked for Mr. Gurley on Sunday nights. It was late when they left. They walked together, Merlin's limp slowing their gait as they dodged cars on Route 66. I watched them from the railroad tracks, backing away as the last freighter moved through downtown. I could hear Merlin talking and the sound of their laughter. I don't think I had ever heard Eliana laugh before. I left the outreach van and followed them, my feet gliding along the railroad tracks, following the two of them the half a mile to their makeshift shelter, built into the precarious sandstone rocks dotting the landscape outside of town.

They made their way into the overhang and started a spindly fire. I stood and watched; my feet perched along the fence line waiting for them to sleep. The fire flickered on their faces in the darkness, the small flakes of dry snow hissing into the flame. Eliana was wrapped in a small sleeping bag, her two hands gripping each side of the broken zipper to keep it closed. Merlin just sat and watched the fire, his thin coat covered in snow, his legs extended toward the flames.

"I can see you out there." Merlin looked out at the darkness and right into my eyes. "Why did you follow us?"

"If you're from the drunk van, we don't want to go out to MRC," Eliana said, her voice a rasp of cold and rage. "We're not drunks."

"I'm here to watch you, to help you." I came into the flicker of the light, unable to feel any of its heat. "You will freeze out here if I let you stay."

"You people are always trying to pretend you're helping us." Merlin took a long drink from his glass vodka bottle and passed it to Eliana, who followed suit. "You people came to kill us and now you're trying to save us? Make up your mind." The two of them laughed. I couldn't help but see their point.

"What if I could help you to leave this place? Right now. Tonight." I looked up into the sky. "What if I could end all this cold, the pain, the illness, the sickness?"

"I don't see how you ever could," Merlin said. He threw a handful of sticks on the fire and watched them burn. "They're wanting to take my legs."

"They want to take your feet, Merlin. Not your legs." Eliana drank from the bottle and gestured toward me. Merlin grabbed it back.

"They might as well take my heart out of my chest." Merlin fell silent. We all did.

"One way or another, the two of us are on our way out," Eliana said to me. "I haven't taken my heart or diabetes medicine in a year and Merlin's feet are turning black. It's only a matter of time."

Merlin had fallen asleep, his arms crossed over his body.

We sat in silence until that fire turned into smoke and the both of them slept together beneath the rocks, their coats and blankets pulled up around their faces. It was one of the darkest nights I had ever seen, but at least the dry snow had stopped. I stood over them, their wheezing breaths in the black. I pulled two needles from my pocket. I moved to Eliana first and pulled her blankets back. When I put the needle in her, she barely twitched, just pulled the blankets back over her legs. I could already hear her breathing slow, her snores becoming labored snorts. Her legs jerked slightly beneath her blankets.

I moved to Merlin, needle poised, the dark guiding my movements. He grabbed my hand in the darkness.

"What are you doing?" His grip was strong, his jagged nails digging into my skin. "What did you do to Eliana?"

"She's moving on, Merlin." I pulled my hand away, then

pushed the needle into his neck. Merlin struggled with me for a second, then lay back and looked into the sky. I could hear the ravens' wings fluttering behind me, all of them watching from the barbed wire fences, scraping their beaks on the metal.

"Look at the stars," he said. I looked up to see the sky pure and clear, every star and constellation in front of our eyes.

"Yes, Merlin," I answered. "Look at those stars."

Just as I looked back up, we saw a streak in the sky, then another following straight after. The life of the stars was just as precarious as our own.

"Those were for us," Merlin said. "Did you see it, Eliana? We're in heaven. Can you feel how warm it is in heaven?" I could hear Merlin and Eliana leaving the earth, flying high above us. They were free.

Two souls. One night. Never spoken of again. I read through the papers every day looking for the names of those I have saved, but they're never there. The messengers have taken them, plated them with platinum armor and laid them at the feet of the angels of God. But here on this plane, they are nameless, ignored. The newspapers don't care about the Navajos on the streets, about Hoskie, my first, or Eliana or Merlin. Their laughter and their faces are already a distant memory.

CHAPTER 15
THE LAST DAY

Sony Alpha 100 35mm (returned) • f/5.6, 1/500 sec., ISO 100

THE CLOCK ABOVE Samuels's door read 6:30 A.M. The entire building was quiet except for a few lights flickering in the main corridor and the sound of a heavy, wet mop sliding side to side in the hallway. I looked into the window of Samuels's office and could see that the files I dropped off last night were gone. Mr. Gurley's ghost was there, sitting in his chair, looking back at me. He didn't say or do anything—just stared. I was sick to my stomach, my muscles aching. I took a seat at my desk and waited for Samuels to arrive.

Detective Salas arrived shortly after. He slammed his newspaper on his desk three down from mine and took a swig of his coffee. My heart raced. Mr. Gurley was in the corner now, near my desk, just watching. I wondered why he was here; he had seemed resigned to death at OMI. But somehow, here he was. He was following me.

"Nothing big happened last night, thank God." Salas sat with a sigh. He seemed tired. "I can't believe it. Not that I'm complaining. I need about two weeks more of this just to catch up on these cases." He wasn't joking. The case buildup was beginning to be counterproductive. When you have only seven detectives and a town booming with crime, some things are bound to be overlooked. Most things.

For me, though, a lot had happened. I felt so sick under that fluorescent light—empty and hollow and weak. I somehow contained my tears. I had become good at pulling my emotions right back into my body.

At last, I saw Samuels coming down the hallway with Detective Whiting, the senior detective in the division.

"Uh-oh. Better be on point. Here come the bosses," Salas said. He straightened his tie and made it look like he was typing something on the computer in front of him.

Samuels and Whiting entered the main office area not looking their happiest.

"Good morning, Detective Salas," Samuels said. "Rita? In my office."

Whiting followed us, shooting me his familiar glare.

Nothing pleasant ever came from a visit to Samuels's office, but today I was ready for anything. I closed the door behind me and chose to remain standing.

"Rita." Samuels sat down and began unloading his leather satchel. He put a stack of files on his desk, my report sitting on top. "Thank you for getting these reports done. I know this is a busy time for us, so I appreciate the effort." He pointed at Detective Whiting, who stood in the corner looking more like a bulldog than a cop. "You know Whiting?"

"Yes, sir." I smiled. "The head of our investigative unit. Hello, Detective."

"It's Sergeant Whiting."

"Excuse me. Sergeant." There was an uncomfortable silence.

"Rita, we have some questions on your reporting, mostly here on the Montaño case." Samuels opened the file in front of him. "How did you come to these conclusions you included in your report, Rita?"

"I'm just relaying what the camera is seeing, Samuels. Nothing more."

"But there is quite a bit more here, Rita. Some pretty major insinuations on your part, don't you think?"

"I am just relaying what I am seeing and hearing on the scene." I looked up at Whiting. "What is the problem with my report?"

"You seem to have your own theory about what happened to the Montaño family, despite the fact that we are still knee-deep in the investigation." Samuels rocked back into his chair. "Would you like to share that with us? I mean, beyond what you have written in your report?"

"You're talking about the photographs in the shed."

"You have accused a highly decorated retired APD officer of molesting his children," Sergeant Whiting said angrily. God only knows how long he had been wanting to snap my neck. "How did you come to that conclusion without any formal investigative crime scene analysis training?"

"There's photographic evidence, sir." I tried to stay calm. "Some of the pictures depicted Montaño together with naked children."

"That proves absolutely nothing."

"We can't jump to conclusions, Rita," Samuels said. "And you're a photo specialist, not an investigator, so the sergeant seems to think you're reaching."

"We don't solve crimes with Ouija boards at APD, Miss Todacheene." Whiting sniffed. For someone of such a high rank, he looked disheveled. His salt-and-pepper mustache had coffee stains on it and there was another yellow stain right above his badge.

"It's Specialist Todacheene," I said. "And neither do I."

Then Gurley reappeared. He rushed up to me, his face suddenly inches from mine. I recoiled and took a few steps back, unable to withstand his energy. His death sickened me.

"Enough of this," Gurley snarled. "Take me home."

"Are you okay, Rita?" Samuels could see that I wasn't focusing. He might not have been able to see Mr. Gurley, but he knew something was here. He had a genuine look of terror on his face.

"We also have reports of you acting strangely at the scene," Whiting said, moving toward me. "Do you have any idea what would happen to our case if the jury heard about how you get your information?"

"It sounds to me like you've been misinformed," I said. "Either that, or you're wanting to salvage your friend's reputation. I'm sure it's not the first time."

"Listen, Specialist. We can pull you from any case that we think you are compromising. This is one of those cases."

I could smell the little girl's breath again, almost like her spirit had blown a kiss in my face. The burning mint and metallic gunpowder. She was there too—her memories and words on my report.

"My report stands," I insisted. "There is nothing you can do to remove those images or that report once I've filed it. Your friend did horrible things, and he will never have to face justice. That is the worst part about this whole situation."

"Rita, we're pulling you from duty." Samuels sat back in his chair and chewed on his pipe. "I think we may have let you come back before you were ready. Dr. Cassler has reported the same thing."

"It doesn't matter how many days she has off, Samuels." Sergeant Whiting stood right in front of me and stared. "She is always going to be a liability."

"So, are you pulling me from duty today?" I peeled off my CSI vest and badge. "I think I might just take off the rest of my life."

"Now, Rita," Samuels said, sitting up at his desk. "I'm not firing you. I just think you should take some time to get your head straight. Get your focus back."

I looked at Sergeant Whiting smirking in the corner and knew that nothing was ever going to change. The department decided what they thought of me the second I brought down Garcia. That was always going to be my fault—this department losing one of its elder statesmen. It had tightened the noose around the necks of all the crooked cops on the force. It made them think about what they got on the take and how it might eventually bite them in the ass.

"No. I'll take my final with Dr. Cassler, and I'm out of the department." I looked at the sergeant. "I'm never going to be okay with what goes down here behind the scenes."

"Rita." Samuels was beginning to follow me out of his office. "We are not asking you to quit, Rita. I would hope that you would stay through the rest of these investigations."

"I told the both of you what happened in that report. Take it or leave it. But I am almost positive that there will be gunshot residue on that man's hands, because he shot his whole family before his oldest son had a chance to save them." I stared at Sergeant Whiting. "And he did horrible things to his family, and you all are covering it up."

"See? She just makes this stuff up. I knew it." Sergeant Whiting was getting his fill. "It just wasn't enough for you to get Detective Garcia killed. How are you getting your information?"

"It was the ghost who told me," I sniped. "Don't you know, Samuels?"

Whiting cracked a smile. Gurley roared up to me again, his body a rough scrape against me.

"It's time to go, Cop," Gurley whispered.

"Go ahead and do the examination. Dr. Blaser knows about all of it."

I slammed Samuels's door and walked right past my cubicle, leaving Gurley's ghost in Samuels's office. Salas spilled coffee on his tie as I stormed past.

"Hey! Where are you going?"

It was on them to figure it all out now. I could feel the heat rising on my face and one small trickle of blood moving from my nose to my lips. I felt suddenly weak, nauseated. I hoped that I would be able to make it home.

CHAPTER 16 | 13°

"For he delivers the needy when they call,
the poor and those who have no helper.
He has pity on the weak and the needy
and saves the lives of the needy.
From oppression and violence, he redeems
their life; precious is their blood in his sight."

PSALM 72:12–14

ANOTHER MEMORY. A prelude to this winter.

The day after I graduated college, I headed back to Delmont on an old Greyhound bus to see what had become of everything I'd left behind. Mostly, I wanted to go to the orphanage, to tell Father Benildus about my plans, about my life of service and to thank him for being a guiding star. The bus ride to South Dakota took hours. In the late afternoon light, the bus station looked exactly like it had the day Father Benildus dropped me off, the signs on the windows faded white from the sunlight. I walked down the dry roads that bordered the fallow fields and the empty houses. I still knew where everything was and could smell and hear the life I once knew.

It had been years since my aunt died. Not long after she dropped me at the orphanage, word made its way to the sisters that she was dead. No other explanation but that. Her house was closer than I remembered; my reappearance in that town reminded me of my own father coming home. How different our lives had been. I had an hour to think of those times, walking the now-paved road through town. I could feel Mama and Wapasha near me.

The sun reflected in the single-story farmhouse's front windows, bristling with red and yellow and heat. The house was new with life, the history of it a distant blur. A young woman shuffled to the door with a small baby in her arms.

"Can I help you?" The baby whined and gripped his mother's shirt by the sleeve. She walked down off her porch and met me at the sidewalk.

"Hello, ma'am," I said. "I'm so sorry to bother you but I'm just passing through. My aunt, she lived here about thirteen years ago with her husband. He worked for the railroad."

"We bought this farm after your aunt passed." Her baby began to howl. "Her husband . . ." She put a pacifier in her baby's mouth. "Well, she's passed, honey. I hate to have to be the one to break the news to you." It wasn't news, but I didn't want to interrupt her or the baby.

The woman's baby stared at me in silence, the pop of suction breaking through his pacifier.

"He killed her, didn't he?" I could feel my face drop, my grief in my throat. I felt shame in the question immediately.

"He tried to tell the police that he was too drunk to remember what happened, but this is a small town." She shifted her baby to her other hip. "We all knew what kind of man he was."

"Is he in jail?"

"No, honey. He's gone too." She stepped just inside the door to sit the baby in a high chair. "He shot himself before they had a chance to take him. Dad bought the farm and we have been here ever since." The baby cried again, his pacifier suddenly missing. "I'm sorry again to have to be the one to tell you."

The slam of her screen door echoed as I stood in front of Aunt Belle's house, the sun setting on the hillside.

I walked on, hoping to make it to the orphanage before the sky had turned completely black. My heart ached. When I finally saw the orphanage at the end of the road, I could see no life coming from it. As I moved closer, I saw that the front gates were closed and locked, and the orphanage was dark. A small security booth sat at the front of the gate, a slight, drowsy security guard sitting inside.

"I hate to have to turn you back but this is private property." He stepped from the booth, reattaching his gun belt.

"What happened to the orphanage?"

"It went under about three years ago," he said. "They're setting it for demolition here in the next month or two. I'm just out here making sure no one gets hurt or gets into any of the buildings, God forbid." He cocked his head as he looked at me. "Are you an orphan?"

"I guess so," I said. "I have been for a long time."

"Well, all I can say is things can only get better," he said. "Pray on it."

"Can I just walk in for a moment?" I stared through the locked gates. "You know, just to say goodbye."

He walked over to the gates and pulled the lock from the bars. "I'll give you ten minutes."

The walls of the old buildings were overgrown with weeds and ivy, the grout and stones black beneath the dark green veins. In the early night air, the orphanage and chapels hovered like phantoms on both sides of me. I could still hear the voices of young boys throwing themselves back, their resonance bouncing from stone to memory. They all walked with me just like they did when I walked these pathways. So much of this was in my blood. It had been the place where I had laid my head the longest.

When I reached the center of the schoolyard, I could see the rectory, its doors curved open by the rot of wood and water. As I bent the rectory door open, I could see that most things had been left just as they were the day the orphanage closed. Moldy Bibles still lay on bookshelves, rusted hooks still gripped a dusty group of vestments, a stole and Roman collar lay over a splintered chair. It looked as if Father Benildus had never even returned to his stone room, not bothering to light another candle or prepare another sermon. I stared at the floor beneath my feet, remembering the pool of blood that I had made when the room belonged to Father Saren and his secrets. The room smelled of anointed oil and dust, the aroma of allegiances.

I walked out into the courtyard and looked toward the old farm pond, just off the rectory stairs. The pond had dried. Only a small puddle of muddy water was left in its center, the last of the day's light reflecting on its surface. I walked to the edge of the old pond, the grass and vegetation growing over the remnants. In my mind I could feel the cold of that night when I took Father Saren to hell. The water settled into my body and into my clothes like hate. I walked into the dry pond, recollecting the water on my chin then over my head until my hair flowed easily and formlessly in the liquid, the blood of Father Saren swirling around me and into the darkness. I walked out into what must have once been the middle of the pond and stared into the sky, the stars only beginning to stare back. Then I saw it.

The old scythe was strangely preserved, with only small hints of rust along the edges of the blade and at the points where the steel met the etched wooden handle. I picked it up, finding it smaller now in my older hands. The blade smelled of iron, of blood, of a million lies. It had called me there for a reason. Although I had spent the last few years studying to have a normal life, I left those lecture halls and libraries still only having a hint of my calling. It had been years since anything had called me as loudly as this blade. I held it, feeling its weight and its consequences. I put it into my pocket, knowing that this was all leading me to where I was meant to be.

IT WAS NEVER my plan to use the scythe I'd retrieved from St. Joseph's. I've kept it at my side, yes, but only as a symbol of my most profound act of vengeance. Many years have gone by, and I've realized that a life of service can leave a bitter taste. As I've watched the daily drudgery of these people on the street, stuffing what little money they have into the mouths of those who hate them most, my hatred for those in power has grown sharper. These men. They run the bars, they run the loan offices, they run the streets—disguised as human beings behind their golden badges and blue polyester suits. They are the ones who really deserve to die.

You see, Father Benildus thought I was sent here to save people from the grasp of death, to help extend their hours and days on this earth through service. Over time, I've found myself going in both directions: saving those who are not ready for the warmth of heaven, and taking from this earth the ones who could not endure one more moment of suffering. But the reality of death and neglect in this forsaken place has brought me to a morbid realization—that I've been tasked with killing those who've poisoned the rest of us with their evil and irreverence.

This winter has tested me. The snowfall has accumulated to

over two feet, the conditions frigid and hostile, unlivable. I've been pulled away from the parish to help full-time with street outreach. But our outreach center is closed for repairs, with leaks in our roof and a destructive break-in behind us. Whoever we are not able to reach on the streets is going to die; it's that simple. The only other place that took people in was the detox center. But the city council had that place closed, too. All I have is my van, which can hardly provide the food people need, never mind the shelter. My helplessness has made me angry and spiteful.

Still, what happened at the Silver Stallion was unplanned— this I promise, and have paid my penance for. I had my eyes on an elder that night. Chayton was his name. As winter descended on Gallup, I tracked his movements more closely. He was to be my first angel of the year. He looked to be at least in his seventies, shuffling around the alleys of Gallup, his arms too tired to ask for handouts. He showed up at the outreach center a few times when we were handing out food and looked like he barely had the strength to eat it. He was the epitome of suffering, walking hunched over with his bowed legs. His gait looked painful, but it didn't faze him. He walked these streets with men a fraction of his age. He stood around the same fire barrels and drank the same clear bottles of vodka that they sold all over town. When you spoke to him, he smiled at you with his few remaining teeth. He was a veteran and that was what he talked about when he told you his history. It was his everything. Too bad his own country didn't feel the same way. When you asked him where he was going, he would always say the same thing. "Nowhere."

But each day he moved more slowly, his feet dragging with the heaviness of pain, his hands curling into dried talons, more like claws than hands. I don't know how he stayed alive through the winter. Maybe his skin was so thick and hard that he had lost the sensation of cold, a coating of the street built in layers. This was a soul that had to be lifted up.

That night, just ahead of Thanksgiving, I waited for Chayton outside of the Silver Stallion around closing time. It was the last bar on the east side of Gallup, straight across from the train tracks whistling through Route 66. A forsaken brown shack with withering wooden shingles all around its perimeter. The neon Coors and Schlitz signs sent a frigid blue light into the packed parking lot, where old, drunk bodies moved in the snow. Every winter, the warm metal of the electric rail line took the lives of Navajos sleeping off their visit to the Silver Stallion, their pillows made of steel. I watched three of them run across Route 66 in the snow and into the darkness behind the train tracks.

A half-hour before closing time, I saw Chayton make his way out of the back door, somewhat oiled by the drinks he had inside. He and another man sat out in the snow sharing a cigarette, the smoke rising into the winter sky. Between two old cottonwood trees, the men began to fill a blue barrel with wood gathered from the field behind the bar, eventually stoking an enclosed bonfire. More customers joined them, their hands orange from the fire's glow. As they passed around a bottle, a roar of laughter shot into the night sky, the moon joining in on the joke.

I watched until the owner, an awful man named Emmitt Gurley, came out to try to run them off. "You fucking Indians need to get out of here. Go home! There is no more hooch for you." Gurley had owned the Silver Stallion for years, one more in a long line of poison hawkers stretching all the way back to the days when they were building the railroad. He was short, with a heavy head of silver curls tamed beneath an old Peterbilt trucker hat. Everyone in Gallup knew him to be one of the most religious haters of Indians in town, a fact he was only glad to prove when he was one of Gallup's mayors fifteen years earlier. He wielded a stout aluminum bat and began pushing the men away from the heat of the barrel until only one freezing Navajo remained. Chayton.

"Get out of here, Chayton." He stabbed the old man in the chest with the butt of his bat, but Chayton just stood there as the snow built a dam on his coat collar. "Chayton!" Mr. Gurley curled back his arm and hit Chayton on the forearms with the bat. As Chayton moved away from the fire, Gurley began to hit him on the back.

I emerged from the blackness of the alleys, enraged. Two nearly white barn owls screeched into the night, sitting in the old cottonwoods above the fire watching and waiting for death. That is what the Navajos believed, anyway. I could feel the owls' power. They were there to witness. They wanted to see my wings too.

I moved into the light of the fire just as Mr. Gurley was about to wield the final blow. He stopped and looked at me, dropping the aluminum onto the concrete.

"You stay out of this. This is none of your business."

I had nothing to say to the man. I watched him melt into guilt. He picked up his aluminum bat and walked toward the rear door of the Silver Stallion, looking back at me through the grate of the screen door.

Chayton rose, limping into the dark street like a wounded dog. I thought for sure the beating had stopped his heart. I should have known better. His hardened hands were only a reflection of the generations of Navajo people who had survived every attempt to stomp them out. He disappeared into the blinding snow and wind, holding the lapels of his weathered coat.

I waited.

Not long after, Gurley made his way out of the bar with his hands full of garbage bags, the glass inside clanging. I watched him walk to the dumpster, out of the light of the streetlamps. The owls above me sent out their gravelly call, followed by a short screech; the ravens were also beginning to collect on the power lines and on the corners of buildings. I followed him, my wheat-rice blade in my pocket. My wing bones moved at my back until one hand rose up and grabbed Gurley around his stubbled chin and my scythe in the other cut straight through his neck. He dropped as the owls cooed in agreement. His blood warmed my arms, steaming into the dark.

Gurley's quiet gasp for air silenced the winter streets of Gallup. Not even the train or the moving cars could be heard. The snow fell on us, the flakes turning red when I looked into my hands. My wings writhed with joy under my skin, and I could feel them all—the winter birds—flapping and singing into the night. I walked back into the alley again, my scythe back in my pocket, and smiled. I didn't want to waste my killing. This was one that had to be done, even if the messengers hadn't told me to do it.

As I returned to my room, I thought of Chayton. I hoped that he had found a warm place to stay and that he had lived through the night. Gurley's blood on my arms took me back to the orphanage, and the gentle warmth of human blood, its stickiness on my body. The memory was like lightning. My body tingled as I sat in the dark of my bedroom, the dried blood now a crackled sheath on my skin. The blood stretched and pulled as I stood in front of my mirror, my body covered in black. I didn't want to wash it off. I wanted to remember.

I could see Father Saren ready to greet Gurley at the gates of hell. I could taste his fear. He was where he belonged.

CHAPTER 17
GOING HOME

Hasselblad 500 C/M 150mm • f/1.8, 1/2 sec., ISO 100, EV 2.5

BY THE TIME I had made it back to Downtown Village, my body was heavy and weak, my leg a constant aggravating presence. I felt foolish in believing that Mrs. Santillanes had been protecting me from the dead. There was nothing that she could do. I could feel the dead all around me, their souls pulling on me. My body was hot, pulsing from the inside out, the images of the Montaños, Mr. Gurley, and Dr. Cassler's dead patient pushing into my memories. I barely made it to my apartment before I dropped from exhaustion.

"Edwin, look at her," Grandma said as I walked in the door. She took me into her arms and held me up.

"Lay her down here," Mr. Bitsilly said. He looked at me, his eyes sturdy, like I was a child, a wounded bird. His hands grasped at his prayer bag. He began to sing his prayers in Navajo, his raspy voice rumbling through my apartment as Grandma brought me to my couch. She held my body close to hers and stroked my hair to calm me.

"Your work is done," she said. "Leave it alone."

I felt my body release. I willed myself to let it all go, to find peace, to leave this strange and empty place behind. My apartment looked nothing like it used to. Stacks of boxes lined the walls and countertops. Irvin stood silent with all of them, his hands against his ears, fending off an invisible screech.

Shanice came from the kitchen and put a glass of water on the table in front of the couch. "We finished packing while you were gone, Rita," she said. I nodded in understanding. They all had a plan and it involved one thing: getting me out of here. None of them would ever fully understand why it was so important for me to finish this work—the incessant haunting that would linger if I didn't follow through. It was so much more than just a paycheck to me. But I had to agree with them now. It had gotten away from me and there was absolutely nothing else that I had to lose. I had never in my life felt so sick with grief.

"You're okay, Rita," Grandma said, continuing to soothe me. I allowed myself to embrace her protection. In her arms, I felt five years old again.

"I . . . I lost my job today," I said. "Or I quit. I don't even know. But I'm not going back."

"Well, there's some good news," Shanice said. "Here, drink your water."

Shanice handed me the glass and I tried to bring it to my mouth, but my hands were unsteady.

"Oh, Rita. You look terrible," Grandma said. She stabilized the glass in my hand and helped to slowly guide the water into my mouth. "Táá hó'ájit'éégóó. You have to listen to us and heal."

"Jesus, girl," Shanice said. "What happened? How did you let it get this bad?"

"Let's get you to bed," Grandma said.

Together they moved me to my bed and Grandma tucked me

under my covers. Everything—the world, their voices around me—felt like a blur. I was slipping away, going somewhere else. For hours I slept, waking only to sip Navajo tea or drink soup. I could only sometimes keep the food down. When I awoke, I could hear them talking about me.

"We have to get her home, now." Mr. Bitsilly had been checking my room every few minutes. "We have to have a ceremony for her whether she believes in it or not."

"I know you're right, Edwin," Grandma said. "She is too sick to fight us."

"This is serious," Mr. Bitsilly explained. "Something has her soul in its grasp. It could be one thing or a lot of things, but it will kill her if we let her stay."

Grandma shut my door gently, but I could still hear her muffled voice behind it. "We'll take her to the funeral tomorrow if she's well enough. We'll need you to drive her car for us."

"Don't worry, whatever she needs." Shanice's voice. "I've got the apartment squared away. If Rita needs to come back, it will be here and so will I."

I knew what Mr. Bitsilly was saying was true. I was dying of a broken heart. The work had kept it at bay for years, but your heart and mind can only take so much anguish in a lifetime. It can only answer questions for the dead for so long. What I also knew was that Mr. Bitsilly would never be able to stop it. He could sing a million blessings into the sky and it wouldn't make what I saw any easier. You have to let go of grief. If you allow it to stay, to build up its own fortress in your body, it will kill you. Your body will never be able to bring your soul back. Grandma was right. It was up to me.

THE NEXT MORNING came, the cold of it unwilling to let go.

The Sacred Heart Church down in Barelas was one of the older parishes in Albuquerque. After the September 11 attacks, the church received a piece of the World Trade Center to rebuild their bell tower, the metal reminding the parish about the sacredness of life. They had a large and faithful group of parishioners. Back when she got around better, Mrs. Santillanes attended church with her friends and then went straight to bingo afterward. I teased her about it from time to time. But I never questioned her faith. She believed in prayer, and in living the life set before her by God. She was a saint.

It was good to see so many people filling the pews to pay respect to Mrs. Santillanes. I felt honor in knowing that I had been a part of her life. I was also glad that Grandma and Mr. Bitsilly were there with me, to keep me strong in the midst of my sickness and loss. Mrs. Santillanes's sisters—it turned out there were two—had arranged a beautiful service for her, complete with huge pots of red chile posole boiling in the back of the parish. I was surprised when her sisters came to us and hugged each of us like we were part of their family.

"Adela told us all about you, Rita," said Flora, the older sister. "She told us about all of you and you are always welcome here. Always." She had the same tenderness in her that Mrs. Santillanes had. I knew that she meant what she said. "We will pray for you," she said. "We will pray for all of you. Now, all of you must eat. Adela would have wanted you to be happy, to sit and eat with her one last time."

I took a seat at the table nearest to me, thankful for the respite from standing. My body was still weak, and hurting, and I had just barely convinced Grandma I was well enough to come. I stared at the food in front of me, unable to eat, unable to even enjoy the scent of Mrs. Santillanes's favorite dish. I searched the corners and the empty chairs for a glimpse of my friend, for one last sign or one last goodbye, but she was gone; it must have been her time. She was already on the other side, I hoped—her skin bronzed in the heat of the heaven she believed in.

As Grandma and Mr. Bitsilly said their goodbyes to Mrs. Santillanes's family, I returned to the church to visit her coffin one last time. A white woven sheet lay over the wood, a photograph of her as a young woman framed on top. I moved over to the altar behind the coffin and lit a candle for her, the red light of the candle glass flickered on the portrait of St. Michael below the windows.

Just then, I heard an echo of laughter in the pews behind me. A chill descended on the church. A familiar smell of blood and gunpowder. They were not finished with me.

"Are you leaving us?" the little girl's voice said. Her hand appeared in mine, then her face made itself known, her gaze dark and sullen. I looked behind her to see the Montaño children in various stages of decay, their eyes black, their skin pale gray, bloodstained. The littlest one began to cry as her ghost feet dangled from the wooded benches.

"Of course, she's leaving us," the oldest girl said. She was angry, resentful—speaking with her fists clenched. Six pairs of eyes barreled into mine. The little girl's hand squeezed mine tighter. My heart skipped, forcing me to gasp for breath, feeling the floor crash against my forehead. My mind spun from the impact, the confusion. Knocked down by an invisible force. I tried to brace myself and rise from the ground, but as I did, I felt rotting hands on my body, fingers tightening around my neck.

"Get away from my children," the dead woman said, her voice a brittle scratch. I buckled against the dark power, my back hitting the floor. It was Mrs. Montaño. Her torso was completely hollowed out; through her center, I could see the church ceiling above us. "Leave us." Her decomposing arm punched into my chest, sewing corrosion into my heart and bloodstream. I stopped fighting the urge to get back up, and quickly lost touch with consciousness. As I did, my world went dark, and the pain disintegrated.

I woke to the sound of footsteps echoing in the church, approaching me. Mr. Bitsilly and Grandma were at my side. The next thing I knew, I was in a car. Shanice was driving us away. I never got to say a real goodbye.

MUDDLED VOICES CRACKED through conversations. Bits and pieces of words leaked into my reality. Shanice drove me home in a car filled with the remnants of my life. Images and memories flew past, a grotesque blur. The gigantic American flag at the top of the west hills of Albuquerque flapped with a sting as we passed it, somewhere between Lost Horizon Drive and my future. The Sandias echoed distorted beauty back at me, their oranges and pinks and reds reflecting off the river as we headed into the setting sun. Soon we'd see the brown and yellow flatlands of Acoma, Mesita and Grants. Sandstone and tall red mesas. I felt suspended between life and death. A switch had been flipped.

"It's going to be okay, Rita. Hang in there," Shanice said, grabbing my cold hand. I could barely lift my head to acknowledge her. My ears filled with the whispers of a thousand voices. Mrs. Montaño's screams echoed in my head. My body was at its limit.

Shanice kept pressing the gas harder, trying to keep up with Grandma and Mr. Bitsilly just ahead of us. I held on to my mother's Hasselblad for comfort, its metal edges pressing into my legs. I snapped a shot of her at that moment, in the driver's seat, her face triangulated by the light of the sun. It was the last lucid thing I remembered doing.

"Where are we?" I managed to say. I looked out the window and saw sparse, popcorn-light snow hitting the windshield.

"We're passing Gallup now. It's snowing, so we're moving slow. But you'll be home soon," Shanice assured me.

Leaving Albuquerque was like passing through a locked door that I'd been struggling to open. I only hoped that a sense of peace was waiting for me on the other side. It'd be even colder in Tohatchi, I knew. Winter had already descended there even though it hadn't reached Albuquerque. That is how it was.

As we approached Tohatchi, we passed a group of Navajo hitchhikers walking on the side of the highway, trudging out of town and into the distant storm that was forming over the Chuska Mountains. Most of them were men, both old and young, coats pulled around their necks. Each extended a hand, dirty, wet, wrinkled—money flapping in the wind—offerings to the buzzing cars that passed them by with blasts of wind and snow.

We could barely see the road by the time we made it home. Wide and heavy flakes came at us like falling stars, their dust filling the windshield in the one-second intervals of the wiper blades. The road was dangerous. The two lanes had yet to be extended all the way to Tohatchi, so every passing car and semi made it feel like we were skirting the edge of a cliff. Tohatchi couldn't appear fast enough. When we saw the lights of the gas station in the distance, it was a relief. A haze seemed to build a halo around it. A light at the end of a very long tunnel.

At last, we pulled into Grandma's driveway. Mr. Bitsilly came to the passenger's side door and opened it. Shanice and Mr. Bitsilly put my arms around their shoulders and carried me through the front door and onto Grandma's couch. My memory, from here, became a blur of sensations. Grandma's warmth beside me. The trail of flames in the fireplace. The smell of sage and the echoes of singing in the dark. Then I drifted into darkness. My world became a room of constellations. I felt such sadness there. The souls of all the men and women who had passed through my lens were with me in that room. They pulled me deeper into the darkness with their contaminated souls.

I SPENT THE next week in Mr. Bitsilly's hogan, listening to him sing for me. I drifted in and out of consciousness for days, trying to understand who was dead and who was alive. I was truly in between worlds, that place where the spirit goes when it can't decide what is next. Lights and warmth appeared from the corners of the room, voices of people that I never knew praying for me to return to life with my soul in one piece.

Days passed and I finally opened my eyes. I was sprawled across the floor. Mr. Bitsilly was there, his forehead beaded with sweat. He was singing into the sky. Grandma and Shanice were sitting next to him, praying. There were others, too—several women, their ghostly silhouettes huddled nearby, their hair and faces lit up by the circling orbs of light that moved in and around the space. At the other end, there were three men engaged in Mr. Bitsilly's song, one of them hitting a small drum and looking straight at me from the other side of the void. He looked like Mr. Bitsilly's grandson, except older. His forehead was wrapped in a thick flowered handkerchief. He turned his attention to Mr. Bitsilly, who was leading the ceremony.

The sensation was too much; I had to close my eyes again. But when I did, I returned to that in-between world. In the vast darkness, at least twenty or thirty of my relatives stood before me. They were dead, most of them in tattered clothes, looking cold and scared, shocked that I could see them there. None of them could speak; they just stared at me in the cold, their breath billowing in the air. Mr. Gurley stepped in front of them, laughing.

"You can't help any of them without helping me first," he said. His voice was a gurgle. Even here, in the middle of this blessing, Mr. Gurley persisted. "The longer you wait, the more there will be."

I tried to cling on to Mr. Bitsilly's raspy voice and his rattle to find my way back. Out here, at the edge of the starry darkness, the songs of my relatives and my family helped guide me; not even Mr. Gurley could raise his awful voice above them, nor the songs and the drums calling me from the other side. Suddenly I knew that if I was to make it back, I'd have to fight my way there. I focused on the songs and prayers. At last, I found a small opening, a distant light that I swam to, pushing the blackness away with each stroke. I followed it until I could see a figure on the horizon—a being of white light that coursed with energy. The light's tendrils reached out for my arms and pulled me through the portal, embracing my body as I passed. I could hear others more clearly; the more they sang and prayed, the louder the voices became. I could feel Mrs. Santillanes's hands on my face, her warmth covering my body; I thought of my mother, now a memory.

When I came to, I was in Grandma's house, the scent of coffee wafting from her stove. She and Mr. Bitsilly were sitting next to me, talking in Navajo.

"Doo bił bééhózin da," Mr. Bitsilly said. "We have to teach her." The sound of the radio threaded through their conversation; ice cracked on the living room window. Grandma stood up and began to walk toward the kitchen.

"Ahwééh shibéézh," she said. The coffee was ready.

I sat up on my elbows and looked at both of them. "They're still here, aren't they?" I looked around the room expecting to see a congress of spirits still in conversation. Instead, there was silence.

Grandma didn't say a word. In her stunned silence all she could do was squeeze me, happy to see me looking back, no longer swallowed by whoever was haunting me. When she finally let me go, she began to cry.

"It is so good to see you, she'awéé'," she said.

"I'm glad you're home, Rita." Mr. Bitsilly helped me to my feet and hugged me. "You can't let yourself get that far away from us again. Do you hear what I'm saying to you?"

"I won't," I said. I owed them some peace. They were too old to be having to take care of me. I went into the kitchen with the two of them holding me at my elbows like a toddler learning to walk. I had let them down. The ghosts were still here, and I could feel it. I knew this sickness was something that the white man's science would relegate to mental illness. My Grandma knew better than to take me to the clinic—even if it looked like medicine would fix it. They knew my sickness was deeper than that. The sickness was in my soul.

Grandma turned on the kitchen light. I could see her age in her gait, each step slow and painful. The kitchen was just as it always was, every pot, pan and holder in its place. The old scarecrow clock was still ticking. It was cold as ever in her house, the linoleum floors absorbing the winter.

"Grandma, sit down. I'll make you some tea." I felt the weakness in my legs subsiding, the nausea finally gone.

"No," she said. "You sit down." I did as I was told.

Mr. Bitsilly nodded in agreement. "Your Grandma is right. You're still healing, Rita." He pulled his chair out, sat down, and looked straight into my eyes. "I saw the man who is pulling you," he said. "It's not him that has the power here. There is a force bigger than him doing it, driving him."

"I tried to tell you," I said. "It's not up to me."

"You may not believe in what I do, but you need to believe in something," he said. "I've tried to help you get rid of this thing, but it has figured out a way to stay with you."

Grandma stood over us, her arms folded, listening to every word.

"You have to stand up to this," Mr. Bitsilly continued. "They can't hurt you unless you let them. You need to learn to live with it, but that requires faith. You can see that our prayers have brought you back again. These things we do are for your spiritual well-being. That is something you have not been able to tend to. But you must. Just as your body needs air and food, your spirit needs to be cleansed and you need to learn to stop carrying things with you." He pointed to my heart, then to my head. "They were all inside you when you came here, and some have let you go. But there will be more of this death coming to you. They told me about it. We will need to cleanse you and tend to your spirit. You must put your faith in something."

I understood what Mr. Bitsilly was telling me. His prayer still echoed in my head even in my sleep. I wondered if he had planted it there.

"Where is Shanice?"

"She had to get back to Albuquerque. She took the train yesterday," Mr. Bitsilly said. "But she never left your side while we prayed for you. She wanted to stay until you woke up, but they called her for work."

"She's a good friend to you, Rita." Grandma set three mugs down on the table. "If she hadn't called us, who knows where you would be or if you would have even been alive."

"I'm so sorry to both of you for lying," I said. "I just didn't want you to have to get involved with all the things I was going through."

"Never leave your family out of your life," Mr. Bitsilly said. "In the end, we are the only ones who will set our lives down for you."

"I'm still going to see them, aren't I?" I felt a lump in my throat, almost knowing the answer.

"Yes," he said. "You are a powerful woman, Rita. This was given to you for a reason. What that reason is, you will need to find out. There is only so much a medicine man can do. You have the power. I don't."

He pulled on a leather strap around my neck, pointing me toward the medicine bag that I had over my chest. The bag had weight to it, the edges bright yellow with corn pollen.

"This is your own tadadíín bag, Rita," Mr. Bitsilly said. "Your prayers are inside of it. All of your protection is in there." He pulled several strands of cedar beads out of his pocket and tied them around my neck and wrists. "These items will protect you," he said. "When you see these things, when they ask things of you or speak to you, you must pray. You must push that negative energy away from you. Just as there are dangerous and angry people in life, there are dangerous and angry spirits in the other world." He held my hand. "When these people died, there was no balance—no hózhó in their lives. Their spirit is caught and that essence—that unresolved want—is what pulls them to you. Do you understand?" He hugged me hard, my ribs folding in. "Always wear your protection. Always. Your ancestors can hear you. They are here to protect you. I've seen it. They will need you again very soon and you'll have to go, but this time you will go with all of us behind you."

"I will," I said. "I promise." I had a renewed sense of protection with me, my soul emptied of the blood in my memory.

"One more thing." Mr. Bitsilly looked right at me. "Never let them know where you live."

"What do you mean?"

"Never leave your footprints behind when you work," he explained. "They will follow you right back home." His words filled me with dread. I wondered how many times ghosts had followed me back home in Albuquerque, my path like a well-worn prison trail back to my apartment.

"I always thought that you would somehow stop this, Rita." Mr. Bitsilly grabbed my hand again. "Now I know that none of us can stop it. So, you will learn to live with it and use every tool in your reach to protect yourself. And never be afraid to pray— to protect yourself. Remember, your ancestors are listening."

The three of us sat in silence around the kitchen table. I sipped at the mug of coffee Grandma had given me, for a moment just happy to be alive. That's when I noticed a pile of boxes in the corner of the living room, my cameras right on top. I walked over and pulled my mother's Hasselblad out from the stack. I lifted it to my eye and positioned Grandma and Mr. Bitsilly in the square frame of the viewfinder. Morning light came in through the window, bouncing off the fresh snow, illuminating both of them. Their faces looked weary, their eyes sleep-deprived. I snapped the photograph.

CHAPTER 18 | 9°

"Be sober-minded; be watchful. Your adversary the devil
prowls around like a roaring lion, seeking someone to devour."
I PETER 5:8

I AM NOT a soulless man. This is what I fear people will not
understand. After I sent Emmitt Gurley to his fate, I paid my
penance in blood. The new *disciplena* was fresh, made the tra-
ditional way with yucca leaves. The warm blood from the welts
made rivers down my back. Though it caused immense pain,
I loved the feeling of penance. The hardening of life on skin.
When I was finished, I washed the wounds on my back in the
hottest water that I could stand, rinsing the red dirt from my
emerging wings. It is strange to me that when I stand in front
of the mirror, naked and exposed, I have no wings. I turn to see
my back, smooth except the scars from my penance, my wings
pulled back into my bones. I can feel that they are getting bigger
and stronger beneath my skin, even if my head pounds right
alongside it.

Thanksgiving kept me busy at my duties, making food boxes
and driving my usual routes, coming back to cook dinner for the
parish. I watched them come to us for sustenance or shelter, their
heartbeats down to a slow simmer. They came with their tattered

blankets, their cardboard boxes, their threadbare pockets—the holiday a celebration of colonization, an ode to theft and backstabbing. I tried to provide for them from what we had, the backhanded guilt of mostly donated bread and nearly expired meat we picked up twice a week at the grocery stores. As the angry weather started up again, heavy and wet snow weighing down every tree and bush in Gallup, all I could think of was the journey—the long and heavy journey of the people on the street.

The following Wednesday, I spotted Chayton again, hands full of the brown bags the church hands out on weekdays: a bologna or peanut butter sandwich, a bottle of water and an apple or orange. He had two of them clenched up against his chest. I followed him to see where he was going. He stopped every block or so to rest his aching legs. He finally ended up at the library right across from the courthouse, where he ate one sandwich, then kept walking toward the train station. It was there that he spent most of his nights under the porch. He had only started that journey to the train station when the sky opened, heavy drops of rain falling on Chayton, soaking his old clothes.

I was prepared. Chayton had suffered more than anyone else on these streets and was twice the age of most of them. I could feel the goodness in his heart, the way it pounded heavy in my ears when he was close to me, almost like the sound of the trains—a scrape and howl of metal.

I pulled my van up into the station once the seven-thirty train headed west out of Gallup, onward to the ocean and dreams far away from this place. Once the sun set, the slow, heavy drops of rain had turned to snow, and the temperature fell with it. It was so cold that I could barely stand to shut the van off, my own heat making a thick fog on the windows. I watched Chayton.

He pulled a bottle from his coat and drank, the snow drifting into him with each push of the wind. He couldn't feel the cold. He kept his mouth to the bottle, frail and quivering, singing in a language that echoed in my dreams, words I would never understand.

The train station grew dark. This was Chayton's cue, his call to stand and say one last prayer into the night sky. A single blue light shone in the corner and illuminated Chayton's last song, his hand raised like he was holding an invisible rattle and sending his prayers up. He sang until his voice broke and he laughed at himself, pouring the last of the liquid down his throat and setting himself back into his small collection of blankets, his tattered coat pulled over his exposed ears.

The Gallup train station had been renovated in 1996 but still didn't have any of the modern conveniences—not even a restroom or a vending machine. It was an interest point for poverty tourism and nothing more. There were no cameras nearby, no record that Chayton slept on the exterior deck of the Southwest Chief after the passengers had gone back to their own warm homes and dinner tables. The oily concrete was Chayton's dinner table.

I moved into the shadows and watched Chayton talk to himself in a blend of Navajo and English, having whole conversations with people who now only existed in his memory. He laughed and cried with the same frequency, his body shaking and moving as he spoke. He pulled another bottle from his pocket, a makeshift container of brown liquid that he sniffed and recoiled from. He then lifted his mouth to the lip of the bottle, coughing and spitting as the liquid went down. His hands were scabbed over on every knuckle, his skin aged and punctured. I stepped out of the darkness and called his name.

"Chayton." I tried to sound comforting, but the sound of my voice startled him. He slammed down his bottle and stood before me. The snow blew in, now piled close to a foot on the concrete and asphalt that surrounded us.

"Who is out there?" Chayton was scared. He did not seem to notice as the wind blew open his thin flannel shirt.

"I am no one," I said.

"Are you here to take me home?"

"Yes," I replied.

"I've been waiting for you. What took you so long to come and get me?" Chayton had calmed down and sat amongst his blankets, looking down at the shattered bottle. Whatever he had been drinking soaked into the snow and left a scent of chemicals when the wind blew toward me. It was "ocean," the poison of the streets—a mix of hair spray and water and anything you could find to kill the taste of the methyl alcohol.

"Do you know where I'm taking you?" I sat down next to the man, seeing the dreams in his eyes.

He looked up into the black sky and pointed into the falling snow.

"Yes. That is exactly where you're going. How did you know?"

"My father was a Pentecostal preacher out in Shiprock. A real believer. He knew where I was, and he tried to come for me, but I'm stuck here." He looked at his hands and rubbed them together. "I will never be able to wash the blood from my hands."

"I think you will make an easy trip into heaven." I tried to look in his eyes, but he refused to look back. "I can feel your door opening. It has always been there for you; you just have to choose to take it."

I pulled my own bottle from the inside of my coat, a mixture of a strong rum and several valium pills from Father Mark's medicine cabinet. I looked at the liquid in the dying light of the train platform, its strength clinging to the sides in swirls. I handed the bottle to Chayton, who still sat amongst his blankets, unaffected by the snow. He took my bottle and drank deeply from it, then nestled it into his chest, pulling his blankets to his shoulders.

"My grandfather was a great man. A healer." Chayton let out a loud sigh. "I was supposed to stay here and become like him. I was supposed to stay." He drank another long pull from my glass bottle and sat back, his breath now heavy.

"You're death, aren't you?" His voice was slurring, his eyes looking past me. "That is what you mean. You're here to take me home. Forever."

"Are you ready to go?" I stared at him as he lay back, his body pressing up against the wall of the train station. I could hear a freight train coming in the distance.

"I'm ready, angel." He smiled at me and gripped my coat. I knew I couldn't let him lie here on the ice. Even if he couldn't feel it, the cold would make him suffer. I pulled a syringe from my pocket. The old priests at Sacred Heart were stocked with pharmaceuticals, their old bodies fighting off every disease imaginable.

I pulled up Chayton's sleeve, his arms already white from the cold, and pushed the needle into one of the many cuts and lesions that covered his forearms. I felt a quick release of his muscles and tendons. I stood above Chayton and watched as his body began to die, his breathing slowing until there was no condensation, just the gurgle of his last breaths. His eyes watched me as he ascended into heaven, his wings carrying him into the sky, away from the rest of us suffering on the earth below.

They would never know what happened to Chayton. To the police and the early morning station employees who would find his body, the death of another Navajo would mean nothing— especially one who had lived his life on these streets, year after year. They would be glad to have him gone, an easing of their own inaction and guilt. Another death from exposure. Another number on their list of statistics.

I can do this forever. Their hate ensures that.

I sat with his dead body and covered his earthly skin with blankets, leaving only his face exposed. The snow blew into him for the first ten minutes of his early journey. The flurries built on his face, white crests forming around his eye lashes, leaving frozen caverns on the creases of his skin. His face was at peace.

I could feel my own shoulders, the itch of the wings beneath my coat. Every time I moved, my shoulder blades shuddered beneath the cloth. As I guided Chayton into his next realm, the sky was preparing for me. Heaven was getting ready for my arrival. But not yet. There was still so much more work to do.

CHAPTER 19
HOME

Hasselblad 500 C/M 500mm • f/4 Distagon Wide Angle lens,
f/16, 1/60 sec., ISO 800, EV 11

THE SNOW, ONCE it began, didn't stop for three days.
Mr. Bitsilly's songs and prayers had brought the moisture to
the Chuska Mountains and everything within her valley. It
reminded me of my dreams, the ones where I ran into the noth-
ingness of winter with Gloria, the cousin-sister who died when
I was a girl, her trip to the other world a harsh recollection in
my heart. I could almost hear her laughter when, after several
days of catching up on sleep, I looked out into Grandma's front
yard and saw a good three-foot blanket of snow, the tires of her
old pickup buried up to the middle of the driver's side door.

When I finally woke, I took my mom's camera around my
neck everywhere I went, waiting for moments to look into the
viewfinder. I found a new sense of purpose with the Hasselblad,
something sublime that slowed the world's pace and allowed
me to heal. It was an adjustment not to be at the call of the
world every hour of the day, waiting for death to arrive so that
I could frame its emergence. Now the camera was here to help
me catalog the death of moments, of memories—to burn them

into the world forever. I took half a dozen shots of Grandma alone—some close-ups of her hands, a portrait of her in front of the stove. I photographed her shelves, all stacked meticulously, and her dog, Barkley, with his one long tooth that jutted out from his whiskers. In capturing these moments, I remembered what made this place so special. The ease with which I could move, breathe and exist here. The pain in my stomach, the ache in my heart that I lived with so constantly I'd forgotten how to be without it—I could only shake it loose when I came back home. Being here in Tohatchi was like imbibing a bottle of oxygen. It felt like I hadn't taken a pure breath in almost seven years. I'd missed it.

"It looks like we're going to be trapped in the house together for a few days, she'awéé." Grandma shuffled on the kitchen linoleum, settling into her chair and taking a bite from the nice sweet roll she had from Glenn's Pastries. I missed those, too. The sticky, sweet white frosting always made it into my hair. Grandma didn't seem to mind being stuck in the house—she had a set schedule in the winter. Get up, make coffee, feed the dog, read the newspaper, then watch her soaps. In the summer, her garden whittled away any morning free time she had, so Grandma would tape her soaps on an old VCR I gave her, using the same shoddy VHS tape over and over. She turned them on midmorning to record, then she would feed her little crew of chickens and tend to her plants. When her work was done, she'd watch the drama that had been unleashed during her stint in the garden.

Grandma handed me a sweet roll then turned her TV on with the remote. As her soap began to play, she looked outside the window distractedly, at the sheets of snow trapping her pickup in the driveway. The sun peeked through the thin clouds above us and pushed its light into the white snow, blinding us both. It had been years since I saw the Chuska Mountains, our mighty bluff, completely covered in snow.

"They've shut down all the roads in and out of Tohatchi. But I need to pick up a prescription later today." Grandma sighed.

I stared out into the white, the world melting into the color of clouds. I doubted that my little car or Grandma's bald tires would make any headway up the road to our little clinic. It wasn't a long walk to make, but I wondered if anyone would even be there. I was also afraid that there may be other things there as well, some ghosts lingering in their hallways or even on the road up to the clinic. Still, I couldn't hide forever. Even Mr. Bitsilly warned me that there was more death to come. My body needed to get outside—to get some fresh air, to exercise my wounded leg.

"I'll walk up to the pharmacy, Grandma," I said. "Even if I dig us out of the snow, I doubt we'll get any traction."

"You're right, Rita," she said. "It won't be long before all this snow melts and the mud traps us in here even worse. Ah, one day, we can put some gravel out on my driveway so that it doesn't get so bad. I've been eyeing that huge pile of rocks the tribe left on the side of the road up there." She pointed across the road. "It's just been sitting there for months. We might as well use it."

There were so many things that still needed to be done out here and I couldn't wait to help Grandma get started. It was going to be months before we could do anything outside with the winter enveloping us in cold. I had saved enough money to do some repairs on the house and get Grandma's truck fixed up a bit, since she refused to get a new one. Maybe I could fix up the garage too. I put on my coat and grabbed my mom's camera from the kitchen table.

"I appreciate you going, Rita," Grandma said, handing me a prescription form. She grabbed my hand and pulled me to her, looking hard into my eyes. "Be careful." Barkley stood vigil outside the door. I pulled my hand from her grasp.

"Grandma, I'll be okay," I said. "Barkley will come with me." The dog turned his eyes up to me, a wag in his tail.

"Watch him," Grandma said, her hands on her hips. "He'll bark at every passing tire." A car passed in the distance and Barkley ran after it, the snow billowing up behind him. "I told you," Grandma said.

I pulled my coat tighter around me as I stepped into the morning snow. The air was brisk, but I felt Grandma at the doorway until she lost me and Barkley to the falling snow. Mrs. Bitsi's house looked abandoned across the street, her fenced-off garden a pile of snow and dead sunflower stalks. An old doghouse sat tenant-less in the corner of the garden, weathered by the wind. The house's windows were covered by aged particleboard that had begun to bow on its corners; the fragile stairway to the door leaned to the left. It had probably been years since anyone had lived there. The house looked like it had died, and no one had bothered to notice. I put the viewfinder to my eye. Barkley ran ahead of me and into the frame as I pressed the shutter button down. I stood and watched the old house, almost wishing that Mrs. Bitsi's spirit had pushed its way into the emulsion.

It took me about fifteen minutes to walk up to the Tohatchi Clinic, dodging a few angry reservation dogs along the way and taking their picture before Barkley chased them away. Nakai Park looked the same, the chains on the swings still as rusty as I remember. So did the Tohatchi chapter house, with its peeling maroon-and-yellow sign to the right of the front entrance. According to Grandma, nothing much had changed inside, either: the same people who ruled the roost when I left still had their feet planted firmly on the necks of every community member. No one got what they asked for except the relatives of the chapter officials. That is how things worked around here, and I guess just about everywhere else. I wondered if they ever looked at that rusty playground in Nakai Park or at someone's house with no running water and thought they should do something about them. No, I didn't need to wonder. The answer was no. They couldn't care less. That's one of the first things I learned when I left the reservation. There wasn't much left out there in the world that wasn't stolen from one person to give to another. It's the same on the reservation. I took a photo of the heavy silver chains on the chapter house door.

I was shocked to see that there were two vehicles up at the clinic and one at the post office. Even in this weather, some people had made it to work, or maybe they'd been trapped here since the storm began. Barkley followed me up to the clinic door and lay down, licking the snow from his paws. There was one nurse sitting inside her little cubicle, a hazy fluorescent light fell heavy on her face.

"Can I help you?" She seemed less than pleased I was there.

"Yes. I came to pick up my grandma's prescription from Dr. Fowler?" I handed her the wadded prescription note from my pocket. She took it and walked off into another room. I sat and looked around as I waited. I remembered the last time I was here, for a nosebleed that wouldn't stop, and an uncatalogued visit from the other side. There were ghosts everywhere then, even if none of them were in the waiting room in its current iteration. I tried not to think about them.

The nurse returned and slid a small bag and piece of paper across her desk. "Sign here."

I signed. With a scowl, the nurse returned to her work. I had forgotten how unpleasant some Navajos could be.

As I left the clinic, I saw more trucks in the parking lot, moving slowly through the snow-covered hills and road. The morning sun had begun to press heavily into the snow, making it somewhat easier to get around but no easier to see. The post office—a small, brown rock building that had been there long before I was born— was only a few steps away from the clinic. I walked in through the glass doors and headed to the PO boxes, which lined two walls in the lobby of the building. There were about two hundred of them, with dials and letters and small knobs beneath them. Grandma had had the same PO box for as long as I could remember. I spun the dial and lined the combination up like I had never left. There are some things that you just don't forget.

"Rita Todacheene!" a strong Navajo voice called out from behind the counter. I only hoped there was a real body attached.

"Yes?"

"You don't seem sure," she said as I turned around. It was Mrs. Peshlakai, one of Grandma's oldest and dearest friends. She let out a welcoming laugh as she approached me, then pulled me in for a hug. Mrs. Peshlakai had worked at the post office or the trading post for most of her life. She was known for her sometimes-dirty sense of humor and her love of professional wrestling. Sometimes, as a kid, I would come to play with her granddaughter when she visited during the summer. She always turned off the television when we came in, embarrassed of her secret love of Rowdy Roddy Piper. We all knew.

"It's been so long since you've been home," she scolded. "Your grandma tells us you work for the police out there in Albuquerque."

"Well, I used to," I explained. "I just quit. My leg wasn't up to it anymore."

"Your grandma told me what happened." Mrs. Peshlakai looked at my leg and sighed. "We're all just happy that you survived. Not everyone can survive being shot, Rita."

"That's true," I said. "I'm blessed."

"So, are you visiting, or have you finally decided to move home like a good Navajo girl?" She laughed with a whine, which made me laugh in turn.

"I don't know what I'm doing, Mrs. Peshlakai," I admitted. "I'm here to heal. Then we'll see what happens."

"Healing." She pulled me in for another hug. "None of us do that enough. Tell your grandma I'll be over on Friday to watch our show."

"You two have a show?"

"We started watching *Criminal Minds*." Mrs. Peshlakai waddled back behind the counter. "She says it's like what you do at work, so we watch it."

I rolled my eyes at this and gave her a smile. "Oh, it was even more exciting than that," I teased. "See you soon, Mrs. Peshlakai."

A matted-looking terrier sat at the west side of the post office, right before the rise in the road and the old metal bridge that sat to the left. As I watched Barkley chase him away, I remembered the picture that Gloria took with her high school class, the one where they all sat around different parts of the bridge, their legs dangling off it. Back then there was some distance between the bridge and the wash below. Now, the worst you could do was twist your ankle or shock the bottoms of your feet in the dry riverbed. Gloria was the only one hanging over the edge of the bridge, one arm grabbing the side of the railing.

I kept walking along the side of the road, absorbing everything that had changed and the overwhelming number of things that had stayed the same. All the houses in the tribal housing units, the cul-de-sac with three or four identical models of houses, each with the dark brown paint on top and the white paint below. Cars slowly passed me, carving out paths along our tiny roads. This made it easier to walk in the snow for the crazy few who headed out on foot. My feet, by this point, were getting wet and cold, my boots offering only feeble protection from this mountain snow.

Once I made my way back down to Grandma's, I could see a truck parked outside her house, a mid-eighties Chevy with two-tone blue paint. The tires had snaked back and forth on Grandma's slippery driveway. Mr. Bitsilly was out there with a shovel, digging Grandma's truck out of the snow.

"Mr. Bitsilly? Here, let me do that," I said as I walked up the driveway. I extended my hand to take the shovel, but he took me into his arms and hugged me instead.

"You're looking so much better. Being home is good for you."

"Thank you," I said. I backed up and raised the Hasselblad to my eye. The viewfinder framed him perfectly—holding the shovel like an axe, his gloves crusted in ice and his eyes squinting from the brightness of the snow. I captured the photo.

We worked out in front of Grandma's yard clearing all the snow and ice from around the cars. There was a path out to the driveway, where the cold snow still provided a temporary barrier above the seas of mud. Every now and then I would peek up from our work to see Grandma in the window with her cat, Ashkii, watching us work. Mr. Bitsilly smiled when he saw me looking up at her. I had forgotten about that old cat.

"The boss is watching us, so you better get back to work." He shoveled a huge scoop of snow and tossed it into the yard. "I need to impress my foreman if I want a hot cup of coffee."

"You need to slow down," I said. "They say shoveling snow is not too good for the heart."

"Life isn't good for the heart." He gathered a huge pile again in defiance.

"I'm just watching out for you."

"It's good to have you here doing what you need to do." He took a break from his shoveling. "You do look better, Rita, but how are you actually doing?"

"I almost feel back to normal. Whatever that is."

The front door swung open, Grandma's voice billowing from the porch, "Okay, no more shoveling for you, Edwin. Get inside." She walked back in and slammed the door behind her.

"Well, you can't fight with the boss."

Mr. Bitsilly rested his shovel against the side of the house and rubbed his gloved hands together. As he retreated inside the house, I kept working. Being outside in the chill air felt good for my lungs, and so did the laborious work of shoveling. I started to make another trail around the house so that we could easily make it around back to the wood pile. Once I made it to the backyard, I lifted the tarp and crammed my arms with as much wood as I could carry. I didn't want to have to come back out here again tonight when the winter wind was at its coldest and the trails we'd made had turned to ice. I dumped a good stack in the garage and went back for more.

The morning sun was moving higher and higher into the sky, leaving a yellow-and-rose-colored hue all over Tohatchi. I stood in the cold and felt the sun on my face, the cool ease of home melting the ice inside me. It was eerily quiet outside, not even the distant bark of a dog or the sounds of semitrucks moving through the highway. It was as still as it could be. I stood in the quiet and photographed Grandma's field behind the house, capturing a perfect symmetry of earth and sky.

Farther out to the east of Grandma's house, I could hear the rustle of partially dried corn stalks moving in the silence. The sound startled me, because there was no wind today that could push them together like that, and I was pretty sure I didn't see any animals out in the field either. It was just the rub, the coarse movement of the leaves moving against each other in that heavy snow. Barkley ran sharply from the other side of the house and sat beside me, his bark intense and the fur around his neck sticking up and ridged. I thought for a moment that it could've been Barkley running around in Grandma's cornfield, but he looked just about as confused by the noise as I was. We looked at the empty field together while Barkley continued his howling. I took my camera and snapped another photo. Once the shutter button closed, the stalks quickened their movement and parted a trail away from us and out into the flats. It made me step back. Barkley barked angrily, eventually growling and running into the rows until I couldn't see him anymore. Something was out there.

I followed him out toward the fence line. As I approached it, two indistinct silhouettes appeared just outside Grandma's fence. As I came closer, I could see a couple, both of them older with tattered coats and weather-worn gloves. Their faces were hidden in shadow, soaked, wet hoods pulled over their heads. They looked lost.

"Can I help you?" I stood just inside the fence, Barkley baring his teeth and growling toward them. They looked like elders, a lost auntie and uncle. "Do you need a ride or a phone to call someone?" They both looked at me, cold and confused. Silently, they turned toward Gallup and walked into the approaching storm. As they went, I noticed that their feet weren't touching the ground. Barkley ran after them, distressed when they vanished into thin air.

I ran back toward the house with everything I had, and in my rapid movement, forgot just how slippery the ground was. I fell forward onto my hands and knees. Barkley came running; his growls and barks had turned into high-pitched whines. We ran into Grandma's house together like we had seen a monster.

"Hey, no wet dogs inside the house." Grandma shooed Barkley back into the garage. "What's wrong with him?" Grandma looked up at me. I was gripping my camera for dear life, limping on my injured leg. "What's wrong with *you*?"

"Nothing, Grandma. It's just cold outside."

She could tell something was wrong. She always knew.

I walked into the kitchen and sat at the table next to Mr. Bitsilly, who was sitting with his coat still on. The room was quiet. Both looked at me suspiciously, holding their coffee still but not offering up a sip.

"I'm fine, really," I said. I tried my best to look normal, to smile, to not let them have one hint of what I had just seen. "The cold just got the best of me today. My leg doesn't like it."

They still weren't buying it.

I stalled. "Mrs. Peshlakai told me to tell you hello." I reached into my coat pocket and pulled out her medicine and her mail.

"Thank you, dear. I was dreading the trip up there."

"It's good to be needed," I said. The silence settled in the kitchen.

"Well, I guess you're just going to have to stay here forever then," Grandma said. "I always believed that there was nothing for you here. But now that I've seen what is out there, I'm beginning to think this is the best place for you."

"It may be," I said. Barkley was still whining out in the garage. I looked out the front window and wondered if anything had followed the two of us back.

"What are you going to do for money?" Mr. Bitsilly always knew what to say. "I hope you're not like my son, who just shows up in between jobs when he has no money. Shíbéésóo ádin ndí."

"I have savings, and I'm going to reapply for my disability payment from APD. I saved that money to help Grandma fix up the house this spring. That was my plan."

"Well, thank goodness," Mr. Bitsilly said. "I'm tired of this generation of young people. They don't want to learn anything about the past, and they aren't in a hurry to help us into the future."

"If I run out of money, I'm sure I could find a job somewhere." I poured myself a cup of coffee and took a sip. "Maybe I can go work at the photo shop, at old Mr. Mullarky's place on the corner."

"They closed it," Grandma said. "It's an art supply store now, but I don't know how long that is going to last."

"What?" I was shocked. "How do you develop your pictures now?"

"At the drugstore," Mr. Bitsilly said.

"Or now they tell us we have to put our photos on a disc or a card or something." Grandma shook her head. "I don't understand it. Besides, I don't take pictures anymore."

"I do," I said. I picked up my camera and took another photo—Mr. Bitsilly at the table, and Grandma standing right behind him. "It's time for me to take the pictures I was meant to take."

CHAPTER 20 | 5°

"But if we walk in the light, as he is in the light,
we have fellowship with one another,
and the blood of Jesus, his Son, purifies us from all sin."

I JOHN 1:7

WATCHING THE RAVENS take Chayton into the sky made my blood hot with want. A part of me wished that I could go with him, feel the cold night sky on my face and the clouds racing through my wings. Chayton reminded me that the work I do is needed. It is not always the easiest thing to do, but it is right. I must give peace to the ones God has chosen.

I saw Rosemary again a few days later. It was the sign I'd been looking for. She was the last one out of the bar, wearing the same dirty brown corduroy coat she had been wearing for the last year, the one with the holes in the elbows. She wore threadbare red tennis shoes, canvas with white laces. I watched her walk up to an aged Oldsmobile that had just started its engine and knock on the window.

"Come on, man," she yelled. "Don't do this to me tonight."

"I can't deal with this right now, Rosey."

The car pulled away as fast as it could, the back end swaying on the ice. Rosemary stood alone on the street watching the taillights until the snow enveloped them. Then it was just her in the snow, with one lonely streetlight above her. And me. Watching. I could almost taste her. She pulled her coat around her neck and walked west on Aztec, maybe to find a friend, maybe to see if one of the old motel owners would let her sit in the lobby until the snow let up. This is what she always did. I knew, because I watched her. I've always watched her.

The heavy snow had begun to build up on the bottom of her pants, covering her red sneakers. I followed her. The deep, fresh snow kept me from making a sound. I moved into the light and called out to her.

"Rosemary."

She jumped, her shoulders up around her ears.

"Oh, it's you." Her eyelashes battled the snowflakes. "You really scared me."

"What are you doing out here in this snow, in this cold?" I looked up into the darkness, watching the snow fall on us like stars.

"My boyfriend." She tried to hold back her tears, but I could see them on her cheeks, the warmth of them rising. "I think he's not my boyfriend anymore. And I'm on the streets again."

I wanted so badly to take her into the shadows right there, to push the needle into her so quickly that she wouldn't know what happened. What alcohol she had in her system would help ease her to sleep. Then she would be off the streets for good, in a place where she could finally find love and acceptance. This was her destiny, I realized then with terrifying fervor, to find her place in the next world, someplace in the universe where her neck couldn't be broken by men's hands. I gripped the needle in my pocket and twisted the top, my heart hovering above my body.

"I shouldn't have told him about the baby."

My heart dropped back into my chest. That was the blood in my mouth. Her blood coursed for two. I could feel it rushing next to me. I looked at her, my eyes welling with fear. The fear I had for that child in her belly had me by the throat. I stared into her eyes, the darkness of them unspoiled in the streetlamp.

"Are you okay?" She reached out to grab me at the elbow. She moved in closer and looked into my soul. It forced me back. "Are you okay?"

"I hate to see you out here like this. I can give you some money for a room."

"Why?" She stepped away from me and from the light. "What do you want?"

"I know what I don't want."

"What is that?"

"I don't want you to die from the cold," I said. "Not tonight."

We walked down two blocks to the Roadrunner Café. Two men mopped the floors and cleaned the small counter with graying wet rags.

"We're closed," a voice bellowed from the back of the kitchen.

"It's Brother Gabriel, Vernon."

Vernon came around the corner in his yellowed apron, wiping his hands on the front bib. "Oh hey, Brother."

"Can we just stop in for some coffee?" I pulled my jacket around my collar. "We just need something to warm us up."

"I can do that." Vernon pulled two mugs from under the counter and poured us the last of the dark coffee that was sitting in the carafe, turning to syrup on the warmer. The men mopped and wiped as the snow kept falling in blankets, the lights of barely moving vehicles peering through the red vertical slats. Vernon came out from the back with one slice of pie on a plate.

"Since we're closing soon, I figured I would let you two have this last piece." He slid the pie toward us. "It's either that or I throw it in the trash."

"Thank you, Vernon," I said. "God bless you."

"Why do you care about me, Brother?" Rosemary dug into the slice of pie, chewing it like she wasn't sure she would like it. "I mean, after all these years you're still taking me to eat." She laughed.

"I don't want anything to happen to you, Rosemary," I said. "That is part of my job in outreach, to make sure we keep as many people alive as we can. Every winter, this is what I do."

"Yeah," she said. "You sure you don't have a crush on me?"

"I love you, Rosemary, as a child of God," I explained. "My thoughts are pure. I only have the best of intentions."

"I have to believe you, Brother. You've never touched me. You just like to feed me."

I had to laugh. I watched her gaze change as she peered out the window, her scarred hands gripped around her mug.

She took a drink and pursed her lips. "It's cowboy coffee." She sat her mug down and poured three packets of sugar into it. She was still a child in her mind, not even realizing the change that was about to come. There was no way that she was going to be able to continue living on the streets with a baby in tow, even if everyone knew she could protect herself.

"What are you going to do, Rosemary?"

She rolled her eyes and ate the last bit of pie off the plate. "I haven't decided." She downed the hot coffee and got up from her seat.

"We don't have to talk about it now." I raised my hands in surrender.

"Can you give me a ride to Mentmore?"

"Not in this snow, Rosemary." I looked across the parking

lot to see if the Roadrunner Motel next door was still open. A small vacancy sign sizzled in the window. It was one of the worst motels in Gallup, but this weather called for a last resort. The roads that veered off Route 66 were a tangled mess of asphalt and hills; anyone traveling in this storm would have been forced to seek accommodations for the night. I began to wonder where I was going to sleep as I tried to imagine myself in the church van, the bald tires turning against ice on the hill up to Sacred Heart.

We walked out of the café and toward the Roadrunner, the snow piling on our backs.

"It's thirty-five, Brother," the man at the till barked, his sallow face behind a box of yellow plastic. "One room?" He leaned his head to the side, staring at Rosemary behind me, her hands buried in her pockets.

"Two rooms, Amir."

"Just checking." He smiled, moving two keys over the counter and through a sloped hole at the bottom of the box. "And no parties or guests." He pointed at Rosemary.

"Don't worry," Rosemary answered. "No one could have a good time in this place. It's disgusting."

Amir pulled back the keys. "You want the room or not?"

I reached through the slot and grabbed the keys, sliding seventy into the slot. It was almost all I had left for the month. We walked out into the snow and found our rooms, three and six, a respectable distance apart.

"I know this place is a dump, Rosemary. But it's warm." I handed her the key to number three.

She took no time to unlock the door. "Thanks, Brother Gabriel," she said. "You saved me again." She shut her door.

I walked down to number six and let myself in. The smell of

stale cigarettes hit me like a board to the face. I turned on the television and tried to forget about where I was. I wished that I could make it back to the parish, but I had to stay focused here and think of my work. I had to make sure that Rosemary was safe in the morning. I would take her to the parish, if my van could make it up the icy slopes. We would find a way to help her there. There was no way that God would not save her from herself. She had to be saved for the sake of the child.

I lay down on the cheap bedspread, my coat still wrapped around my body, and drifted off to sleep. I woke up early in the morning and walked to door number three. I knocked a few times before looking through the open curtains. Rosemary was already gone.

FOR DAYS ALL I could see was Rosemary's face. Her skin and her smell followed me into my dreams. It wasn't good for me to think of her this way. I was having trouble focusing on the plan—figuring out how to get her to the one place where no one could hurt her anymore. I thought about her snow-soaked tennis shoes and her tattered, thin coat. But mostly I thought about the man in the car, the one who had planted himself in her mind and her body and then left her to die. Being pregnant and homeless is common in a town like this—a freeway of poverty and the women who make up its traffic. Gallup has no place for men to practice their proclivities, no strip clubs or whorehouses. They had to drive to find that. Here they can just go to the streets and take who they want.

The man who had abandoned Rosemary deserved a slow and cold death. After she left me at the motel, I turned my attention to him. I watched him for several days, following his path to work at the trading post up on the hill, seeing him step into the liquor stores after-hours, sometimes going straight to the bars. In that time, I only saw him eat once. One evening, he went to the pawn store on old 66, most likely to fund the trip to the bar that he made afterward. I wondered what Rosemary saw in him. I wondered if his blood would smell like liquor.

I followed him from the pawn store to the American Bar on Coal, where he sat and wasted away for hours as I watched the American flag above the entrance twist in the cold wind. Every now and then the door would open, and music and laughter would escape from the opening. Warm bodies usually followed. When the man emerged from the orange doorway of the bar, I was happy to see that Rosemary was not with him. She deserved her place up in heaven, far away from the hands of this man.

His maroon Oldsmobile sat under one of Gallup's deep yellow streetlamps. Dry snow sprinkled like dust along the top and windows. I followed him as he staggered to the car, his feet flapping on the cold sidewalk. He began to hum as he walked, something familiar but not placeable. I lost music a long time ago. I would rather have complete silence.

He seemed to hear me following behind him and turned. The humming stopped, leaving the whistle of wind and the sound of an approaching train in the distance. He was tall and had a hard and sturdy face—not handsome or even pleasing to look at. The yellow of the streetlamps did nothing to soften him. I think he almost saw me in the shadows, our eyes connecting. I tilted my head to see if he would notice. He squinted into the darkness.

"Who's there?" After a frozen moment he lowered his head and said to his feet, "Aw, Henry, you're hearing things."

I realized that I hadn't even known his name. *Henry.*

He picked up his song again, and started walking. I followed.

I waited in darkness under the marquee of the movie theater

as he opened the back door of his car to pull out a paper sack–dressed bottle. He got in the driver's seat and the Oldsmobile rattled to life, the heat from the exhaust sending clouds into the air. Through the snow-speckled glass I watched him rubbing his rough hands together and blowing into them, cupped up to his face. I emerged from the darkness of El Morro Theatre, the night shrouding my movements, and opened the heavy back door.

"Hey. Get the fuck out of my car, man." He turned to me, his eyes sleepy and red. His breath was soaked with alcohol. I gripped the wooden handle of the scythe in my pocket.

"Hello. It's Henry, right?"

He struggled to see me in the darkness. "Who in the hell are you?" He lunged for me in the backseat, but my body was just out of his reach as he punched.

"I've been watching you for a while, Henry." I used a soothing voice. "They're waiting for you. Did you know that?"

"Who is waiting for me?" The veins in his face contorted in confusion.

I thought about telling him why I was there. I wanted to give him context, to help him to understand that Rosemary was an angel, and that he had no business being a part of her life, and now the life of her baby. I knew I didn't have to explain.

"They're done waiting."

I plunged my blade into the side of his neck and watched the blood pump from his body, the warmth moving into my hands and down my arms. He grasped my blade and tried to pull it from his neck, but his slippery blood made it impossible; he was no match for the strength of my hands. The heat of his life pooled onto his shoulder and down the front of his pillowed jacket, soaking into the foam of his old car seats, flecking the windows like the gentle snow falling outside as I watched him die. He reached out for me again, his hands covered in his freezing blood, then surrendered.

It only took a couple of minutes for the snow to shroud us in darkness.

His eyes leaked tears and drops of blood as they stared at me. As I watched them settle into death, I swear I heard the laughter of Rosemary's children. I saw those gentle souls' futures on the earth. I blocked them out. She was much too good for a world like this. Her children, too. This I knew.

I had to pull hard to release my scythe from his neck—the bones and muscle still holding the steel and wood. When I finally freed the blade, the man let out a loud and intense growl that startled me, then settled his heavy body into the front seat. My job was done.

I opened the Oldsmobile door and walked out into the night. There was an unkindness of ravens sitting on the marquee of the movie theater. They cawed and gurgled into the night, their beaks clapping together in unison. They began to speak to me, their tones high and shrill, then low and chirping in celebration. Once they started their songs, more and more ravens began to collect on the street around my feet, swirling around my coat in the silence of late-night Gallup.

I left Henry with no guilt in my heart, though penance would have to be paid. This man was colonization personified. He was the bottle and the drugs; he was the man who pulled money from the land and blood from the water. He was their death and the love that they lost. He was all of it and now he was nothing.

I hoped that his descent to hell was long and full of pain. I also hoped that his death would finally set Rosemary free.

CHAPTER 21
SLEEP

Hasselblad 500 C/M 80mm • f/4, 1/125 sec., ISO 6400, EV 5

I ENJOYED SEVERAL nights of dreamless sleep with nothing but blackness at the other end. There was no end to the amount of sleep that my body called for—it seemed like I was catching up for years of restless city nights, of unsummoned ghosts inserting themselves into my subconscious, ushering me into their world. Here, I couldn't stop sleeping—and nothing, for a gracious stretch of time, disrupted that peace.

Until, that is, the dreams returned. The night Gloria came to me, she brought with her the nostalgic familiarity of home. I was walking the paths among the cornfields behind Grandma's house, in a humid haze of summer sun and gentle rain. The smell of wet dirt filled my senses as I approached the fence that lined the southern end of Grandma's property. Barkley was at my side, running and barking at the wind. That's when I spotted her, Gloria, walking toward me. She appeared there in the same way she'd always lived in my memory—her blue jeans and sneakers and T-shirt with blue rings around the collars and sleeves. Her hair flowed like it was under water, a gentle, fluid movement back and forth. When she was within reach, I couldn't help but touch her face.

"Hey, kiddo," she said to me. "You're home."

"What are you doing here?" I reached out to her and took her in my arms. I hugged her so hard that I'd convinced myself this wasn't a dream at all, but a real, warm, gripping embrace.

"I never left," Gloria said. "I've always been here, even if you didn't need to see me."

"But I see you now."

"Yes," Gloria said. "You see me because you need me. You don't know it yet, but you need me."

Suddenly, the dreamscape changed. A dark storm gathered behind Gloria, her hair picked up by the sudden wind. Grandma's cornfields clattered and swayed. Gloria stood beside me as we watched the squall build into tall spires of clouds.

"A storm is not all that's coming, Rita," Gloria said, her voice raised above the thunder and wind. "The storm has been here for a long time, but now it's coming to life and bringing death with it."

"I brought this here, Gloria," I said. "It could put everything and everyone in danger."

"You didn't bring it. It's been sleeping, but it's been here. It's ready to take all of them into heaven."

"Who is it taking?" I felt a surge of fear.

"I'm here to protect Grandma," Gloria explained. "I've kept every single thing away. For years and years. That was my promise and I kept it."

"How?"

"I push the spirits away from here," Gloria said. The storm began to rage behind her. She looked toward it, her hair suspended above her like snakes. "There is an evil that is coming for them and they need your help. You won't want to do it, but you have to. If you don't, more will die."

"Who are they and what do they want me to do?" The storm was moving closer, the lightning flashing into the entire landscape. "What do they want from me?"

"The longer you wait, the more there are," Gloria said. "That is what they keep saying."

"This is about Gurley, isn't it?" I said. I hated to say his name out loud.

"There are more than just him. All I can do is keep them away from Grandma. All the rest is up to you."

"What if I need your help?"

"I'm always here," Gloria said. "You may not see me, but I'm here."

The storm was getting closer, the harsh wind at my face, the cold on my skin palpable even in my sleep. Gloria smiled as the storm surrounded her, the wind pulling her hair and her voice away from me.

I awoke from the dream in a panic. It was still dark outside, early morning. I heard Barkley's howling in the distance, on the other side of the house. I tried to lie in bed and process what I had just heard and seen in my dream, my fear building as Barkley's concerned baying grew nearer. It didn't take him long to get to my window. Did he know I was awake? He called me with his bark over and over until I finally rose from the bed. I put my coat and shoes on and headed out into the cold, grabbing Grandma's old square flashlight that she always left by the door. Barkley was standing just off the front porch, his bark quieter now, his paws running back and forth on the cleared snow path. I followed him up the path, Grandma's one streetlamp illuminating the snow in a strange bluish-white haze. We walked back to the cornfields, almost to where Gloria and I had just stood together. I pointed the old flashlight into the cornfield and saw nothing but swaying stalks and snow.

"I don't know what spooked you, Barkley, but I don't see anything out here." I panned the flashlight through the fields again, shadows lying long on the trees behind them. When the rustling started, Barkley barked wildly again, running back and forth at the front rows. I frantically pointed the light into the fields, looking for anything in the darkness. At the middle row, I could see what looked like eyes peering out from between the stalks. When I pointed the light toward it, Barkley growled.

"Barkley, get over here." I patted my leg and pointed to the ground. He came over and sat at my side, barking and growling at the corn.

"What do you want?" I called out. No one answered. "You're not welcome here."

Barkley was completely silent now. He stared at the rows as we backed up together toward the house.

"What do you want?" I said again. The two hazy figures appeared, their backs to me. Their translucent fingers entwined together, their bodies emerging out of the snow. The two ghosts hovered south toward Gallup, a trail of light like heavy blankets dragging behind them. I followed them with my flashlight, which started to flicker in the dark. It must have startled them. They turned their faces to us and screeched, the snow kicking up all around them.

A horrifying whisper came through on the wind. "They are dying from your silence." It didn't sound like Gloria's voice to me; instead, it sounded like the growl of death, the grumbled and scratchy renderings of severed vocal cords, an eerie force, coursing through my ears. I retreated, Barkley by my side, my heart racing inside my chest. I turned and ran back toward the house as fast as I could move.

"Don't worry, Barkley," I said once we were inside. "It was nothing."

Barkley looked at me as I turned off the kitchen light. He wasn't so sure.

AS THE SUN rose over the Chuska Valley, I walked through the front yard with my camera in hand, Barkley cautiously following me. We went around back to the cornfield again and looked out on the snow-covered expanse. Our parallel footprints were still in the snow from the night before, but no others—not in the rows or where I'd watched my own fears dance last night. There was nothing—the ghostly Diné figures who'd appeared before us, hovering inches above the ground, were gone. Only my memory of them remained, the echo of their awful whispers. I knew that something was approaching.

It started to snow again as I walked up to the top of the hill above Grandma's house. I took my camera and framed the view in the early morning haze. The thick flakes moved fast, creating falling sheets in the light of the still-rising sun. I took four photographs, thinking of the camera's square frame and how they might piece together as one image. As I looked out, I witnessed a changing Tohatchi. Other residences had begun to encroach on the acre where Grandma's house sat, two houses on the sides and one at the back of the hill. They were literally closing in on us, obscuring our view of the Chuskas.

When I went back inside, Grandma was sitting in the kitchen, her long cotton socks pulled all the way up to her knees, her stained slippers still curling up at the toe.

"Good morning," she said. When I sat down next to her, she smiled at me and pulled me in close. "You look tired."

"I'm okay," I said, happy to be there at that moment. There in her kitchen, I was safe from everything.

"You needed the rest, dear." Grandma rose to her feet and grabbed some tortillas from the stove and put them in the center of the table. "I warmed up some mutton stew for breakfast, and there's some coffee on the stove."

I poured myself a cup of coffee from the saucepan on the stove, and as I filled it with grandma's canned milk, a constellation of coffee grinds rose to the top. Grandma moved in the kitchen, soft and graceful, pulling bowls from the cupboard and opening the steaming pot with her handmade potholders. The two bowls of stew I brought to our table flowed with licks of steam. My mouth watered.

I went to the doorway and grabbed my camera out of my bag. I put my eye to it and framed Grandma in the shot, a wide smile on her face, the steam curling around her sweater. When I advanced the film, the cartridge clicked, then the final thin section of film wrapped itself around the roll.

"You finished it," Grandma said.

"I have more film somewhere," I said.

After breakfast Grandma shuffled to tend the fire in the living room, soap operas beckoning her from the television. The boxes of my life still stacked in the hallway were unruly and disorganized, large boxes on top of small ones. I searched a dozen before I finally found my tank and rolls for the Hasselblad, then hid myself in the hallway closet, pulling the negatives from the roll in the dark, my memory of the maneuver guiding me. My eyes measured the mixtures as I stirred the developer into swirls in the container. The chemicals rolled back and forth in the tank as I counted down the seconds in my head. I clipped the negatives on a thick string I'd found in Grandma's drawer; the plastic bindings barely able to make their way around the thick cotton. They all swayed in unison in Grandma's bathroom, where I hung them up.

It felt good to be doing this again, to bring back the memories buried inside my muscles. I could see the images on the film, the dark gray shadows proving that I still had my mixtures right, bringing the camera sketches into reality. My fingers ran along the edges of the film, pulling the images up to the light. In the light of the window, I could see the streets of Albuquerque; the woman from the laundromat, her basket heavy with clean clothes; the long, desperate alleys of downtown and the self-portrait I took at the bus stop on Central, the whir of passengers creating blurs around the edges of my body.

The second section of the roll held some photographs I had no idea I had taken, a distant and obscured view of things passing by, the corners of window frames invading the screen. None of it was clear through the prism of window light, my unsteady fingers holding them to the sky. I dug through my box again until I located my eyepiece, an old tool that had lived on my desk for all the years I worked at APD, still finding its usefulness in the prison of digital. One thing I didn't have was a light box. The last one I owned met its end under the boots of Garcia's men and I had never bothered to replace it.

I brought my negatives to the window. I had a strange desperation to see what was in the photos; my fingers trembled as I stuck a small piece of masking tape to the window to keep the roll from curling. I pressed against my eyepiece, bringing the negatives into focus. They were there as I remembered them, the mountains, the cold streets of Albuquerque, the beams of light and adobe edges, the white window frames, clean and perfect in the downtown windows.

As I moved through the negatives one by one, I began to see the darkness in them, shadows crawling in from the corners of the negatives. On the streets, beams of odd, ghostly light stirred among the living, some beings reduced to dusty shadows, the grays and blacks elongating their necks and mouths. On the fifth negative I could see the woman grasping her laundry basket, her face worn and tired, with three small ghosts behind her, their fingers tangled in the pockets of her heavy sweater. Nearly all the negatives had some sort of anomaly, glitches that made themselves known somewhere between the air and the burn of the lens.

The eighth photo was my self-portrait. My body was circled by a mass of black, a shawl of curled smoke filling the frame. My eyes strained to make out faces in the black of the negative. Blurred and angry, their stomachs filling with what they'd taken of my soul. Toward the end of the roll, Grandma and Mr. Bitsilly sat in Grandma's kitchen, their eyes and bodies filled with worry. Around them, bright lights hovered in clusters, shining gray-blue down on them. But behind them, the slight outline of a man, his slender body in the corner of the room, his beard and his neck still caked with blood. I knew that face. I dropped my eyepiece on the bathroom floor.

"Are you okay, Rita?" Grandma stood in the bathroom with her arms full of folded towels. I felt the rage and fear on my face, a quick turn of blood rushing through my body. In the photograph, right behind my grandmother, stood Mr. Gurley, staring back at the frame directly, his body a darkened haze of gray, his mouth open, mid-speech.

"I'm okay, Grandma," I said. I stood back and stared at the negatives: twelve blocks of ghosts backlit by snow. "Don't worry."

"I think I hear someone coming up the driveway," she said.

It took me a second to pry myself from the negatives, the feeling of dread they now gave me. We both went to the living room window. Grandma was right—two vehicles were pulling into the icy driveway, and even as the heavy snow obscured our view, I could see that it was two cop cars.

"What did you do?" Grandma looked at me and closed the curtains.

"I haven't done anything," I said. "What do you mean what did I do?"

There was a knock at the door.

Grandma gave me another concerned glance. "Are you sure you didn't do anything?"

"Grandma, open the door." We peered out into the cold.

There were two officers standing there on Grandma's front porch. One was wearing a Gallup Police uniform, the other a Navajo Nation uniform. We were getting a visit from two jurisdictions at once. The Gallup officer was a woman—someone I recognized. Detective Arviso. She took off her hat and shook off the snow, showing her long black hair tied into a tsiiyééł.

"We're sorry to bother you this morning," she said, then looked at Grandma. "I'm Detective Arviso, from Gallup PD. This is Officer Hale, Navajo police. I worked with Specialist Todacheene on a case a few weeks ago, and I wanted to talk to her."

"Are you here to arrest her?" Grandma glared at the officers.

"No, ma'am," Arviso said.

"Thank you, Grandma," I stepped in. "Detective, it's great to see you again. What can I help you with? And . . . what are you doing here in the middle of this storm?"

"Come in," Grandma said. "You're letting all our heat out."

The officers came inside, and Grandma ushered them to the kitchen. "Sit, sit," Grandma insisted. They knew better than to say no. They both took their seats, stiff and uncomfortable with their duty belts still wrapped around their torsos.

"How do I say this? I'll cut to the chase," Detective Arviso said. "Rita, we're . . . looking for an investigator. We need help. We called OMI in Albuquerque to put in the initial report and Dr. Blaser told us to contact you. He said you'd moved back to the reservation, that maybe you wouldn't want to come back. But he speaks very highly of you."

"I see. And how did you find me?" It was shocking to me just how small the world had become. I thought I was going to be able to at least hide from the living out here on the reservation.

"We asked for you over at the Thriftway and they told us you lived here, next to the old police station, the white house with red trim."

"Well, I guess those guys at the Thriftway really have our number, Rita," Grandma said, irritated. "Tohatchi is full of gossip."

"We don't have enough investigators in Gallup and the Feds sometimes have to cover. But it's just taking too long," Arviso said, resting her hands on the table before her. "We've been taking our vics to Albuquerque for processing and autopsy, as you already know. We've had an uptick in deaths recently and we're trying our best to keep up. Our crime scene unit is severely understaffed right now, and I don't even have to tell you about the tribal police and their own staff issue."

"I'm sorry to hear that," I said. There was a long silence. Grandma brought her kettle and three mugs over to the table. I thought of what that voice in the field had whispered to me. There were more coming. I didn't know what to think now, what I should do. Grandma poured tea in our mugs.

"Thank you, ma'am," Arviso said. "Ahéhee. Officer Hale here is with me because we were having to inform family out in Sheep Springs today and this is his jurisdiction."

Officer Hale stood up at the table and shook our hands sheepishly, embarrassed that he hadn't done it already.

"Ya'at'eeh," he said. "I live up in Nakaibito so this is my beat at the moment. My dad used to work for El Paso Gas, so I've been here my whole life."

"Well, I'm sorry you came all this way, Detective Arviso. Officer Hale. But I'm retired." I took a sip of my tea and looked at the two of them. I wasn't about to jeopardize all the work and sacrifice that it took to pull me back from the abyss. I couldn't just go out and invite it all back in. But still, I couldn't stop thinking about that whisper. There were more coming.

Detective Arviso swallowed. She seemed to expect I'd say as much. "We had a second murder in Gallup, a body discovered in a car. It was a little too close to our case at the Silver Stallion, the Gurley case. It looked to me like the same kind of wound, the same kind of weapon. Of course, that's all preliminary, but aside from where the bodies were found, there wasn't much difference."

"That murder," I said. "The one in the car. When was it? I didn't see it in the paper. You'd think it would be front page."

"It was early this morning. They were getting ready to tow a car along Aztec when they found the DB inside." Arviso nodded toward Hale. "We called OMI and they suggested we talk to you. So, here we are. We're still making efforts to remove the body."

"The body is frozen inside his car in front of El Morro Theatre," Officer Hale said. "The victim was also wanted on the reservation for drug trafficking and sexual assault."

"Oh my God," Grandma said. She had one hand over her mouth, the other holding on to the table.

"I apologize, ma'am," Arviso said. "We really need help. That is all I can say."

The room went quiet, save for the distant voices from KTNN coming from Grandma's room. When I looked at Grandma, she was staring straight at me. She wanted me to say no.

"What would you need me to do?"

"We really need an investigator with your kind of credentials, Rita. We're not just looking for someone to take pictures."

I stood up and looked out the window. "What else did Dr. Blaser tell you?" I had been wanting to ask that question since they got here. Something about the way Arviso had just phrased it—*your kind of credentials*—made me weary. I didn't trust that they were just recruiting for the Gallup Police.

"We heard some . . . rumors about you, Rita. I'm not going to lie. We know that some people at APD say you can see things. Things that help solve cases. And that is why you quit."

"Even the girl at the Thriftway knew," Officer Hale said.

"That may or may not be true, but it's not why I quit," I shot back. "I quit because I was tired of working for a bunch of criminals. It was draining beyond belief. Some of the cops at APD are as bad as the criminals themselves. I almost died last year."

"We didn't mean to upset you," Detective Arviso said. "I . . . Dr. Blaser warned us you might feel this way. I understand, Rita. I do."

I thought about all the trauma I was carrying with me. I thought about what Mr. Bitsilly had said, about how more death was on its way, about how none of it would stop until I did the work. Now, I had the tools to protect myself.

It was the thought of Mr. Gurley appearing in the photo

negatives, though, that made my choice easier. "I'll—I'll come, but not permanently. Just to see if I can understand what's happening."

There was still Grandma to convince. She stood up, nearly blocking my way to the door. "Rita?" Her eyes said all of it. "Think of what you're doing. Remember everything that you just went through." She turned her attention to the two officers. "How are all of you going to make it back to town in this snow?"

"Don't worry, ma'am." Officer Hale pulled his coat around his ears. "We do it every day."

"Thank you so much, Rita," Arviso said. "I'll wait for you in the driveway. Take your time. Whenever you're ready, we can head to Gallup." The officers stepped out, filling the room with one more arctic blast.

Grandma stood by the kitchen table, furious with me. "Nothing is going to change with you, Rita," she said. "Remember what Edwin told you. Don't forget to pray. Don't forget everything he gave you." She looked me in the eye, then began cleaning up the mugs.

I retreated to my room, grabbed my tadadíín bag from a hook in my closet. I pulled it around my neck and tucked it in my shirt. "You heard what Mr. Bitsilly said, Grandma. This is never going away," I said as I walked back to the kitchen. I avoided eye contact with Grandma—the only person who could convince me to stay. She was probably right, too. It was too early to go back. Too quick. "He said it's coming, and I believe him. This will not end unless I end it." I pulled my coat off the chair and dug around one of the boxes still stacked in Grandma's kitchen for my Nikon camera bag.

"I still don't understand why you do this, Rita," Grandma

said, and hung her head. "I just don't want this to kill you like it almost did last time. Please tell me it's not going to kill you."

"It will kill me if I try to ignore it," I said.

I walked out into the snow and opened Arviso's cruiser. Mrs. Santillanes's rosary, my monster beads and my tadadíín bag all dangled around my neck. I didn't feel the weight of death on me yet. This time, I had to remember to keep my balance.

CHAPTER 22 | 15°

"But those who won't care for their relatives, especially those in their own household, have denied the true faith. Such people are worse than unbelievers."

1 TIMOTHY 5:8

I LASHED MYSELF twenty times when I got home, the yucca whip encasing my body, joining my hands, which were still sheathed with the blood from the man who had impregnated my Rosemary. I could still smell his blood on my body, the stain of it like long gloves encasing my arms. Our blood mixed with every lash, the yucca mixing with every heave.

As I stood up from the chair in the corner of my room, I heard something—a creak of the door, a gust of wind, a ruffling of feathers. Something. I felt a slow undoing of my sanity, my mind playing tricks on me. The darkness was following me, taunting me. I focused on the things I could understand, solid objects here on earth: my desk with a ream of paper and two pencils, the photograph of Archangel Michael on the brown wall. I thought of my private altar under my bed, thought about visiting it for safety, laying my scythe below St. Michael and praying to him for guidance. Then I felt a chill.

"Hello?" I called out. "Is anyone there?"

Nothing replied, but I felt it in my bones. I wasn't alone.

I needed to get out of there before I was swallowed whole by the darkness. Blood dripping from my back, I gathered a bag of my things. My needle with its poison, my scythe, a change of clothes, the retablo of St. Michael. I'd go to the abandoned outreach center, I decided. Nobody would find me there. I'd be safe. Before I went, I mopped up some of the blood from the floor and tried to wrap my wounds in bandages. It was a makeshift job, but it would do.

I looked into my humble room, almost afraid to leave the quiet and security of my home. The sisters wouldn't be there to forgive me, to share in my secret and my devotion. I would move forward alone. I unlocked the door to my altar and kneeled before St. Michael, my offering filled with the images of all the souls I had sent him, and begged for forgiveness. I could smell the blood in my chalice, my offering of life, and opened up my hand once more, adding my own blood to the sacrifice, consecrating all that I was leaving behind. This altar was my last and best offering before moving to the next world, before holding open the gates for Rosemary and her unborn child.

I headed out into the cold, into the van. Gallup was encased in ice, a beautiful infusion of frigid cold and silence. Only the sound of the train echoed through the city. Not a soul was on the streets as I wove through them. The alleys seemed abandoned, no tents or people sleeping under blankets. I wondered if somehow this was my heaven, if I was already there, living my final dream of mercy, where no one was left to suffer. Rosemary was nowhere to be found.

As I made my way to the outreach center, I clutched the

retablo for guidance. Archangel Michael had commanded the army of God; it was his job to bring those close to death straight to the heavenly gates, especially those who were cruel and evil during their time on earth. Good and evil, he brandished his scales, ready to make the final judgment. All those I have taken in mercy are there with him right now.

Killing Henry was more than just bloodlust. I know this now. I wanted to put a weighty fear into all the rest of the people in this city, to make them sick with the smell of alcohol and money. I wanted them to take a hard look at how they lived their lives. They needed to know that their choices would not go unpunished. They needed to know that when they looked out into the night thinking they were seeing a sky full of stars, they were really seeing the reflection of a thousand raven eyes looking back at them, ready to send them to the shadows and the gutters.

Down by the El Morro, I saw someone standing under the marquee, arms crossed over their chest. I slowed down and lowered my window to see who was behind the blinding snow. No one was there. The snow hypnotized me as I made my way down every road and alley looking for her. I stood outside the van and looked up into the sky, feeling the snow on my face. There was no one there with me. No messengers. Nothing speaking from the fence lines or the rooftops. The voices had stopped, the urge to move out into the cold and the rage and all of it felt miles away.

I yelled out for Rosemary. The words never echoed back to me in the thick of that snow. The streets absorbed it all. I can't describe the feeling I had, like awakening from a coma after years of sleep. I've had other moments of clarity before in my life, and I knew that it wouldn't last. I prayed for Rosemary and for her baby. I prayed that I had saved her and her child from a lifetime of beatings and suffering. I prayed that I had saved her life by taking Henry's.

When I finally made it to the outreach center, anguish threatened to consume me. Pain was screaming in my ears now, as water leaked in from the ceiling, sending me deeper and deeper into my visions. I clutched at the fresh wounds on my back, the bandages wet from blood. I stared at St. Michael, the gold leaf around his wings shimmering in the streetlight. I cut my arm open and watched the blood pool into the gold, the borders of black filling with my blood.

The ravens were already at the window, pecking their beaks against the glass, wondering when their next offering was coming. They wanted another innocent.

"You are not finished with your work," one raven said. It flew inside the building; it spoke to me from the back of a wooden chair, its eyes following my every move.

"I know I am not finished," I said, "but how much more of this would you have me do?"

"Two deaths now were not born of mercy," the raven said. "Those kills were born of rage, your own weakness. They were a product of your sin. Your lust."

"I have given you what you wanted," I said. "Their souls have been given to you."

"We didn't ask for their souls, Gabriel." The raven's eyes were red at the corners.

"How many more must I take for you to finally let me go?" I needed an answer. I needed my wings. I needed mercy and to move on from this world. This world had brought me nothing but lies and terror.

"We don't just want one more soul. You must take two."

"How can you ask this of me?"

"You must take the woman. We can feel her power." The ravens all began to croak, their bodies turning the tree in front of my room black. "We were surprised that you let her go."

"You're talking about Rosemary." At that moment, I knew. The ravens had heard.

"Yes," the raven answered. "But it's the baby we want."

CHAPTER 23
207 W. COAL AVENUE, GALLUP, NM
Nikon D2X • f/16-f/2.8, 1/500-1/250 sec., ISO 400

THE FROZEN BODY sat in its car in front of El Morro Theatre, boxed in by a triangle of yellow tape along Coal Avenue, between Second and Third. A few people stopped and stared as we arrived on scene, but the weather kept most of the gazers looking out from the nearby stores, their faces framed in the windows. It was a dark, cloudy day, more like night than morning; the wind made the temperature almost unbearable. Last night's snow created heavy waves of ice dust blowing along our path. The maroon Oldsmobile was as Arviso described, snow and ice concealing the body inside.

"The car was partially pulled into the fire lane here," Arviso pointed to the sidewalk out in front of the El Morro, the red paint peeking out from the snow. "An officer drove by this morning and put a parking ticket on the window. A tow truck came by later, and the driver saw our man here. That's when we got our morning wake-up call."

"Whoever did this did humanity a favor," Hale said. "This guy has been killing kids out on the rez for years with his drugs."

Hale stood and stared at the snow-covered car, darkness in his eyes.

"Has anyone actually opened the doors yet?" I asked. We stopped outside the tape. I took initial shots of the scene as it was, making sure to cover the sidewalks and streets for footprints. It looked like the snow had continued to fall after the man died, for hours most likely, a good six inches was piled on the roof of the car. Any prints were going to be at least partially covered.

"Yes," she said. "The first officer on the scene opened up the passenger door and looked inside." Arviso pointed to him sitting in his unit on the other side of the street. "I came in as well and closed the unit back up. I saw his neck and sealed off the street. That was about six o'clock this morning." It was now 9:35 A.M.

I walked with them, noticing the trail of footprints from the officer's unit to the victim's vehicle, and another set of tracks, smaller, coming from the same direction. I took establishing shots of the scene and pulled in tight to the footprints. The tread was muddled by fresh snow, but you could still make out the back and forth of a deep boot tread. I moved around the vehicle and found another trail of prints along the sidewalk, which led right to the car. They looked to be about a size eleven and were different from the prints on the other side, which must've been Arviso's and the other officers'. I pulled my pocket open and laid my tape down on the ground beside one, then took another photo. Photos twelve through fourteen.

I turned my attention to the car, a frozen steel coffin. From my vantage point, I could only see the outline of a body, a deep gray shadow beyond the frost. My eyes moved around the scene to check for any lost souls standing on the sidewalk. I saw no one. I put on my gloves and slipped into the paper suit Arviso had given me when we arrived. A gust of wind swept through, kicking up fresh snow dust from the car. It was colder than I ever remembered. I wondered if I could even do it.

"You okay, Rita?" Arviso said. She'd sneaked up on me. I recoiled, grabbed my camera a bit tighter.

"Sorry. Didn't mean to scare you."

Arviso was right—I was scared. I held my chest, pressing my tadadíín bag tight to my heart. My body tingled with anxiety. Was I wrong to return to the job so soon? "Let's open the doors and get this started," I said.

Arviso opened the passenger's side door, revealing a man frozen in the front seat, palms up in his lap, dead eyes still open and fixed on the ceiling. His body contorted, his clothes twisted haphazardly around his legs and torso, his feet tangled under the brakes and throttle. I imagined he'd put up a fight, then dropped his hands to his lap when his throat was slashed. I pulled the camera to my eye and began my work, first documenting the trashed interior of the vehicle. The oily handprints on the roof and dash, the floors scattered with empty bottles, crushed cigarette butts and old burned squares of foil and paper. Photos fifteen through twenty-eight. I trained my camera on the vic's face—lifeless and disturbed. It was frozen in horror, his yellowing teeth exposed through a mouth that yawed open like a hungry bird's. His coat and lapel were black with blood, the brutal neck wound gushing thick, frozen gore all down his corpse. The smell was putrid, coming straight from the wound framed in my close-ups. It opened like a flooded river, the banks bursting with flesh. His neck was cut through to his spinal cord, the muscle and tendons a morbid swirl of color and frost. Photos twenty-nine through fifty.

I scanned his body with the viewfinder. The blood had traveled all the way down his corpse, his half-exposed torso revealing a silver rodeo belt buckle that pressed into his stomach and bore the words: 1993 LIONS CLUB RODEO CHAMPION. His open palms held small ponds of dried, frozen blood. Photos fifty-one through sixty.

"That wound does look familiar, Detective Arviso," I said as I continued snapping photos. "I can see what you're saying."

"Yes," she confirmed. "It's almost exactly the same. A left-to-right neck wound with that little ridge at the opening of the cut." I focused on the start of the wound again and remembered Mr. Gurley's neck, loose and open, the jagged entry wound right below his ear. "It even goes just as deep and wide. He almost cut the head completely off." Arviso made her way back around to the other side of the car. She opened the glove compartment and pulled out some crumpled papers, a small handgun and a clear plastic bag. She examined them one by one.

"Any idea who this guy is?" I asked.

"Yeah. We all know Henry," she said, holding up the registration paper she'd found.

"Who is he?"

"Henry Duran. He's one of our local drug dealers," she said. "Not a real great guy. He's been in and out of city jail more times than I can count. Hale here was hoping to pull him in on some federal charges."

"Guess he's gonna get out of that one, too," Hale said from the sidewalk.

"His registration is expired," Arviso added. "Big surprise."

I could hear an ambulance approaching. It was most likely the only way that they were going to get the vic out to Albuquerque in this weather. I was surprised that OMI or one of the field investigators hadn't agreed to come to help take his body away. That's what they did for Mr. Gurley.

"No investigator for Henry?" I asked.

"He wasn't the former mayor of Gallup," Hale said. "I say no special treatment for a woman beater."

Arviso came beside me again as the EMTs unloaded the ambulance and pulled a gurney close to Henry's car. "Do you have everything you need?"

"I have enough of the body," I said. "Just need to get a few more once they take him."

Henry's body was so stuck to the icy seat, the EMTs had to forcibly pry him out of the car. His legs remained frozen and oddly twisted. They couldn't even close the body bag properly.

When the body was gone, I took a few more of the car interior, making sure I didn't miss anything for later analysis. Spatter everywhere: on the dashboard, the seat and headrest, the floor and on the steering wheel, some dried into the Oldsmobile logo at the center. Photos eighty through ninety-nine. When I moved to the backseat, I could see a trail of tiny blood spots, almost invisible among the oil and dirt. Foam escaped from the top of the ripped seat cushion, stains of red on it. Photo number 127. This was where the killer had sat when he cut Henry Duran's throat. There was a darkness to sharing that space with him, his ominous energy very much alive. We might never know if the killer had sat and waited for this man or had entered another way, and we didn't know yet if they knew each other or how their paths had crossed.

I stood back from the car and looked at my image count— 134. I raised my camera one more time and framed the scene wide—the car with the doors still open, the movie theater behind it. That's when I noticed the man standing at the trunk of the car, pointing to the backseat. Henry Duran. He stared silently as my finger dug into the side of my camera in fear. He opened his mouth, as if to yell, to scream at me at the top of his lungs. But no sound came—only black blood, spilling from his mouth. He stood and waited. I didn't know what he wanted.

The EMTs rolled his corpse into their vehicle and pulled away, driving off in the direction of OMI, where Dr. Blaser would begin his work. By foot, Henry's ghost slowly followed the ambulance. I didn't know what he was doing—perhaps he was seeing if he could somehow chase down his body and reenter it—but I didn't care. I was just thankful he didn't seem interested in following *me*.

DETECTIVE ARVISO DROVE me back out to Tohatchi that night. I think we were both exhausted, spiritually hungover from spending our day with Henry Duran—then recording and cataloging the scene back at the Gallup Police Department. I was feeling that familiar rush of anxiety from being back at work, even though it felt good to investigate alongside her. I could trust her, I found. I felt free of judgment and fear around her.

"Thank you so much for your help, Rita," Arviso said, breaking the silence.

"I'm glad I could help," I said. "I'm sure you'll have no problem finding out who did this. Gallup is a small town."

"That's true," Arviso said. "Gallup is a small town. But violence has always lived there, in the corners and shadows. You know that."

Arviso, of course, was right. Gallup was a place where dreams, and Navajo people, went to die as far as I was concerned. Death and disappearance were endemic. It was still a far cry from Albuquerque, but it was linked to that city through spilled blood. It was a border town.

"It's even worse on the reservation," Arviso added. "Hale and I have seen some things that no one should ever see."

"Listen, I know you were hoping that I might be able to give you some direction, or maybe some clue to this whole thing . . ." I paused, unsure of what to say. I had seen Duran's ghost, but he didn't engage, and neither did I. He probably didn't know any more than we did about who slit his throat. "But I have nothing helpful to offer. I'm sorry."

"You did a lot for us today, Specialist," Arviso said.

We drove the rest of the way home in silence, listening to the radio cut in and out. It was 11 P.M. when we got to Grandma's. As I expected, she was still awake. She sat on her rocking chair, the television on, crochet needles in her lap. Mr. Bitsilly was there too, watching the news and drinking coffee. The cat was on the couch next to him, only passively acknowledging my presence.

"Your grandma told me what happened today," he said. "We've been waiting for you to get back."

I sat down by the fireplace and poked at the flames, preparing myself for a scolding.

"I told you that more death was coming, and here it is," he said. "I was hoping that it wouldn't be so soon, but I have no control over that."

"This is you welcoming all of that back into your life," Grandma said. She was upset still, barely looking my way. "We've been through so much, and you're already back out there. I just don't understand why you can't say no, just commit to not listening to these spirits."

"Rita is going to have this ability no matter what," Mr. Bitsilly said, reasoning with her. "She can't help it. We can't do anything about it but pray for her safety."

"When they asked me for help, something inside of me told me it was important," I said. "If I waited, I knew there would be more. More bodies, and more ghosts. I can't explain anything other than that. I was ready to let it go too, Grandma. I know you never wanted this for me. But there is something here telling me that they will keep dying if I don't help them."

"Who is saying these things to you?" Grandma said, finally looking my way. I understood her anger and fear. But for me, it wasn't about the money anymore, or even justice. Now it was life and death. More would come if I waited. More people would die.

"She's right," Mr. Bitsilly said. "I could see that this was coming."

"You will do this one investigation and it will be over?" Grandma's voice was shaky. "I don't believe it. You've said that before, but it's never over."

"I went to help the detective, Grandma, because I knew her," I explained. "We worked on a case together before I came here, and she needed me. It's not like I'm working for the police now. I just went to help, and nothing happened." I looked at Mr. Bitsilly. "The ghost of the man stood on the sidewalk and stared at me. I don't know how, but he knew not to approach me. I can't explain it. His spirit was in shock. I did everything you told me to do, to protect myself, to keep them from following me home."

"I'm glad to hear that." Mr. Bitsilly rose from his chair. "Both that nothing happened and that you aren't working for the police department. Just be careful."

MR. BITSILLY'S WORDS weighed on me as I tried to sleep.

I dreamed of them that night, Emmitt Gurley and Henry Duran, their necks swaying as they tried to wedge their fingers into the bottom edge of my bedroom window. I sat on the other side of the thick windowpane watching them, my Hasselblad on the tripod next to me. I framed their rotten bodies with the camera, taking photograph after photograph of their panic. They couldn't reach me, their fingertips bloody from trying. They screamed, but I couldn't hear them. They slammed their bodies up against the glass. I framed them over and over until the roll was finished, then I removed it from my camera.

Suddenly I was in the darkroom from my early days—the red light of my university photography studio. When the images appeared in the enlarger, they were exactly as I'd captured them—the two of them, their desperation, their frantic moving in and out of my frame. But when I transported the paper into the developer, rocking the liquid back and forth in the tray, the two men became surrounded by eerie, translucent silhouettes of several other beings, their outlines surrounded by light. I couldn't make out their faces. The photograph was still moving, coming to life in my developer tray as I continued to dream.

CHAPTER 24 | 9°

"The generous will themselves be blessed,
for they share their food with the poor."

PROVERBS 22:9

THIS STORY HAS been told before, the battle of good
and evil, of angels and demons, of gods and humans. Humanity
doesn't learn, or care, about the inequities of heaven. I am still
tethered to the messengers that God continues to send. I am
not the angel that God sent. I am a horrible human still. Please,
St. Michael, hear my prayers. Confirm for me that the voices
that I'm hearing are coming from you. Assure me.

I waited for nightfall to search the streets for Rosemary
again. The bars were still open and I circled their dark perim-
eters, stepped past their loud jukeboxes to peer into their dim
restrooms. The dark alleys were alive with firelight. I drifted
through the old hotels with rust-stained walls and chipped vinyl
flooring. Rosemary was nowhere to be seen.

It was past eight o'clock when I gave up, figuring Rosemary
was miles away in Mentmore or some other distant place.
Hopefully she was staying warm and being loved. I went into
the pharmacy, feeling the sting of dried blood beneath my coat.
I needed to change my bandages. The blue light of the drugstore

drowned all of us unfortunates in the color of death. The pain in my back was becoming unbearable, a meager price to pay for my wings of death, but still a price nonetheless. A fever was rising in my body. Infection. My back crawled with it. All I wanted to do was dig deep into the soft black virus and pull it from my body, toss it into the dark with the broken glass and garbage. For now, in that crypt of a pharmacy, I sought relief. A few hours of peace before the pain kicked up again.

I walked the aisles until I found what I was looking for—a box of painkillers and an ointment to smother the agony I felt. I stood in line, anonymous. I had three or four crumpled bills in my pocket, but I couldn't wait any longer. The nausea pooled in my throat, the thick bile and stinging acid. I threw them on the counter and headed out into the cold.

There was a woman outside, a Navajo, her body wrapped in a cheap Stuckey's poncho, approaching people as they left the store. At first, I thought I had found my Rosemary, there in the darkened parking lot of the pharmacy, but it wasn't her. An older white woman passed by me with a brisk march, her knit cap topped with a red ball that bounced with her gait. She was holding her hand up. I couldn't quite hear what the woman in the poncho said, but I figured she was asking for money, a little something to help her get in somewhere for the night.

"I don't work my ass off so that I can give you money," the older woman said as she entered the pharmacy. "Get away from me." The Navajo woman in the poncho moved quickly toward the street, her wet hands counting some tattered bills. She squinted at me between the flakes of snow. I had never seen her on the streets before.

"Do you need some help?" I swallowed the bile in my throat and wiped my mouth, unsure if I was presentable.

"I was just trying to get back to the other side of Gamerco." She pointed with her lips toward the north side of town. "The snow is too heavy to get a ride, I guess."

I dug out a couple of vouchers from my coat pocket, about forty dollars of motel credits from what I could see.

"Go over to the Lexington and tell them you have a voucher." I handed her one of the coupons. "I'm sorry you had to get yelled at."

"It's okay," she said. "I saw who that was after I asked her if she could give me a ride." We both watched the woman inside the store as she directed the cashier with her finger in front of the cigarettes.

"Who is she?" I looked toward the drugstore, the neon lights blinking under the snow.

"It's that cheap lady," she said. "She's the city councilor who made that anti-panhandling law. I sure asked the wrong person." She laughed and walked into the snow, her silhouette lost once she crossed the street.

I knew exactly whom she was talking about. Over the years, Arlene Ryder had made a name and a way for herself in Gallup. She'd opened a children's clothing store and started the community policing organization in town. On the city council, she proposed a new crusade every week to save Gallup from itself. I read about them in the newspaper. She claimed to be a God-fearing woman. I didn't know where she went to church, but it wasn't at Sacred Heart Cathedral. Even in my work in community outreach, I'd never spoken with her. She hated being asked for money only slightly more than she hated Navajos. Over the last year she managed to close MCI, the one and only place in Gallup that helped those fighting addiction and homelessness. She filled the business owners with lies about taxes funding methadone clinics. None of it was true. But they got rid of it anyway. This woman was one of the reasons people would be dying on the streets tonight.

I stood under the dark eaves of the grocery store on the corner and watched for her puffy red coat and sparkling white snow cap with the red ball at the end. She was easy to spot through the pharmacy window, her face contorted by anger, saying something to the cashier and to the man in front of her. Since giving up on my search for Rosemary I had imagined a quiet night for myself. My plans were going to have to change.

Arlene Ryder walked out of the drugstore with two heavy plastic bags in her hands. I pulled myself from shadow to shadow until I was right behind her at her car.

"How many times do I have to tell you people to stay away from me?" The woman turned and stared at me. "What in the hell are you doing?" Her eyes fell to my neck, my collar exposed from under my coat. "Jesus, Father, you're bound to give someone a heart attack."

"I didn't mean to startle you," I said. "I have a question for you."

"What?" She opened her car door, throwing her heavy shopping bags onto the floor. "I don't have time to stand around and talk in this weather."

"Are you a Christian?"

"What? Of course, I am. I attend First Baptist." She looked me over again as she sat down in the driver's seat. "Is that where I've seen you? You look familiar."

"Why do you fight against giving to those less fortunate than yourself?" I moved in front of the door, my leg pushing it back.

"Oh, you're one of those Navajo-rights people. No comment." She grabbed her door to pull it closed. "Get away from me or I'll call the police."

I forced the bent end of the scythe into the side of her neck, feeling the muscle and ligaments drag against it. She just sat there, her hand gripping the wheel, and stared up at me, her eyes blacker than ink. I could feel her pulse slowing, the blade turning a little with each beat. The hot stickiness of her blood spilled slowly, soaking into her blouse and the thick wool scarf that lay loose on her neck. I let my hands feel the heat of her blood, aroused by the touch of her blood on my skin. I pulled the scythe back, using the wool of her scarf to wipe the blood from the blade.

I hadn't really thought about who might be watching us, but snow was falling thick and heavy, as if to cloak my actions. An elder, her hands gripping a wooden cane, shuffled out of the pharmacy with a woman who might be her daughter. They came within feet of Arlene Ryder's departing soul, but never looked up, staring at the ice on the sidewalk.

I closed the car door, hearing the councilwoman's head thump against the glass. In this weather, she would be frozen solid by the time morning arrived. I came around the passenger side of the car and got in so I could prop the woman up in her seat.

Her purse was nestled between the console and the seat. It was heavy. I pulled everything out, every coin and every dollar. I was surprised to see so much cash. I found a quiet pleasure in the thought of giving it all away. Her dead eyes looked straight ahead, the blood a web of striations on her neck. I couldn't help but trace the blood with my finger, craning my neck to get a view. I put her hands on the wheel of the car and stepped out, methodically pouring a circle of coins around her car. No one witnessed the blessed iteration of my mission. No one except the ones who always watch—who always know.

By the time the last coin had been dropped, the flapping

wings had begun to emerge from the dark. They cheered for me, loud and unruly in that parking lot, surrounding the car, slapping the snow with their feathers. I was back on the streets, my wings throbbing as I moved through the most intense and dangerous snowstorm I had seen in the years I lived in Gallup. That night I saw twelve people on the streets, covered in blankets and huddled around fire barrels or tents. I took that woman's blood money and laid it in their hands.

Arlene Ryder's death had done nothing to lessen my pain. I could smell the iron in her blood. I rubbed it into my skin, trying to harness that feeling again, the one that would arouse my sense of purpose. I was sure that St. Michael would anoint me with oil for this deed when I arrived before him, that it would be the thing that made my final transformation complete.

I came back to the cold outreach center, the dark greeting me and the blood on my body. One last raven waited for me as I neared the darkened corner by the abandoned outreach center. "We are still waiting for our two angels, Gabriel. That kill back there has earned you absolutely nothing."

CHAPTER 25
1101 CAMINO DE SALUD

Office of the Medical Examiner

Nikon D2X • f/8, 1/500 sec., ISO 200

MY BODY STOOD outside in the cornfields, my bare feet buried in the snow, my hair blowing in the wind. I watched nine beings, undefined and faceless, stare into my grandma's bedroom window. The sounds of a million locusts hovered over our heads in the darkness. I shouted at the ghostly faces to leave us be. I marched toward them and used my full strength to push them back to wherever they came from. This did nothing. The ghosts just stood there and stared into Grandma's window. Somewhere, maybe beyond the locusts, I heard a dull ringing. I covered my ears and went to let out a scream, and—

When I awoke, I half expected to be alone in my old Albuquerque apartment, ghosts at my bedside. It took me several seconds to remember that I was at Grandma's. It was early morning, and snow continued to fall outside. My dreams were tangled up in my hair. I picked up my phone, which had been ringing off the hook beside me.

"Hello?"

"Hi, Rita. It's Detective Arviso. We got some reports back in from OMI and I was hoping you might come with me to the main office."

"In Albuquerque?" I didn't feel like going back already. There still wasn't enough distance between me and that city. Maybe there never would be.

"Yes," she said. "Is that okay?"

I thought of my dreams and the voices and the eyes in Grandma's cornfield.

"I'll come, yeah," I said. "When's a good time?"

"I'm finishing up some paperwork now in Gallup, so whenever you can get here . . ."

I knew what that meant. It meant now. I looked down at all the protections Mr. Bitsilly had given me, rolling the cedar beads along the tips of my fingers. All of it was coming with me. I tried my best to pray, to hold on to something that had brought me back from death and that would push me through the rest of my work.

Grandma stopped me in the kitchen, startling me. I hadn't heard her wake up.

"Grandma, is everything okay?"

"I had dreams about you all night, Rita." She looked out the window. She took my hand and pulled me out onto the front porch. There, in the cold, in just her windbreaker, she prayed for me, placing a pinch of corn pollen in my hand. We prayed, laying pollen down on ourselves, seeing the last of it swirl in the uplift of winter wind. It blew right into us, the corn pollen yellow on the edges of Grandma's hair. I could taste it on my tongue.

GALLUP POLICE DEPARTMENT – 7:30 A.M.

When I walked into the station, Detective Arviso was talking to an officer in her office. I knocked on the door and tuned into their conversation as it spilled out into the hall.

"There was no way to know how long the meds were missing," the officer said. "He called us this morning to make a police report, but they hadn't restocked in six months, so the window is wide open."

"How much is missing?"

"He didn't know," the officer said, checking his notes.

"Thank you," Arviso said. He tipped his hat to me as he left the room, his hands full of files. "Can you and Officer Baje go down there and get a full report? Don't forget to take pictures." A wide yawn spread over the officer's face as he walked toward the station's back door.

"The vet clinic was broken into, well . . . sometime in the last six months," she said, gathering her gear for our trip to Albuquerque. "I hope the meds don't end up in the wrong hands."

The detective ran her lights all the way to Albuquerque, driving us into town in record time. I dreaded seeing OMI again, the familiar sounds and smells, the metal reflecting into your face. We walked in the door, my camera bag at my side, and it was like I had never left. The receptionist waved me in like usual. I tried my best not to limp, but long rides made my leg feel like it was on fire.

"Hello, Rita," the receptionist said. "Good to see you here again."

"Thanks. This is Detective Arviso from Gallup PD. We're here to see Dr. Blaser."

We walked through the glass doors, Dr. Blaser in his green scrubs, still working, his eyes fixed on the microscope. He saw us out of the corner of his eye and waved us into the examination room.

"Couldn't stay away, could you?" Dr. Blaser said.

It was good to see him, but I couldn't shake the connection he had to this place. Maybe someday I could see him at the store or at the library and it might break the cycle.

"Thanks for getting back to us so quickly, Dr. Blaser," Arviso said. "Things are heating up and they are pushing us hard for answers."

"I understand." He walked over to his report on the table and the green body bag lying on the gurney. When he unzipped the bag, Arviso stepped back, gripping her files closer.

"Sorry, this never gets easier for me," she said.

Dr. Blaser pointed to the severe cut on Henry Duran's neck. "This is definitely the same tool and likely the same killer," he said. "The initial contact of the blade is almost identical in both of these cases. A deep cut then the pull through to the rest of the throat."

"You say 'tool,'" Arviso said. "It wasn't a knife?"

Dr. Blaser clicked on a file on his computer, bringing one of the photographs I took of Emmitt Gurley's neck to full screen. "Look at the similarities." He pointed to the edge of the wound. "That initial hook ridging the corner of the wound and tearing the exit. It's definitely one of these." He pulled up a catalog of farming tools, pointing to two tools in the corner of the page he'd highlighted. "I think you're looking for a daruma sickle or a billhook sickle. It's like a hand scythe that farmers use for clearing brush. It's a strange wound, a much different cut than one from a knife or a razor. And whoever used it had it sharpened so well that it actually cut into the bones in their throats."

I thought about my dream, Mr. Gurley holding that ghost and cutting its throat.

"Like, something used to harvest small crops?" Arviso asked.

"I suppose so, maybe lettuce, herbs, that kind of thing. I haven't been able to find the exact tool. I think it may be a bit older, something with a different design than what is readily available in a hardware store now."

I looked at Henry Duran's wound again, the blood dried around the hardened skin.

"And you're sure it's the same in both?" I snapped a shot of the man's neck as he lay on the gurney. Detective Arviso scribbled in her notes

"Yes," he said. "Same tool, same left-to-right cut, same degree of strength." He pulled the bag down farther and showed us Henry Duran's arms, bruised and poked with needle holes. "He probably would have died eventually given what he was taking. Tests came back with heroin, cocaine and a significant amount of alcohol."

"I guess someone just wanted to make sure he wasn't gonna make it," Arviso said. "This guy was a known dealer in Gallup and pushed out on the checkerboards. He's been up to no good for a long while."

"Now all you have to figure out is how he was connected to your other vic," Dr. Blaser said.

"How much strength do you think you would have to have to cut a wound this deep?" I bent down to look at the orbital side of his head. The wound really went through to the man's spine, the nerves like blossoming vines at the end.

"A lot," he said. "Whoever killed these men was able to subdue them and make this cut at the same time. It was quick and measured."

Detective Arviso and I looked at each other. Fear was in Arviso's eyes, and probably mine too. Someone capable of such force was still walking the streets of Gallup. It was the worst of nightmares in a town already haunted by a violent history. Dr.

Blaser walked over to Duran's body and pulled the zipper back over his face.

"We also processed your DB from last week," he said. He walked back toward the morgue and pulled on the long silver drawer. A file sat on top of a translucent storage bag. "A Mr. Chayton Tso, found at the train station in Gallup. No one ever came to claim him."

"Oh, the exposure death." Arviso looked at the paperwork. "I remember him. He was a veteran, so I'm surprised that no one has made arrangements."

"Me too," Dr. Blaser said. "Also, not an exposure death. This guy had metabolic acidosis. Poisoning, most likely. Not something you get from drinking too much or freezing out in the cold."

"Antifreeze?" Arviso said.

"The tox screen shows that he had quite a bit in his system. Mixed with the alcohol, he probably went into a coma and died."

"Do you think he was taking it of his own accord?" Arviso looked down at the man's body, frozen beneath the thin plastic covering, his skin blue and green.

"I doubt it," he said. "But you never know. If someone is desperate enough, they'll drink anything, including antifreeze, to stay warm."

"That's about as grim as it gets," I said. "Can I see his face?"

Dr. Blaser pulled the plastic back to reveal an old Navajo man, scars on his face, but oddly at peace. He looked familiar to me, like an uncle I never met. It made me sad to think that his frozen body had to make this city morgue its home, unable to move into his next world. Now that he had been here over a month, I wondered if anyone would ever come for him.

"This one was listed as an exposure death when it came in,"

Arviso said, glancing at his files. "Why did you do a tox screen on him and not the others?"

"Most of these deaths that come in here in the winter time don't look suspicious," he said. "We classify them as exposure deaths almost immediately. We had twenty exposure deaths in Gallup this past year alone. I can't count how many I've seen in the past decade. When I see an older homeless person come in frozen with obvious signs that they've been drinking, we can pretty much see the cause and release them to their families." He looked toward the back of the morgue. "Back there we have people who still haven't been claimed by anyone. It's up to the state now. The NamUs system is nearly established, but it's going to take a while before we're able to keep track properly." Dr. Blaser cleared his throat. "This man was different, though. He had a sweet smell. Something wasn't quite right, especially considering how many deaths there have been. So, we did the testing just to make sure," he said. "Good thing we did."

"So, the rest of these deaths . . . we don't investigate them?" I had to ask.

"You mean the other exposure deaths? I doubt it. Look, if these deaths look suspicious or there was injury involved, we do our examination. But for the most part, we don't waste our time. These victims in Gallup were practically frozen when they were found. I'll let you all know if there were any more tox screens that came back with MA. I'll run the tests and get back to you."

WE WERE BACK in Gallup before lunch, our minds reeling with new information. There was an immediacy to finding out who was walking around town with a strange weapon, waiting for another victim. I wondered about the man in the drawer and his familiar face.

"Can I ask you a question, Detective? How do you do it?"

Arviso's eyes stayed glued to the road. "You mean, because we're Navajo and death and all of that?" she said. "I guess I can ask you the same question."

"Yes, that's what I mean," I said. "Does it ever haunt you? How do you cope with the everyday of it?"

"I pray," she said. "Don't you pray?"

I felt too embarrassed to admit that I had a hard time believing. "I've had to start. I'm trying to learn to trust that it will work."

"I was raised that way," she said. "I think it kind of helps me stay healthy. I'm not going to push anything on you, but I think it might help you."

"Maybe," I said.

"Is it really true what they say about you?"

I listened to the road, the tires on the bumpy asphalt, the cracks filled with tar. "Yes," I said. "It's true."

There was a long silence.

"Is it something that happens all of the time?" She shook her head. "I'm sorry. I guess I shouldn't be asking questions."

"I understand that," I said. She reminded me of Shanice in those early days when she tested me on the daily. "It's something that I've dealt with my whole life, and I can't get rid of it. Believe me, I've tried it all."

"Do you see every single . . ."

"No," I said. "Although, after I died for a second last year, there have been a whole lot more of them."

"You died last year?" Her voice dropped.

"The worst part for me is not how it affects me, but how it affects my grandma, my family," I said. "I feel like they are facing this with me now that I'm home. It was easier to hide it when I lived in Albuquerque."

"Someone needs to say some prayers for you, Rita."

"They have," I said. "That's why I'm still standing here today."

She nodded.

"Don't tell anyone. This is just between you and me."

"Well, I'm not sure I'm the only one who knows," she said. "People talk. Especially out here."

"That's fair," I said. "Don't feed it."

"I won't," she said. "Thank you for doing this. I'm sure it doesn't make your life any easier. We're stopping in on the parish offices up at Sacred Heart, if you don't mind. A missing persons call came in that we need to attend to."

THE GUTTERS ON Second Street had turned into rivers of black sludge. The trains bellowed off the brick buildings as we moved along the simple, slanted houses that perched along the steep concrete slabs. On the top of the hill, Sacred Heart Cathedral stood like a monument, as if the rest of the city had been assembled outside of its brick walls. As we moved closer, we could see that Christmas loomed, the sparkle and light of ornaments and decorations along the fence lines, the old red-and-white tinsel candy canes hanging from the top of the city light poles.

We walked to the rectory to look for someone to talk to. At this point, I wasn't sure why I was tagging along. I was here to help with the connection on Emmitt Gurley and Henry Duran. Beyond that, I could have just gone home, but something inside of me thought that Detective Arviso shouldn't be alone, even if she was walking into the church.

"Hello, Officers." A young nun came out from behind one of the rectory doors, her hair lightly tucked behind her habit. She moved her hand in front of us, guiding us into the rectory offices and out of the cold.

"Thank you so much to the two of you for coming up here," she said. "I'll go get Father Mark."

We sat in the parish offices on some stilted plastic chairs and waited. The room was filled with dusty piles of paperwork, the burnt coffee smell crawling into my coat fabric. Father Mark came into the office, his voice loud and booming like he was projecting from the pulpit.

"Hello, Officers," he said. He extended his hand to Arviso.

"Hello, Father," she said. "I'm Detective Arviso and this is Specialist Todacheene, who's helping me with a case right now."

"Good to meet the two of you. I wish it was under more joyful circumstances." He sat at his desk with a thud, the leather and wood creaking beneath him. "Brother Gabriel Jensen, our community outreach coordinator here at the parish, is missing."

"How long?" Arviso took out her notes and began to document the details. The nun in the corner stood quietly, her hands beneath her habit, her hood digging into the side of her cheek.

"From what we can glean here, I would say about two days," he answered. "Is that right, Sister?"

"Yes, Father," she said. "We haven't seen him since he prepared dinner for the parish staff on Wednesday night. He went back to his room and we never saw him come back out. When I, and the rest of the outreach group, went to get him before our lunch service down at the Indian Center, he was gone."

"This is very unusual for someone like Brother Gabriel," Father Mark said. He sifted through the drawers in his desk and retrieved a photograph of a man, a large soup ladle in his hand. "This is the only picture we could find. This is from a few months ago, at our outreach center."

"How old is Brother Gabriel?"

"He turned forty-three this year," he said. "We had a birthday celebration for him here at the parish. He had no family to speak of, so we tried our best to make him feel welcome."

"I've met Brother Gabriel before," Arviso said. "He's been here at the church for a long time, hasn't he?"

"Yes," Father answered. "He's been with us for thirteen years. He lives a quiet life. He's a good man, works our soup kitchens and does outreach for the homeless here in Gallup."

"The man is a saint," the nun said. "I'm worried that someone may have done something horrible to him. He does a lot of work on the street, and you just never know."

Father Mark seemed a little perturbed by her interruption. "He is like clockwork," he said. "He is here every day, cooking in the parish kitchen without fail. When we woke up and he wasn't already booming from the kitchen, we knew something was wrong. We thought maybe he had an appointment or some other engagement he had to tend to. But when it turned to two days, we figured we had to let you know. Like I said, the man had no family."

"We will get right to this, Father. Do you know if Brother Gabriel ever had any kind of issues with anyone? Any confrontations?"

"No," Father said. "But I'm not out on the streets with Brother Gabriel and the sisters every day. I know they face violence here and there."

"Is there anywhere that he might be, maybe another parish or doing outreach somewhere here in town?"

"In the last month, we've had to move most of our work to the Indian Center or here at the parish hall," the sister said. "Our outreach center in town is closed. The leaks and damage to the building forced us to close it down a couple of months ago."

"We're fundraising for the new center now if you'd like to

donate," Father said. "We can always use support from our police department."

"I'll be sure to make a contribution, Father," Arviso said. "I've seen some of the good work that you've done."

"In the meantime, we will pray that Brother Gabriel will walk through the doors with an explanation of why he made us worry needlessly." Father Mark pressed his hands into his desk and stood up. "I don't think anyone would ever try to hurt him."

"He's the sweetest man," the nun said. "Everyone loves him."

I watched as Father Mark glared at the young woman. It wasn't quite a look of complete hatred, but he looked as if her voice scraped at his ears.

"Thank you, both," Arviso said. She shook Father Mark's hand and so did I. "And thank you, Sister . . . ?"

"I'm so sorry. I'm Sister Yolanda. Please let us know if there is anything we can do to help you find him."

We walked back to Arviso's unit. I could see that something wasn't right with her, but she didn't want to say it out loud. Once she started her cruiser, she let out a sigh and looked out the window as though exhausted by the sight of snow.

"Something is strange with those two," she said. "Is it just me?"

"Father Mark doesn't seem to like Sister Yolanda. That was pretty obvious," I said.

"Yes," she said. "Or they're not telling us everything. Sister Yolanda looked like it was sitting on her tongue."

We rounded the corner onto Broadbent. The police station was fully enshrouded in untouched snowfall. I hoped that the snow hadn't really begun to stick as I had thirty minutes on the road home ahead of me. I looked toward the mountains to the north and could see that the clouds were slowly moving toward the Chuskas.

"Thank you again for coming with me, Rita," Arviso said. "I'll let you know if I hear anything else about the case. Are you sure your career as an investigator is over?"

"It's never over, Detective," I said. I knew that I had to tell her; right there in that moment, she deserved to know. "Remember our investigation at the Silver Stallion?" She stared at me in silence, almost waiting for me to say it, her eyes glassy with fear. "He was there."

"Who was there?"

"Mr. Gurley. I saw his spirit." I looked out the window, hoping that no one was watching. "He made me so sick that it took me to the very edge. I don't know how to explain it."

"I remember that day. You looked like you hadn't slept in weeks. You almost fell over. Why didn't you tell anyone?"

"When you spend years working so hard to hide it, it becomes part of your life."

"I'm sorry," she said after a long silence. "Why did you agree to come here? Why have you decided to help me?"

I looked into the rearview mirror. Arviso followed my eyes. I think she was afraid to ask.

"Mr. Gurley is here now," I said, looking at the mangled ghost in the backseat. He was staring at us, listening to our every word. I hadn't seen him in some time now, but I knew, in some sense, he had never left. He was smiling. Angry, but smiling. "And he will stay until he gets what he wants."

"What does he want?"

"He wants justice," I said.

CHAPTER 26 | -2°

"Consider the ravens, for they neither sow nor reap; they
have no storeroom nor barn, and yet God feeds them; how
much more valuable you are than the birds!"

LUKE 12:24

I STRIP MY skin and stand in the cold, whipping my back
in penance. I deserve to die with them. I know now that there is
nothing left for me but death.

I could see them moving through the windows, a webbed
screen of ice separating me from the other side. My fingertips
were still sticky with blood. I tried to feed my body two old
hard-boiled eggs, but they weren't enough. When I licked my
fingers, a desperate act to not lose one single morsel, I could
taste the evil woman's blood. The bitterness made me spit white
and yellow all over the dirty wet carpets. I was sick with worry and
want. I had come this far, and now the years of investment are
about to disappear. Where do I go from here? I didn't have the
strength to tell the messengers that I had failed. They would
surely pick my bones clean with their beaks. I could hear them
talking about me, just out of sight of the ridges of bricks and the
heat of the power lines.

I had lost my way. The easy targets I had found, the ones
who begged to die, they are dead. I was sure more would show

themselves and this city would continue to need me. But the messengers have betrayed me with promises they cannot possibly fill. Because of my own questioning, my own insecurities, I believed them when they told me that I could earn such a thing as wings and fly to heaven with them. I was a fool.

That night, after I spilled the councilwoman's blood, I screamed to the ravens in the darkness from the rooftop of the outreach building. The snow fell harder and harder as I told them that I saw through their lies. I showed them the bleeding scars on my back, the semblance of growth now just scabs and tissue. No matter how hard I atoned or gave my life and body in service, nothing would ever come from it. My eyes were swollen with tears when a voice finally spoke up.

"You will have what you seek when we have the woman and her child," the voice said, a flutter of shiny black in the darkness of night. The snow fell on all of them, the wind a blinding and stiffening cold. I strained to see the beasts and their beaks in the dark. I stood in that cold, my skin bared and open. The night stung me deeply.

"You're all liars!" I screamed. "I don't believe that you'll keep your promise!"

"We're waiting for you, Gabriel," the ravens grumbled. "You will be one of us." The shining black of their feathers flew toward me, surrounding my body with their flapping wings. Their chiseled claws pulled at my skin and my hair, yanking me from the rooftop with their collective strength. My body was flying above the town, the vibrant grid of the streets below. We flew right over the street corners, swinging low and fast, my arms bruising in the strength of their claws. I loved the feeling of flight on my face, my movements beginning to join with the darkness. They held on to my body, covering my bare skin from the cold, masking the pain of my penance. We flew past the edge of town, past the white flat lights of the refinery, the blinking red lights from the towers along the side. I let my body become part of their wings, blood and flesh. I didn't want my human body anymore.

I wanted a taste of her. I wanted to pull her skin and her flesh with my beak and taste her in my mouth. I wondered if her baby would taste the same.

CHAPTER 27
TOHATCHI VALLEY

Nikon D2X 50mm • f/2.8, 1/500 sec., ISO 400

BY THE TIME I rolled over the last hill on the outskirts of Tohatchi, the snow had capped our mountains, sheep and cattle peeking out of makeshift barns on the sides of the road. My old car rumbled along as always, held together by the prayers my mother had put into it. Grandma's house had several cars in the driveway, golden light pouring out of every window. I forgot that it was Grandma's movie night with Mrs. Peshlakai. I was hopeful that they had cooked something delicious to go with it.

Grandma was sitting with Mrs. Peshlakai and Mr. Bitsilly at her kitchen table when I entered. They were camped out there watching the sink intently: two legs jutted out from beneath, two arms above them twisting a wrench back and forth.

"Rita, you're home," Mr. Bitsilly said. The mood was much lighter than it had been in previous days; it felt like something closer to normal.

"Hi, everyone. Mrs. Peshlakai, nice to see you again," I said.

"Rita, this is Charley Marris, the new math teacher from over at the high school," Grandma said as if she'd practiced a million times. "Charley, this is my granddaughter, Rita."

Charley got out from under the sink and waved hello with the wrench still in his hand. "Nice to meet you," he said. Grandma and Mrs. Peshlakai giggled like schoolgirls. "I would shake your hand, Rita, but mine are filthy."

He raised the palms of his hands to me and smiled. He was a tall man with a strong build, and still carried his accent with him—a slight twang, though you could tell he was starting to lose it. His hair was longer and stuffed up into an old hat that didn't suit him. There was a sweetness about him. I couldn't place it, because I'd never encountered it before.

"After what I've seen today, my hands couldn't be much cleaner." I put my hand out toward him, and he took it. His shake was firm and warm.

"Thanks for looking at that pipe," I said, taking a place next to Mrs. Peshlakai at the table. "We've been worried about it for a while."

"He's been looking around the house and told me there is a lot to be done around here," Grandma chimed in. "He says he can help."

"I've told your grandma that I am at her service," Charley said. "If y'all need anything, I can certainly do my best. I'm only a few minutes away."

Mrs. Peshlakai elbowed me in the rib cage.

"That's very generous of you," I said. "But we are going to get a lot of that taken care of this spring. We wouldn't want to impose on you."

"Well, I just moved here last month," he said. "I get bored easy when school isn't in session."

"Isn't that terrible, Rita?" Mrs. Peshlakai said. The three of them were smiling at me.

I laughed, changing the subject. "I forgot it's movie night. Are you still going to watch something?"

"Oh, she's right," Grandma said. The two took their mugs of tea, ready to head to the living room.

"You better let him come over here if he wants to, Rita. Don't say no to a man willing to help. Especially out here," Mrs. Peshlakai offered.

Mr. Bitsilly and Charley laughed, and I had to join them. She was right. We were lucky to have our pipe fixed in this cold and without an exorbitant bill from the plumber.

"Let me go turn the water back on." Charley walked out to the garage and the three elders stared at me, pushing their agendas.

"What?" I shook my head.

Charley was back in a minute. "Okay." He turned on the kitchen faucet and peered down below to check for leaks. "Everything looks good now." He scribbled his phone number on one of Grandma's legal pads and handed it to me. "Please call me if it leaks or for anything else."

"Thank you, Charley," I said. "It was good to meet you."

"Well, you're gonna stay for dinner and a movie now, aren't you?" Grandma stood up and went to the stove. She was warming up her stew from the night before.

"Thank you, ma'am," he said. "But I can't tonight. Maybe another time. I have some work to do before the semester is over."

"Maybe another time, then," Grandma said. "I can cook a mean stew."

"She can," I offered.

"I just might take you up on that," he said. He shook my

hand again. "It was good to finally meet you, Rita. I've heard a lot about you."

I looked over at Mr. Bitsilly, who was sitting innocently at the kitchen table, then at Grandma and Mrs. Peshlakai, who were avoiding eye contact with me.

"I bet you have," I said.

I WAS STILL awake when the phone rang, after only a few hours of being home. It was Detective Arviso. They'd found another body in a car, and she wanted me back in Gallup as soon as I could get there. I could hear the cold in her voice as she directed me to the east end of Zecca Plaza.

I slipped out of the house without even telling Grandma, my mind buzzing the entire drive there. More bodies, a relentless killing spree, the beginning of sleeplessness. I was becoming entwined in this case whether I wanted to be or not. But I had to stop it—they'd never leave if I didn't. It brought me back to those negatives from the other day. Mr. Gurley standing in the kitchen, just behind Grandma and Mr. Bitsilly. The space I thought would always be safe had been invaded. It had to end.

"I guess I can't just get enough of your company," Arviso said, shaking my hand when I arrived on scene. "Everything, okay, Rita?"

"Yes," I lied. My mind was still on what I saw in those negatives. I tried to shake the thought away. "What was that? Maybe five hours off? I'm sorry, but I can't believe I'm here again so quickly." I pulled a camera out of my bag and followed her to the car.

"I understand," she said. "I have never seen so much homicide in all my years here in Gallup. Violence, death, horrible things, for days. I can't even sleep." She opened the passenger side of the silver car, ice lining the edges of the steel. "We haven't opened the other door. I think she is frozen to it. She's been here for a bit."

The woman's neck was open like a mouth of flesh, the fat and blood mixing in her throat. There was blood spatter all over the interior of the vehicle but especially along the driver's side door, the windshield and along the dashboard, a wide and fine spray that coated every surface. We knew as soon as we looked that it was the same killer. The cut to the neck was almost identical.

"This cut is slightly higher up, moving up into the jaw when it exited," Arviso said. "I think he was probably standing right outside the door when he did it." She pulled out her phone and showed me the few pictures she took before I'd arrived. "There was a lot of de-icer on this side of her vehicle since the mainte-nance guys were clearing snow out of the parking lot, but on the other side the snow is still pretty thick. We have a partial foot-print in between the coins." I hadn't noticed the muddy pennies, nickels and dimes on the ground. They went all the way around the car in a strangely perfect circle, the snow hiding most of them in the thick, shaded areas around the parking barrier.

A crowd had developed in the pharmacy parking lot, and I saw the woman's ghost among them, looking on with the living, the color completely drained from her face. She seemed confused by her death, almost as if she were still putting it together that it was her own body that was inside the car. I looked away.

"The victim is Arlene Ryder, a city councilwoman here in Gallup. She owns all the kids' stores. You know, kid clothes." Arviso aimed her flashlight at the woman's face. Her bloody skin was covered in a thin coat of ice, her eyes a cold, hollow white. The rest of the car was clean, two heavy shopping bags lay in the backseat, some drops of blood on the edges of the bleach bottle inside. I took a few photos of the shoe print on the other side of the snowbank, my ruler lying alongside of it, though most of the detail inside was lost to the thaw.

"How long has she been here?"

"She might have been here since that snowstorm a couple of days ago." Arviso stepped back. "It took some time for that thick ice to fall away from the windows enough for security to see it and a whole extra day before her beloved husband decided to report her missing."

"It's number three, isn't it?" I looked at Arviso, who nodded.

"The deputy field investigator is on his way." Arviso looked toward Albuquerque. "This case just got bigger than us."

One of the officers walked up to Arviso, two women in tow, wet blankets wrapped around their coats. One was smoking a thin cigarette; the other, a bit younger, was shivering.

"Detective, I have a witness here," he said. "She saw the woman in the store. They have one security camera inside and we're getting the footage."

"How do you know who's in there?" Arviso asked suspiciously.

"Everyone knows that car," the older woman said. "It belongs to that lady who hates Navajos." The two women laughed quietly until they met Arviso's stare.

"I asked her for money when it was really snowing the other night," she continued, taking a deep drag on her cigarette. "I was looking for a ride back to Gamerco. When she turned my way, she started yelling at me. I know who she is. If I would have recognized her in time, I wouldn't have asked."

"And when was this?"

"It was late last night, or maybe the night before." Her face lit up orange from her cigarette.

"And what about you?" Arviso pointed to the other woman,

her hair pulled back in a bun. She was beautiful and looked like she was too young to be living hard alongside her friend.

"I don't know anything about this," she said. "Jacinda's cousin is giving me a ride out to my auntie's house later."

Detective Arviso turned back to her witness. "What happened after she yelled at you?"

"I don't know," the older woman said. "I walked away. I didn't follow her or anything. I just left."

"And that's it?"

"Yeah, that's all." The witness looked down at the ground, pulling her blanket closer. "Down by the sidewalk, I talked to a man who asked me about her, who she was. He was nice. He gave me a voucher for the motel down there, the Lexington." She pulled her blanket over her head. "Good thing too, I would have froze out here."

"She must be talking about Brother Gabriel. He paid for me to stay at a hotel too," her younger companion said. "He's the outreach coordinator over at Sacred Heart."

"That's right," she said. "I knew he looked familiar. He was in a big coat with a hood, so it was hard to see him, especially in that snow."

Detective Arviso and I looked at each other.

"You saw Brother Gabriel on the same night as your confrontation with the victim?" Arviso stared hard at both women. "How did he look?"

"He looked, normal, I guess? He gave me the voucher and I left. I didn't want to be out there that night, or tonight either."

"Brother Gabriel is a good guy," the young one said. "He's helped me a lot of times. He's helped a lot of people."

"Did you see what direction Brother Gabriel went after you headed to the Lexington?"

"No," she said. "I remember I turned around to say thank you and he was gone. He just kind of went into the snow. I tried to thank him and here he was just gone. So, I turned around and kept walking."

"Thank you both for talking to us." Arviso gave them her card. "Did you give your information to the officer?"

"We did," the younger woman said. "I gave her my auntie's number out in Fort Wingate. Jacinda's going to move out there with me at my auntie's trailer."

"Thank you, Jacinda," Arviso said. "And what is your name?" She looked at Jacinda's friend as the woman's thin arms reached out to shake Arviso's hand.

"Rosemary."

CHAPTER 28 | 8°

"And do this, knowing the time, that now it is
high time to awake out of sleep; for now our salvation
is nearer than when we first believed."

ROMANS 13:11

MY EYES WERE heavy with sleep, the stale air in the abandoned outreach center making my body stiffen with cold. I slept
in the back storage room, blankets over my bare skin. My bare
feet stepped through the wet, cold carpets, the melting snow
leaking through the ceilings. The mirror in the bathroom framed
my back, the wounds sticky with blood under the bandages. I
pulled the adhesive away from my skin and poked the wounds
with my finger, searching for a hint of hardened cartilage or a
wisp of feather, but there was nothing. I scanned the rest of my
body, half expecting to see my arms pocked with claw marks.
My skin looked untouched, fresh with life, suddenly reinvigo-
rated by the promise of last night, my flight high above town.

I watched from the windows of the outreach building—the
cars and trucks moving about their business, Navajos doing
their shopping, some young kids coming out of the movie theater. I would never find her this way, standing in this cold, dead
building. I held on to my rosary and my small, bloody retablo
of St. Michael and kneeled, offering my prayers to God and to

the legion of angels. I was still a little unsure of myself, waking in that cold building, my body sore and battered. I prayed for strength. That was all I could do.

It didn't matter to me that my new kills were disregarded by the messengers. That blood was shed as a sacrifice for the ones who will still be here on these streets after my soul has left. Those evil ones will not be able to touch them, to lure them with their wickedness or trample them with their hatred. They are gone.

I will move on too, taking Rosemary and her angel with me. We will enjoy our fruits in heaven, where I will finally be able to see my mother again. I wanted to remove the memory that I carried all of these years: her face dismantled by blood, lying there in the rich earth, the sun on her eyelashes. I will give Rosemary to her, to show her the woman I could have loved. Even though I don't know where Wapasha's soul has traveled to, I hope that I will see him again too, will hear the assurances in his voice.

I walked until my feet became heavy with water, checking every place that Rosemary was known to frequent, the bars and the cheap hotels along the edges of town. The messengers gave me the vision, our wings high above the ground. I remembered her, the yellow trailer, surrounded by a small corral with four sheep inside, the silver car that pulled away from the alley in Gallup. But there were no markers in our vision; there were no signs.

Zecca Plaza was surrounded by the police; the red and blue of their sirens pulled me closer. I am proud of what I have done. I don't deny that. I am the one who destroyed that evil energy so that we may reinstall the real teachings of our Lord and savior, to love and be loved. Even if the messengers don't agree, the angels will relish her banishment.

I watched the police move around the car, the flash of lights bleeding on the streets. I felt that Rosemary was near, the smell of her skin hanging in the air. I drifted closer, standing at the edge of the police barrier. The investigators rigged the council-woman's body, getting ready to remove Arlene from her frozen shell. At the corner of East Aztec and Mollica, the two women I'd seen investigating Gurley's death stood outside a running car. One policewoman, a pad of paper in her hand, was talking to two other women in wet coats, their hands stuffed under their arms, shivering. I plodded to the other corner, trying to get a better look. That's when I saw her, standing silent by the other woman, whose hands pointed toward the road. Rose-mary's sweet smell traveled with the stiff, cold breeze. I could feel the warmth of her heartbeat and the flutter of the baby's on the center of my palm. I wanted to move toward her, to pull her from that moment, to consume her and take her into me. I nearly lurched out of the darkness, my body straining, but I pulled back at the last moment. I would need to wait.

I watched the two of them move around the side of the building and into the alley behind the shopping center. I fol-lowed. I could hear them laughing as they walked through deep yellow patches of streetlight, the occasional car splitting our paths. Between the gas stations and Earl's restaurant, I knew there was an empty block where neither woman would see me coming toward them. One of the first innocents I took slept in the very alley we walked. I tried to remember his name. I could only remember his wheelchair, the handles missing from the back. I imagined his ghost watching me from the darkness, his eyes like blue gems.

As I stepped into the street to cross Aztec, the splash and hiss of a car broke my gait. The silver car emerged from the darkness behind Earl's, pulling to a stop in front of Rosemary and her friend so they could jump into the back seat. I ran after the car's brake lights until my heartbeat pulsed in my tongue. I looked to the skies as the red lights pulled into the darkness, my dearest Rosemary disappearing again, the two heartbeats now only a whisper.

IT TOOK FORTY lashings to pay my penance, for being so close and letting her slip through my fingers. The messengers cawed and flapped at the sight of my blood, my third day of fasting making me weak but steady in my conviction. My wounds had to be stripped again, an example of my own failures, a reminder of the continuation of Rosemary's suffering. I stood on the roof of the outreach center. The winter pressed down on me, my *disciplena* wet with blood. I begged for the messengers to show me again, to lead me through to their path. I needed to know where Rosemary had gone.

I had never seen the messengers like they were this night, their eyes red with rage. They had grown tired of my incompetence, my lust and my hesitance. There were three at first; they appeared to me in the outreach center, their black feet perched on the kitchen counters, their bodies still and hardened. They startled me with their outstretched wings, landing on my back and pulling flesh from me with their beaks. Then there were more than three, multitudes, their beaks joining in, a thousand voices in my head. In the flash of pain and longing, I finally saw what I needed to see.

The ravens had already led me to her. Last night they had flown me low right over where she was staying, on the outskirts of town along I-40. I remembered the small community of handmade homes and trailers that sat just on the other side of the old water tower, FORT WINGATE in black letters on the side.

I awoke from my hallucination, the pain still alive, my body still in human form. The town still stirred outside of the windows. The world still turned without me. Inside, my fasting set my body on fire, but it gave me strength and longing. I couldn't wait to be able to hunt like the ravens, the world a feast of flesh and glitter. It would be tonight. This will be one of my final chapters.

I returned to Sacred Heart, seeing the outreach van still sitting inside the chain-link fence. I knew the church would forgive me for my moment of weakness. I knew that no matter what happened tonight, the van would find its way back home. With or without me.

It was still dark by the time I arrived in Fort Wingate. I knew it wouldn't take me long to find her there. I started on the north side of the village, behind the trading post, tracing the dirt roads, ragged dogs nipping at my tires as I peered into the night. I could see the blinds of windows splitting, fingertips and eyes watching the passing lights in the darkness. Up past the graveyard and the ghost of the boarding school buildings, a cluster of homes interrupted the landscape, plumes of smoke rising. I took the first right and followed the tree line until the road ended, my headlights stretching out into nothing.

I turned around, sure I had taken a wrong turn, when I saw the yellow trailer at the edge of the rise, away from the rest of the homes. I turned off my lights and approached the trailer from the opposite side. There was no silver car, but I recognized the ramshackle corral with four sheep in the backyard. Through the thin window on the corner, I saw a woman inside drinking water from an amber-colored glass. It wasn't Rosemary. Not yet.

CHAPTER 29
415 E. GREEN AVE.
Sacred Heart Cathedral
Nikon D2X 50mm • f/3.2, 1/250 sec., ISO 1600

DETECTIVE ARVISO AND I sat in her patrol car and watched the field investigators process the scene, the OMI vehicle pulling up to the edge of the parking lot. The investigators eventually managed to pry open the iced-over driver's side door. The woman didn't move. I could see the frozen blood on the open door; her face had been frozen flat against the window.

Arviso let out a big sigh. "So, what do you think, Rita?"

At that moment I wish the ghosts had made it easier for me, had walked up to me like the gunpowder girl and led me right to the evidence.

"There's definitely a connection here." I watched them pull the woman from the car, her body stiff just like the ones before. "All we can hope is that there is not a number four. The state investigators don't seem to be too worried." We watched as the body was loaded into the transport vehicle, the two investigators slamming the door.

One of the deputy investigators came to our window and took off his gloves to knock on the glass. "I'm sure they're going to be processing this quickly," he said. "We'll have to have your initial report by the end of the week. The mayor was going to issue a warning during his press conference tomorrow, but we asked him to wait. We have to make sure it's the same perp doing all of this before we actually announce a serial killer to the public."

"The two of us have seen all three of these cases so far," Detective Arviso said, staring him down. "Even if you all are taking over, our investigative work stands. We've seen that cut before but go ahead and pick at it in Albuquerque. I'm sure OMI will tell you the same thing."

"Detective, you know we have to include all aspects of the investigation before we can make any kind of assumptions."

"There is a man on the streets of Gallup right now who is murdering people," Arviso shot back. "People should know." She rolled up the window and pulled away from the scene, her face contorted in anger. "I really hate to be cut out of cases like this."

She pushed the gas pedal hard, heading out toward the north edge of town, where the Indian hospital provided Gallup's only skyline. "I feel like Sister Yolanda and Father Mark need to know that their missing outreach coordinator might still be out here somewhere."

Sister Yolanda was the first to greet us when we arrived at the parish. She caught us at the front gate, a huge ring of keys in her hand, her robe pulled tight over her neck. "Is this something that could have waited until tomorrow?" she said quietly, a marked change in her demeanor from our previous meeting. She opened the exterior gate and led us into the parish offices, careful not to wake Father Mark or anyone else sleeping in the rectory.

"I'm sorry it's so late, Sister," Arviso said. "We spoke with someone tonight who may have seen Brother Gabriel. We were hoping that he may have returned or contacted you."

"Please come in," she said. "We have the archbishop here from Santa Fe as our guest. He is preparing to do Mass for our anniversary celebration. I don't want to wake him."

"So, have you heard from Brother Gabriel since your report?"

"Of course not," she said. "We would have contacted you immediately."

Detective Arviso cut right to the chase. "Does Brother Gabriel have a life outside of the church?"

"What do you mean?" Sister Yolanda said, shocked by the question.

"Does he ever leave, or have friends or interests outside of the church?"

I could feel something behind me, a distant chill that moved into my body as I stood in the rectory. I walked to the hallway quietly as Sister Yolanda and Arviso continued to talk, my body feeling the heat and chill I had felt before. The collective hands at my spine pushed me to the end of the hallway, where I found a heavy wooden door. The word KITCHEN was carved into a sign on it. They pushed me on, their deaths filling my heart with dread.

"Open the door," the voices chimed. "Open the door."

"Excuse me." Sister Yolanda stood at my back. "You're not allowed back here."

Detective Arviso gave me a questioning look. "Rita, what's going on?"

"I'm sorry, Sister Yolanda," I said. "Where is Brother Gabriel's room?"

"I can't allow you into Brother Gabriel's quarters," she said. "That is his private space."

"Sister, if you don't allow us in his room, his life might be in danger." I never broke my gaze even when she tried to avoid it. She pulled her key ring from her apron and opened the kitchen door. When she turned on the light, I could see that the kitchen was spotless, every shiny pan and tool in its place. The kitchen was huge, with four large ovens and ranges and every tool that you would need to cook for hundreds of people. Sister Yolanda used a skeleton key to open a humble door in the far corner of the kitchen, which led down four steps into a tidy apartment.

"This is Brother Gabriel's room," she said. "Please don't disturb his things." His room was meticulous, the bed made so tightly you could probably bounce a quarter off of it. All along the walls, blue-and-gold portraits of St. Michael hung in perfect four-inch intervals. There were portraits of St. Michael at St. Mary's in Tohatchi, but they weren't as beautiful as these. A gray outline on the wall told me one of them was missing.

"Where did Brother Gabriel spend most of his time, Sister?" I knew that Brother Gabriel was the key to this whole thing. Everyone we spoke with so far had nothing but nice things to say about the man. I wondered if he had met the same fate as our victims, his body frozen somewhere in Gallup, waiting to be found.

"He spends most of his time in the kitchen and down at the outreach center." Sister Yolanda opened his door, ready to usher us out of the room. "He does a lot of street outreach, and drives the meal van to our remote locations."

"You'll have to show us the van," Arviso said. "Maybe there are clues to his whereabouts."

Sister Yolanda watched from the door as we searched the entire room, its brushed and clean appearance a perfect reflection of the man who was now missing. Clean and untraceable.

Arviso stuffed her notepad into her vest, shaking her head. "Thank you, Sister," she said, walking past the nun and out into the kitchen.

I followed as Sister Yolanda shut off the lights. Out of the corner of my eye, I caught light coming from beneath the bed, a perfect square of yellow.

"Sister, what is that?" I pointed. Yolanda turned the light back on and Arviso and I moved Brother Gabriel's small bed aside, revealing a trapdoor sealed with a small silver lock.

Detective Arviso stood up. "Do you have the key to this door, Sister?"

"I've never seen that door before, Detective." Sister Yolanda stood with her hands in the pockets of her robe. "Maybe I should wake Father Mark."

"I have a crowbar in my unit." Arviso hurried out after Sister Yolanda, leaving me alone in Brother Gabriel's room, the smell of death and blood filling my nose. The ghosts remained, their cold breath at my neck. They didn't want me to leave. They wanted me to see what was locked beneath that floor.

Arviso returned from her vehicle, crowbar in hand. She was prying open the door beneath Brother Gabriel's floor when Father Mark arrived.

"What is going on here?" he said. Sister Yolanda stared anxiously behind him. I thought we were in for a scolding, but the two of them joined us in a ring around the trapdoor. Arviso finally got it open, revealing an odd shrine at the bottom of four steps. Sister Yolanda looked down into the hole and gasped. Each wall was adorned with gold-and-blue portraits of St. Michael, even more intricate than the ones in his room. On the center of a pedestal sat a small chalice of blood, its coagulation black and putrid. I stepped down into the altar, and could see it clearly: several photographs were stacked in rows, with nine of them framed. Each photograph was of a different person, some of their white-edged portraits dirty with clay and blood. I pulled my camera from my coat and began to take photographs of all of it. My leg creaked into the bend.

"I had no idea any of this was down here, Detective." Father Mark stood at the top of the stairs at the altar, his soft hands over his mouth. "Brother Gabriel is such a sweet, quiet, humble man."

"Who are these people in the photographs?" Arviso was already grasping her radio. "Have you seen any of these people before? Don't touch anything. We will need to process what is down there."

"It looks like the residency photos we used to take down at the Indian Center back when we had the housing program." Sister Yolanda peered down to the altar through her glasses. "Most of these people have died. Some of them years ago. Except for those two." She pointed toward the last two photographs—a man and a woman. "That is Merlin Etsitty and Eliana Begay. They stopped coming to outreach a while ago. We figured they had moved back to the reservation."

I had recognized their faces immediately, thinking of their legs and feet disappearing into the Tohatchi snow. I knew it was them the moment I filled my camera frame with their faces. I took photographs of the photographs, wondering why these faces were in Brother Gabriel's altar. As I zoomed in, I spotted another photograph underneath the chalice of blood.

"Do you recognize her?"

Detective Arviso peered down at the opening of the altar, looking at the face from above. She pulled a pair of gloves from her pocket and reached down, moving the chalice off the photograph. Under a ring of dried blood was Rosemary, the woman we'd met earlier that day.

Arviso pointed to the row of photographs. "How did they die?" she asked Sister Yolanda.

"From exposure," the nun said. "They were all found dead over the years, frozen on the streets."

"May God rest their souls," Father Mark said, making the sign of the cross.

I pointed toward the third photograph in the row and looked at Arviso. "Is that Chayton Tso?"

She jutted her face closer and we shared a glance. At that moment we knew.

"We're going to have to close off Brother Gabriel's room until we can bring a unit down here," Arviso said, helping me out of the portal and closing the door to the altar in the floor. "No one touch anything until we process this." She pointed her flashlight at a trash can in the corner. "Is that blood?"

We stepped forward to look. In the trash were several square bandages, soaked with a good amount of blood.

"Those are Brother Gabriel's bandages," Sister Yolanda said.

"How do you know?" Father Mark looked drained, confused about everything happening around him.

"I've helped him change them." Her shoulders were slanted like a guilty puppy's, her lips pinched in a look of abject shame.

"What kind of injuries did Brother Gabriel have?" Arviso used her pen to move the top bandages aside, revealing layers of dark, soaked bandages beneath. "That looks like a lot of blood."

"He had . . ." She hesitated, looking at Father Mark again. "He had cuts on his back."

"From what?" Father Mark moved closer to the nun. "Tell us what is going on, Sister."

"Brother Gabriel was whipping himself," she whispered. "At first, he hid it well. For years, I think. He had deep scars under the new wounds. I saw blood on his back in the kitchen once, years ago. He brushed it off when I asked him. But lately, he has been drenched." She began to cry. "When I helped him two weeks ago, his back was covered in blood."

I thought of the couple's photograph inside Brother Gabriel's secret shrine and knew at that moment that Brother Gabriel had been the one they warned me about. Now I knew what they meant when they said there would be more death, more victims to be found. A heated panic filled my face as I thought of how many more there could be at the hands of this man. Rosemary's photograph spoke to me, her eyes full of life. If we didn't move quickly, she was going to be next.

"Didn't you say that Brother Gabriel drove the outreach van?" I said. "Where is that?"

"Out back, by the bay doors of the kitchen."

Father Mark led us around the to the back door and opened it. The alley was empty.

"We used it to move donations this morning," Sister Yolanda said. "I have the key."

"Anyone else have a key?"

"Brother Gabriel," she said.

It only took seconds for Arviso to call it in. Everyone for miles was going to be looking for that white church van. We had no idea what we would find if we tracked it down. We had nothing to go on except for what was on that altar.

Arviso and I went back to our cruiser to wait for the investigative unit to arrive. I couldn't wait to say it out loud, to release that truth into the air. I spoke in a panic.

"There is a connection here—Rosemary is connected to

Brother Gabriel. She knew him," I said. "She could be in danger. Everyone else on that altar is dead."

Arviso turned in her seat to give me a hard glare, half worry, half dread. "How do you know that?"

"Before you even came to find me, I saw that homeless couple, Merlin and Eliana, out past the cornfields at my grandma's house. I didn't know it then, but they were ghosts already." I grabbed her hand. "I wouldn't lie to you, Detective."

Arviso started the car. "I know you wouldn't."

"He's going to kill Rosemary next. That was a cup of blood sitting on her photograph."

I think Arviso could feel my panic. "Here comes a unit." She pointed to the approaching lights. "Let's get them settled processing the scene, then we'll head out to Fort Wingate to find Rosemary. I'll get her number from the Ryder report."

As I watched Detective Arviso talk to her officers, I sat in the unit and called Grandma's house to check on her. The phone rang without an answer. I thought about the negatives again, and my blood ran cold. I called Mr. Bitsilly, frantic for answers, but he also didn't pick up. I tried both of them several times. Nothing. I looked through my bag, finding Charley's scrawl written on a small corner of yellow legal pad, and called it. He answered.

"Hello? Charley?"

"Yes?"

"It's Rita. Rita Todacheene."

"Hi, Rita," he said. "Everything okay?"

"I'm worried that my grandma isn't answering her phone, and neither is Mr. Bitsilly." Arviso was already walking back to the cruiser. "Can you please check on them?"

"Mr. Bitsilly is in Window Rock today, I think," he said. "But

I'll go straight over now and make sure everything is okay. I'll give you a call."

"Thank you," I said. "I really appreciate it."

"No problem," he said. "And Rita? Be careful out there."

Arviso got into the driver's seat and pulled the car into gear as I hung up.

"Here's the number that Rosemary gave us at the scene." Arviso handed me her business card, a number written on the back. "We can hopefully get her on the phone." I called the number as we drove down Aztec. No one answered.

"I guess we're taking a drive to Fort Wingate," she said, and switched on the headlights. The snow was starting to fall in thick waves. My stomach began to sink as I thought of Grandma and the snow and her phone sitting in the corner, unanswered.

CHAPTER 30 | 3°

"And God shall wipe away all tears from their eyes;
and there shall be no more death, neither sorrow,
nor crying, neither shall there be any more pain:
for the former things are passed away."

REVELATION 21:4

THERE IS SO much evil in the world. My father had only
shown me the edges of it when he struck my mama down with
his axe. He'd shown me hate and violence. I saw other facets
of it at St. Joseph's; I saw predation and cruelty. At university, I came to understand selfishness and greed. By the time I
graduated, my path forward had become clear, because I knew
there was no going back. Now I know what Wapasha said was
true. *They're watching you*, Wapasha said to me. *They watch you
always.* The ravens were watching when he said those words.
They still were.

I won't be on this plane much longer. Rosemary, her baby and
I will be vanishing into the skies above. The world in its current
iteration would have to wait a million lifetimes to see all of us
again. This story I have told here is all of it. It is all that I have
chosen in my life and all that has been chosen for me. I am
ready for the pain to end. I have resigned even my own doubt.
I have to believe that what the ravens have shown me is real. I

must trust that the last years of my life have not been wasted on delusion or weakness.

I was determined to finish my work before my earthly body died. It was already dying, my back infected with death and guilt. The fever of infection never left me. It took me back to my life with Lozaro, before the pain was unbearable, before my fate was sealed. I felt the infection was my punishment, my sins never confessed, the blood on my hands. A faith like Lozaro's was unequaled, but I worked as he taught me, and I took that work to Gallup, building an altar of my own, a space of devotion beneath the floorboards. I may never have become the man that Wapasha wanted me to be, never what fate had prescribed, but I always remembered that I had a purpose in this world.

The trees around the trailer are full of snow, their drooping branches making a perfect place to hide and wait. In the thin window above the sink, I see Rosemary walk by on the other side of the aluminum skin of the trailer, her hair a halo under the kitchen lights. The sheep are watching me. I can feel it.

I'm going to take Rosemary to the water tower to finally offer her to the messengers. I hope that she doesn't fight too hard when I take her. I don't want to hurt her. I will deliver her to heaven, untouched by the rage of this earth. I cannot wait to feel my wings, to have the air piercing through my feathers. I can already feel the earth beneath me, the roads and trails laid out before me.

I have my needle with me, but I hope that I won't need to use it. Rosemary will trust me. She will follow me, and we will push our bodies out into the dark and fly up to heaven, our bodies rewarded by the blood I have spilled, our souls met in heaven by all the angels I have sent before us. St. Michael will see our souls, heavy with adoration for him, our reverence exposed like bare flesh. The weight of our pure souls will open the gates of heaven. Rosemary will love and trust me enough to go.

The messengers will never let me rest without Rosemary; I know this. It is what drove one foot in front of the other, up that dark path and into the shadows. I'm watching her now in the kitchen, opening a can then dumping the contents into a pan on the stove. She's looking out the window into the dark, never meeting my gaze. It will take nothing to put her in the van. She will beg me for her life. But I will explain it to her. I will tell her why it is her time. She will sit on the thrones of angels, her baby at her side. She won't get away because my eyes have blackened. There is nothing left of me. I am ready for my transition.

My end has come. I will make my way to her door, where I will wait for her to step out into the dark. High up on the water tower, we will make our final journey, we will fly into the next world. The thought of it makes my mouth wet with blood.

CHAPTER 31
122 PAGE ROAD, FORT WINGATE, NM
Nikon D2X 50mm • f/1.4, 1/250-1/500 sec., ISO 200

THE FOURTH TIME that I called Rosemary's number in Fort Wingate, someone finally answered, their breath in a panic.

"Hello, Rosemary?" All I could hear was a panicked cry.

"She's gone," a woman said. "The priest just came and took her."

"Are they on foot?" I braced myself against the dashboard as Arviso wove in and out of traffic.

"No," she said. "I can still see his taillights at the end of the road. They're in a white van."

"We're on our way, ma'am."

"I just called the police," she yelled. "Where are you?"

"Unit Fifteen, come back." Dispatch was already calling as Detective Arviso raced us out.

"This is Arviso."

"We just got a call from Fort Wingate," the dispatcher said. "A Rosemary Nez was just abducted from behind the Navajo housing unit. Her aunt called saying a man in a van had her by her neck with a knife. I heard 'white van' and thought of you."

"Copy," Arviso said. As we made our way over, we could see the van heading away from Fort Wingate, past the old horseshoe and out into the canyon.

We sped over the roads, trying not to make it too obvious we were following. The van pulled into the canyon, continuing past the parking barriers and up toward the foot trails. We stopped at the park entrance and watched as two figures headed up toward the Fort Wingate water tower. There was no way Arviso's unit was going to make it up that rocky trail.

"We may need to come in on foot," Arviso said, pulling her gun from her belt. "Do you have a gun?"

"No," I said. "I take pictures."

Arviso pointed to the revolver in her console. "Take that with you."

We headed out into the dark and toward the water tower. We had to feel our way around the park; flashlights were sure to give us away. We could hear Rosemary screaming in the distance and ran toward the sound as fast as we could. The uneven ground shocked my leg with pain, the adrenaline numbing the terror.

Once we made it to the edge of the trail, we could see Brother Gabriel forcing Rosemary up the ladder of the water tower. They were already halfway up to the top when the snow began to fall.

"Stop right there, Gabriel Jensen," Detective Arviso said, her gun aimed straight at his head. "Step down here and let us help you."

"Don't you see them?" One of his hands was raised to the twisting clouds in the sky. "Don't you see them coming to get us?"

We looked into the sky but could see nothing. Brother

Gabriel laughed into the dark. Arviso started up the ladder after them and I followed, painfully dragging my humming leg up each step.

"We are here," Brother Gabriel screamed to the sky. "You promised to take us. We have a deal."

"Brother Gabriel," Arviso repeated as she pulled herself up. "Come back down toward me. Leave Rosemary right there."

"You promised me," he roared. He pushed Rosemary up the last rung of the ladder. She continued to twist and writhe away from him, but each time he pulled her back, her strength no match for his. The nerves in my leg growled, but I kept going. Arviso was nearly to the top of the tower.

"Please, Brother Gabriel." Rosemary's shriek carried through the blasts of snow. "Don't hurt me. You always said you would never hurt me."

Gabriel stilled, his arm around her neck. Even from where I was, I could see that he was battling something inside himself. But then he took a step, dragging Rosemary with him. She gasped in the dark.

"You promised me if I brought her to you, you would give them to me!" Brother Gabriel cried out to the sky, his throat cracking under the strain. "Now, here she is, her baby's heartbeat inside of her. Let me go!" He climbed onto the platform of the water tower and took hold of Rosemary's neck, her hair twisted in his fingers. I was frozen on the ladder below them, watching her buckle on the platform, her bare feet sliding off the edge. "I can feel them! They're finally here." Brother Gabriel shouted.

I looked up to the sky again, half hoping for a glimpse of the thing that Brother Gabriel was talking to through the falling snow. There was nothing there but the cold.

"Brother Gabriel," Rosemary pleaded, her fingers prying

fruitlessly at his. He was tall and strong, an ominous presence in the dark. "Don't hurt my baby, Brother."

Arviso was on the platform now, her gun aimed at his head. I watched her hand steady as I climbed onto the platform. I could see Brother Gabriel was crying now. She inched closer, careful not to provoke him. Rosemary dangled like a rag doll, her hair blowing back, her bare arms red and frozen from the cold.

A smile flooded Brother Gabriel's face. "You're coming with me." He encircled Rosemary with both arms, his breath in her face. He was shouting into the snow. "We can show you mercy. We can wrap your child in the warmth of God."

Detective Arviso was powerless, with the hostage between her gun and her target. But Rosemary, slender, hungry Rosemary, was not. I watched as she grabbed his pinky finger and wrenched it back so hard he cried out, releasing her. Her frozen red feet gripped the ice and ran toward us, leaving Gabriel, his tears and his hallucinations at the end of the walkway, a smile on his face, his arms outstretched.

"Do you see them? Aren't they beautiful?"

"Brother Gabriel, don't—"

"I love you, Rosemary," Gabriel said. "I just wanted what was best for you. Do you understand?" The wind and snow curled up around him.

"Brother Gabriel?" I shouted. "Come back to us. You'll be okay."

He looked at the three of us, the snow building, the red-and-blue lights of the patrol cars arriving on scene. He smiled again.

"God forgive me," he said.

Gabriel launched his body off the water tower, his expression completely unafraid, his arms outstretched like wings.

Detective Arviso, Rosemary and I watched him fall. He landed with a deep, hollow thud below, his last breath squeezed from his body in a wheeze. I could hear Rosemary crying. Brother Gabriel lay in the snow, his red blood spreading into the white.

Arviso gave Rosemary her jacket and slowly helped her down the water tower. Gabriel had taken her from her aunt's trailer wearing a T-shirt, sweatpants and no shoes. The cold had already turned her skin a deep and dark red. It was hard to get her down with her feet numb, her skin on the verge of frostbite. They took her into the ambulance the second she made it down, wrapping her up in blankets and checking her vitals. Her aunt was there waiting for her, her eyes wet with tears, happy to see her alive.

Arviso and I walked over to Brother Gabriel, his body face down, his neck a warped coil. His face was fully twisted to the side, a haunting grin on his face. His coat lay open, a black leather-bound book spilling out of the pocket. I walked to the unit and pulled my camera from the backseat. I began to photograph all of it, just as it was laid out before us, the snow working against it.

Arviso pulled a white tarp from her car and I helped her cover him as more sirens approached, red-and-blue lights turning their way through the night. My leg twitched from pain and I stopped to lean against the ambulance, where the paramedics continued to connect wires, to push needles into Rosemary's skin. She never flinched. When she opened her eyes, it was like she knew I was watching her. She smiled at me, a tear sliding down her cheek. We couldn't even speak.

CHAPTER 32
HOME

Hasselblad 500 C/M 80mm • f/5.6, 1/250 sec., ISO 100, EV 13

WHEN MARGARITA MONTAÑO came to visit me, she didn't have blood on her breath anymore. She was still wearing her favorite pink pajamas, the fabric untouched by blood or the burn of hot bullets.

"Can you come with us?" She smiled as she said it, standing there in the dusty morning beams in the living room. "Can you come with us and play with us?"

"I can't go," I said. "I have a lot of work to do here." I pointed toward the beams of sun. "They are waiting for you." The dream was warm, a reassurance of what was meant to happen. The little girl had come to say goodbye. I watched until she disappeared into the haze before me, elongated lights guiding her into the clouds.

It had been two weeks since I had been called back to Albuquerque for my deposition. The Jude Montaño case had moved quickly through the juvenile justice system in Albuquerque. They had been eager to prosecute the boy, the headlines in the papers drumming up the faithful followers of the "Montaño

Massacre" case. Albuquerque Police were not able to hide what they found inside that storage shed on the Montaño property. My report only helped to back up Jude's story, to actually raise enough doubt in the scenario that the police department had presented. Once again, one of their own officers had become the subject of a huge department investigation. My deposition lasted an entire day.

I hadn't heard the news yet, but I knew that Margarita's appearance to me meant something. The children had been lingering to make sure that Jude Montaño would not be punished for the sins of his own father. Thanks to their direction, the police had the evidence right in front of them. All they needed to do was follow the law.

Tohatchi was different in the spring. The valleys came to life, splitting the red clay into sections of sagebrush green and bright yellow rabbit bushes. In early April, Grandma and I drove up the back of the mountain and spent the day in the thin, crisp air. This time, I stood Grandma in front of the piñon and juniper bushes and took her picture. She put her hand in the camera frame.

"Don't, Rita." She laughed. "I haven't done my hair." It was curled with bobby pins under her hairnet.

We sat out at the edge of the mountain and watched the valley below turning green, the highway in the distance reflecting back to us. We ate tuna fish sandwiches and drank Black Cherry Shasta. The wind was gentle to us, the sun not yet hot and punishing. As we sat out on the tailgate of Grandma's truck, she grabbed my hand and smiled. She didn't have to say a word. Memory was funny that way. We could see each other, almost thirty years of memories rewound, the skin of that five-year-old still mine.

It had been four months since Brother Gabriel met his end. Dreams of his last minutes followed me for weeks, nightmares that had the man confessing to me, following me through streets—whispering to me in bed. But I knew what to do this time. I knew how to protect myself.

When I came through his door, Mr. Bitsilly already knew why I was there. He sang for me right there in his kitchen that night. He started a ceremony that lasted four days. Grandma and Mrs. Peshlakai; Charley and Darius, Mr. Bitsilly's grandson; and Shanice sat in the hogan and prayed for me, and for once prayed *with* me. I didn't expect that any of Gabriel's victims would be making their appearance again since the man who killed them was now dead, eaten by his own horrible history. That night I heard more than just our voices rising with the smoke of prayer. I could hear whole generations of my ancestors singing the songs with Mr. Bitsilly, pulling their prayers from the next world into this one and wrapping me in their protection. I was finally ready to believe in all of it.

Reservation gossip fueled the fires in Gallup as the scandal of Brother Gabriel was laid bare in the newsprint of the *Gallup Independent*. Investigators began to look into the church and into all of the allegations that had been filed throughout the years. It was only the beginning of a reckoning. The archdiocese would be dealing with the fallout from this scandal, and others, for years to come.

Sacred Heart redirected the blame at Brother Gabriel, citing his mental health, his untreated descent into madness. But investigators found out that Brother Gabriel had begged for help for years, consulting doctors about his headaches, planting more than a few red flags when he was seen at the local hospital for hallucinations and confusion. But the system found it easier and cheaper to turn a blind eye; an institution can overlook an occasional spell or strange proclivity in exchange for good, free and faithful labor.

They found Brother Gabriel's harvest blade in the pocket of his black coat, the handle soaked with blood. His journal claimed that he had been killing people for years, listing their names in his pages, a twisted history of death undiscovered. The photos linked him to the murders of our homeless relatives, each of their deaths now rewritten as homicide. Using his journal, Detective Arviso's team finally found Merlin Etsitty's and Eliana Begay's bodies, mostly decomposed in the water-carved caverns outside of town. They had traces of the same poison that was found in Chayton Tso, the old vet whose body had been discovered at the train station. Dr. Blaser had linked the scythe we found in Gabriel's pocket to all three of the slashing murders from that winter. The syringe in his pocket contained the same toxic solution that had been found in Chayton's, Eliana's and Merlin's remains, but beyond that, not much could be proven in the rest of the exposure deaths we had seen over the years. Even Gabriel himself had confessed that he couldn't remember how many lives he had taken. He was here for thirteen years. Who knows how many really died at his hands?

It made me wonder about the multitudes we had lost by hidden homicide, the mystery forever shrouded in the apathy of the police. No one cared when these nameless faces made their final journeys; the most important thing was to keep those victims—those people—out of our eyelines.

In March, Detective Arviso came out to see me in Tohatchi. She brought Brother Gabriel's diary with her and we sat out at Grandma's picnic table, beneath her cottonwood tree. That was when spring was just beginning.

"Some of it is hard to read, isn't it?" Arviso watched the traffic pass through Tohatchi, sharing some of Grandma's sun tea with me. I paged through each story, Gabriel's handwriting meticulously describing his journey through his own madness. All of the text was in perfect form, not one sentence obscured, or one word crossed out. It was one long stream of consciousness that haunted me. What a horrible life he had led. There was a logic and a purpose to what he did right until the very end. He truly lived a righteous life in his mind. He brought mercy to the suffering and justice to the downtrodden. Some passages were streaked with blood, and a black feather was pressed between the pages.

"I'm just glad that he is gone," I said. "One more terrorized soul off the streets."

"That's the worst part," Arviso said. "There are plenty more already taking his place." She was right. Here on the reservation, right now even as flowers bloomed in our valleys and the melting snow brought our creek beds back to life, something horrible was happening somewhere. It wouldn't be long before they would call. Addiction and greed would make sure that my phone would ring again. There was so much more work facing me, so much more justice to find.

The April wind welcomed Grandma and me as we watered her corn, pulling the truck bed up to the rows and irrigating it with our hauled water. The big blue barrels filled the back of the pickup. The work strengthened me, my muscles building themselves up in Grandma's fields. She was right. It was going to be a great year for the corn, with deep green stalks already sprouting from the rich earth. Grandma still scolded me when I hoed the rows, pulling weeds and goatheads.

"Pull harder," she yelled. "Get the root from the bottom."

It was a blessing to be home again. It wasn't the same as it was when I was young, not knowing what lay ahead, the terror in what I was dealing with at that young age. It made me stronger. But what I learned more than anything by coming home is that I had people. I don't know how to describe how alone I had felt out in the world. There was so much pressure to do all the work, to tend to the living and the dead in equal measure. I forgot to take care of myself and to stay strong. Here I had constant reminders. I had people around me, to help hold me up and keep me safe.

Charley and Mr. Bitsilly had supervised as a cement mixer arrived last week, creating a perfect large slab on the southwest side of Grandma's house. Charley and I planned the layout of it, so much more room for Grandma to store her garden stuff or park her old truck out of the elements. More importantly, we were going to tear down that old garage at the beginning of the summer and unharness the view that Grandma always wanted, the two windows below the scarecrow clock ready to lay the flats out before her.

It had only been a few months, but Charley had become a big part of our lives. Grandma loved him and that was important to me. His total adoration had surprised me. I had never had that before, and it took someone like him for me to realize that, and to realize it was something I deserved. He made sure that I felt safe, but more importantly for me, he made sure Grandma was safe. He was there every day after work, helping to resurrect Grandma's garage, changing Grandma's oil, chopping her wood—whatever she asked. I joked with her that she was beginning to prefer his company.

For now, all I had to do was help Grandma with dinner. Mr. Bitsilly and Grandma's favorite math teacher were coming. The kitchen was filled with warmth and the smell of steaming mutton stew. I was sitting at the kitchen table when I caught Grandma staring at me.

"I'm so glad that you're home, Rita," she said. "I mean really home."

"Me too, Grandma," I said. Mr. Bitsilly and Charley walked through the door, Charley's arms full of flowers.

"Are those for me?" I asked.

"No," he said and handed my grandma the biggest bouquet I had ever seen, marigolds and sunflowers draped in greens. "These are for you." My grandma grinned, a half-moon of her pearly white teeth.

"And these are for you, Rita." A nice, perfect balance of roses wrapped in thick, green paper.

"You sure know what you're doing." Mr. Bitsilly laughed and grabbed Charley's shoulder. Grandma looked for a vase for her flowers, Mr. Bitsilly for Grandma's coffeepot.

"Thank you, Charley," I said.

"Always bring flowers," Charley said, smiling. "My mom taught me that."

"Not just for the flowers," I said. "Thanks for taking such good care of these two."

"They take care of me, Rita," he said. "Edwin told me about you. He says you're special and you're not to be messed with."

"He did?" My face ached with laughter.

"So be gentle with me," he said. I don't think we had all laughed that hard in a long time.

The food was headed to the table when Charley and I went out to the backyard and stared toward Gallup, the sunset turning the mountain a light purple. Grandma's cornfield was being reborn, the world coming back to life. For once I felt hopeful that I was in the right place. I could see that I had a future ahead of me and it wasn't always going to be filled with death.

Finally.

ABOUT THE AUTHOR

RAMONA EMERSON IS a Diné writer and filmmaker originally from Tohatchi, New Mexico. Her debut novel, *Shutter*, was longlisted for the National Book Award and the Bram Stoker Award, nominated for the Edgar for Best First Novel, a finalist for the PEN America Open Book Award, the PEN/Hemingway Award, and the Macavity, Barry, and Anthony Awards for Best First Novel, and winner of the Lefty Award for Best First Novel. She has a bachelor's in Media Arts from the University of New Mexico and an MFA in Creative Writing from the Institute of American Indian Arts. She resides in Albuquerque, New Mexico, where she and her husband, the producer Kelly Byars, run their production company Reel Indian Pictures.